Laura C. Holloway

Howard

The Christian Hero

Laura C. Holloway

Howard
The Christian Hero

ISBN/EAN: 9783337195779

Printed in Europe, USA, Canada, Australia, Japan

Cover: Foto ©Andreas Hilbeck / pixelio.de

More available books at **www.hansebooks.com**

THE CHRISTIAN HERO

BY

LAURA C. HOLLOWAY

AUTHOR OF "THE LADIES OF THE WHITE HOUSE," "AN HOUR WITH
CHARLOTTE BRONTE ; OR, FLOWERS FROM A YORK-
SHIRE MOOR," ETC., ETC., ETC.

FUNK & WAGNALLS

NEW YORK   LONDON
10 & 12 DEY STREET   1885   44 FLEET STREET

CONTENTS.

VI.

VII.

VIII.

IX.

X.

INTRODUCTION.

The difficulties which beset the path of a biographer, even under the most favorable circumstances, are well known ; they are by no means lessened when the subject of the memoirs is still living. Presentation of a man to a public composed of his friends and enemies is a task of extreme delicacy. The time has not yet arrived to publish all the facts of General Howard's career ; he is still in the active pursuit of his profession, and full of promises of future achievements.

Even the strictest sense of justice will not save the biographer from disappointing the expectation of friends and hurting the feelings of others who have taken part in the drama of Howard's life. The purpose of the present volume is neither to chronicle the military events with which the name of General Howard is connected nor to criticise the different personages with whom he has been associated. General O. O. Howard, the Christian soldier, is the subject of this biography, which, it is hoped, will tell those who know him more about his eventful and distinguished life, and introduce to those who do not know him a character well worth study.

General Howard has been called the " Havelock of the American Army," and been likened to Palmer, to Vicars, and latterly to Gordon, whose fine spiritual character was akin to his own. The comparison with Chinese Gordon, of all others, is best sustained for both ;

"Peace hath her victories not less renowned than war;"

Gordon's peace triumphs in Africa and China find striking parallel in Howard's services to the Freedmen and his missions to the Indians of the West. Unlike Gordon, Howard had the opportunity of not only fighting to free the enslaved, but also to be the leader in establishing them under altered conditions of life. To pursue the comparison further, the religious element has been intensely strong in both; but religion with them has been a living sentiment, which has refused to bend the knee to any ecclesiastical system. The large-hearted catholicism of both has called forth repeated criticisms from sectarians. Although it is unfair to compare and contrast the religious tenets to which they hold, it may be safely asserted that the general effect on their characters, produced by deep religious convictions, has been similar. In all acts of life each has been first the Christian, and then the soldier or administrator. They were also alike in this, that they have not looked upon honest poverty as a reproach, but have estimated wealth at its true value— as a means to noble and manly ends. Nor must the dissimilarities between the two characters be overlooked; each has a strongly marked individuality of his own, which even a superficial observer will not fail to note. But while both are products of the same conditions in our civilization, Howard's Pilgrim ancestry and his temperament, curiously at variance with accepted theories regarding heredity, render it impossible to class him with this other eminent character. It is needless to establish further parallels, as the qualities in which the subject of this memoir resembles the illustrious names we have mentioned, as also their points of dissimilarity, are too striking to escape observation.

The progress of civilization, and the influences brought to bear upon war by science, have altered the character of the soldier's life, and have eliminated from the profession the possibilities of physical heroism which once existed. War has lost much of its savage and romantic character as well : it has been reduced to the level of a gigantic play of chess, involving frightful massacres of the rank and file, but requiring of leaders more intelligence and quick observation and less strength of arm. In modern times military achievements, however brilliant they may be, rarely allow a soldier to acquire glory as the slayer of numbers of his enemies ; but at the same time it has removed from the soldier's character that stain of murder which attaches itself to even such a heroic personage as King Arthur. It is curious to note how Murat, afterward King of Naples, and one of the finest cavalry officers that Europe has ever seen, fought two hundred battles without having himself taken a single life. The very fact that the difficulties of gaining glory through military achievements are now so great, adds additional lustre to the fame of those who have won renown for brave leadership in battle. General Howard at Fair Oaks and Atlanta affords striking examples of dashing bravery carried to the verge of recklessness through self-made opportunities.

The growth of enlightened public opinion and humane feelings, which prevent the development of a modern Alva, does not render it impossible for a soldier to be also a philanthropist. Of course war itself, considered from the highest moral standpoint, is a violation of that law of love which the philanthropist instinctively recognizes and joyfully obeys. But, as Cowper says :

" Such men are raised to station and command,
When Providence means mercy to a land.

> He speaks, and they appear ; to him they owe
> Skill to direct, and strength to strike the blow ;
> To manage with address, to seize with power
> The crisis of a dark decisive hour."

The defence of the innocent and the oppressed is looked upon, in all lands, as the highest privilege of the pure and strong.

Since the introduction of artillery in warfare, the actual havoc made on the hostile ranks has ceased to bring glory to the soldier. The student of military history looks for different elements of greatness in a general than mere personal bravery or the fury of destruction. Life has become artificial, and every natural quality which can be simulated by art has ceased to attract any especial attention. Our intellectual civilization will deny recognition to the thundering arms of an Ajax, and put the laurel crown on the head of a mutilated Nelson. The whole tendency of the last few centuries has been to suppress the personal element in every department of life. Manners have felt this depressing weight the most, and have robbed the world of the charm of a sincere expression of feeling, which no age or country can well afford to lose. Nor has personal courage and bravery escaped the newly-introduced influence. To judge from the past, it does not seem impossible that before long a day will arrive when active courage will not be regarded in the light of a merit, as the necessity for it slowly disappears. Each age but admires most that which it needs. As the true value of life comes to be recognized, the reckless exposure of it, which the savage possesses in such great abundance, will be deservedly looked upon as a crime. True bravery consists in risking one's life in the performance of a duty ; throwing it away for any other purpose is self-murder.

Public opinion has given unmistakable indication of its decision by refusing to recognize aggressive courage as noteworthy unless accompanied by other specially intellectual gifts. No historian in these days will give the precedence of heroism to one whose sole merit lies in slaying a number of adversaries at a single combat in competition with one whose skill baffles a stratagem of the enemy. Ours is a pre-eminently intellectual age ; even the fine arts show the influence of the intellect, which seem to have carved the forms of beauty with which the centres of civilization are filled out of solid blocks of gold. The same intellectual eye regards with admiration the moral power in a soldier, his foresight and faculty for combination.

One effect of these forces upon the character of the soldier is traceable in the fact that hardly a general of any celebrity has been produced since the last years of the past century who has not distinguished himself also as an administrator. In a marked degree has the dual character of soldier and administrator distinguished Howard, who, whatever may be the eminence assigned to him as a man or as a soldier, is a child of his age and country, and these general remarks find a good illustration in his biography.

HOWARD: THE CHRISTIAN HERO.

I.

"An indefatigable man" was the remark once made
by Major J. H. Taylor concerning General Howard—a
remark which, in the opinion of those who most thoroughly know him, best expresses his leading characteristics.

By nature impetuous, ardent, and impulsive to a
degree, he has evolved, through a long course of self-dis-
cipline, that resultant quality defined by his friend as
"indefatigability." His military training was an important factor in his work of self-development, and this,
combined with his inherited religious tendency, enabled
him, early in his career, to gain an ascendency over himself, which is the secret of his moral influence over
others.

Unlike Vicars, whose Christian character Howard
chose as a model years ago,* he early gave evidence of a
religious bias, and we find him at the age of nine years

---

* Hedley Vicars, of whom Charles Reade wrote : "Here you have
a fighting saint, a religious red-coat, a man who cuts down a Russian
with the Gospel of mercy in his mouth."

standing up in a church-gathering, to which he had gone
alone, and, in response to the usual invitation of the
leader to hear from any one who had a word, speaking a
verse from the Bible.   It was the admonition, " Children, obey your parents, for this is well-pleasing in the
sight of the Lord." This selection, we may well believe, was not due to his own judgment, or chosen with
any special fitness to the occasion, but seized upon at the
moment because familiar, and perhaps for the reason
that his mother's teachings had indelibly impressed it
upon his memory, or perhaps because it referred to children and he wanted to say the suitable thing.   The excitement he labored under caused his limbs to tremble and
his cheeks to flush ; but he had done his part, and was not
at all disconcerted that the grave, elderly men about
observed him in silence.   It is not difficult to imagine the
effect it produced upon them, but the circumstance impressed itself upon the lad's mind, and was never forgotten.   His desire to do something impelled him to the belief that the leader wished all to speak who had anything
to say, and he did so, as unconscious of effect as if
he had tendered the use of his jack-knife to a companion.
He went home to his sick father and busy mother, who
had not noticed his absence, and reported the part he had
taken in the meeting.   His father eyed him curiously,
and expressed surprise that a little boy should have
spoken at such a time.   The child said he was invited to
speak ; and the father hesitated to point out to him the
difference between the literal and the conventional invitations of people, seeing the happy trust of the lad in the
matter.   He was interrupted in his revery by the question, " Father, do you ever pray ?" The sick man
looked out of the window over the moonlit scene, so
quiet and restful, a long time ; he could not at once

gather strength to conquer the choking sensation in his throat. The sober-looking little boy waited at his side, leaning on his arm-chair, and when the sick man said, " Sometimes, my son ; would you like to have me pray ?" he instantly responded, " Yes, father." The hand of the man held that of the child as they knelt for the first time together, and when the simple, earnest petition was ended, the boy was sent to bed with his father's blessing. A few weeks subsequent to this event Mr. Howard died, and the boy never forgot this occurrence. He came to look upon himself as in some way responsible for his father's death, and all that related to him he naturally remembered vividly.

On the day that Mr. Howard was taken ill young Otis had been sent to watch the cattle in a field some distance from the house. It was Sunday, and only the most urgent work was done on the Sabbath day on that New England farm ; but there was a field of growing corn, and it was important to keep the cattle out of it. The lad was sent to guard them while feeding near by, and was having a pleasant time with the dogs at play when he heard his father's voice. It was church time, and he knew why he was summoned ; but he did not know then that it had been a great exertion for his father to make him hear. The wind was blowing briskly in an opposite direction, and he strained his lungs in the effort he made to be heard over the fields. The family went to church, leaving Otis behind, and at noon-time Mr. Howard was brought home exceedingly ill. While in church a hemorrhage came on, and it was with difficulty that the weak man could be removed. The doctor who attended him attributed the attack to the violent exertion he had made that morning. He lived an invalid for eight months, and the little boy, who fully realized the

cause of his long illness, grieved contritely for him. To
his mother he tried, in his childish way, to make atonement for the loss of his father, and his love for her was
intensified in consequence. Years afterward he wrote
these words of him in a story for boys,* which is to some
extent autobiographical :

"Donald now learned about his father's early life :
how promising a young man he was ; how he was rising
in the world, when he was obliged to return to his father
(Donald's grandfather) and to take care of him, as the
old man had fallen into misfortune and embarrassment ;
how he had been engaged to the most beautiful of young
ladies of a high family ; and how, with diminishing
prospects, his father had offered, in sorrow (so it was
reported), to break off the engagement ; but that, Ruth-
like, she was too constant to permit it. Be it teacher,
merchant, or farmer, with him she had cast her lot.
They were married. Farmer Woodward, by constant
labor, always helped by his good wife, had paid up the
old debts, supported his father all his life, and had now
a nice farm and property all clear, and some money in
the bank. How much real poetry there is in almost
every life, if one could but find it ! These self-denials,
these unremitting efforts, these thrifty ways, such as
Farmer Woodward and his wife had followed from day
to day for years, were a *real* inheritance, better than
gold to their children."

Young Howard's attachment to his mother was not
only unusual in its strength, but was based on appreciation of a real worth. He was thoughtful of her from
his earliest youth, and now in her ripe old age she rejoices in the fulfilment of the promise that "her chil-

* "Donald's School-Days."

dren shall rise up and call her blessed." He has penned
many beautiful things of that beloved parent and of all
mothers. These are some of his tributes :

" She never appeared untidy, even at the hard work
of cooking. . . . Isn't it wonderful that these mothers
hold out so long in their ceaseless routine of daily duty !
. . . Every afternoon of a week day, when the work
of the dinner was over, a brief time was given to the
demands of her toilet. Then you would have noticed,
for a few moments, her woman's adornment—a profuse
spray of hair, glossy, brown, and flowing to the waist.
Very quickly it was rolled and flattened, and became a
crown to her head, fastened by the high-crested comb.
She was remarkable for two excellent qualities of mind
and heart—forethought and self-possession."

It is pleasant, as well as instructive, to quote what he
says of her characteristics, for they give his own por-
trait. Writing of these early days, he introduces an
accident which occurred to his brother, and makes this
allusion to his mother :

" The boys used to say, when older, it was almost
worth while to be hurt or sick to find out mother's real
heart ; for she seldom at other times used expressions of
tenderness to her children, not after they had passed
babyhood. . . . She gives him a fervent kiss—those
mothers' kisses, what meaning ! how they last !"

Soliloquizing over the value of this beloved parent, he
says :

" Boys do not seem to notice the pains a mother takes
to show her love for them ; but when years have gone
by, when the mother's eye is dim with age, and their
own children are receiving the same attention from
painstaking, self-denying, tireless mothers, then the old
picture comes back, and their hearts catch glimpses of

real mother-love, and warm up with grateful affection
that did not perhaps at the time find any coveted expression."

And these are his reflections concerning parents'
counsel and its blessing to the young :

"If a boy had the power to forecast the future, and
could look the consequences of his outreachings clearly
in the face, he might be very content never to roam
from his father's counsel and his mother's care, and he
might snuggle down in his soft bed, fully satisfied with
the present ' well enough.' "

The love and sympathy he entertained for his mother,
greatly strengthened by the feeling that he had been
instrumental in hastening his father's death, increased
with years.   She was equal to any sacrifice for her children, and self-denying to a degree, while just to herself
in her government of them.   She would walk a mile in
the deep snow to carry him a message which it was important he should know, but would require the perform
ance of the more trifling duty with rigid determination.   Her children's education was her first ambition,
and she almost overvalued a college training.   She
willingly saved and denied herself that her sons might
have the advantages she wished for them.   The ambition
of her boy gave her infinite pleasure, and she heartily
sympathized with him in his decided disinclination to
take up farm-work for his livelihood.   Where a mother
wills she usually wins, and the clear-headed Mrs. Howard
had a well-balanced character, which sustained her in
this as in all other duties, however difficult and long-
continued.   It accordingly pleased her to hear the lad
discuss plans and project ways and methods of raising
himself to a different sphere of life beyond the severe
and unremunerative occupation of a farmer.   Once he

returned from a Fourth-of-July celebration full of the
desire to be an orator ; mounting a chair in his enthusiasm, he repeated the words and imitated the gestures of
the speaker of the day, while his mother listened in
silence, mentally resolving that Otis should have all the
advantages she could secure for him.

There were elements, she saw, of a good and useful man in him ; his pedigree was unexceptionable, and
his inheritance of blood, brains, and purpose ought to
insure success. After years proved the correctness of
her judgment.

The Howards were an English family settled at
Bridgewater, in Massachusetts, where they remained for
several generations. When the Revolutionary War
broke out Seth Howard, the head of the family then,
went into the army with the rank of captain, leaving to
his youngest son the care of the farm, where he resided
with his mother. This youngest son, also Seth Howard,
was the grandfather of the subject of this biography.
During the latter part of the war the son joined the
father in the army, and saw service in the field.

Seth Howard the younger, many years after this
time, removed from Massachusetts to Leeds, Kennebec,
now Androscoggin County, Maine. He was a man of
family, and when he made this change of homes his son,
Rowland Bailey, the father of General Howard, was
ten years of age. Seth Howard was a noble specimen
of manhood, who commenced life with no other fortune
than his character. His was a generous, convivial
nature, fond of life and his fellow-creatures, and full of
hope and good cheer. He built himself a granite house
at Leeds, solid and substantial, like himself, and owner
and house were known far and wide. The name " Seth
Howard " was carved around the border of its ample

hall, and its thick walls were reared to stand for years to come. It was a spacious dwelling in its day, and long remained an imposing reminder of its owner.

Mrs. Howard, his wife, was a daughter of Dr. Rowland Bailey, of New York, and their family consisted of nine children, the youngest of whom, Rowland Bailey, was, as we have said, the father of General Howard. This young man had for his inheritance a delicate constitution, and he appears to have been the bearer of heavy family burdens from his early manhood. During the latter part of Seth Howard's life he became embarrassed, and upon this son, who had gone out into the world to care for himself, devolved the burden of his relief.

The worldly ambitions which he very naturally entertained were blighted by the heavy pecuniary cares that were upon him, and when he married his first love it was to take her to the old farm, where he was struggling to free himself from debt. His bride, Eliza Otis, was the daughter of Oliver Otis, of Scituate, Mass. Mr. Otis was a rich farmer, and as remarkable in physical appearance as Seth Howard. He was a man of fine ability, and possessed of those sterling qualities which secured for him the respect and affection of his neighbors.

Of this grandfather, his namesake says : " He was one of New England's sturdy sons, who in his youth started out, with a strong body, a stout heart, and an axe on his shoulder, almost penniless, to hew his way to fortune." The sum of his earthly wealth was five dollars and his useful axe. In those days woodmen were very essential members of a community, and Mr. Otis had no difficulty in making a start in the world. He became a wealthy and influential citizen, and lived to see the second genera tion of his name rejoice in his presence and prosperity.

The young couple had many tastes in common, and

both were refined and ambitious. Mrs. Howard was a self-educated woman, for schools were not always convenient for farmers' daughters, and in her early womanhood she taught school ; she was unusually well-read, and possessed a strong liking for art, poetry, and music. Her husband shared with her in these likings, and the two were exceedingly happy in their marriage, though both would have preferred to have had less hard work of an uncongenial kind. They were young, and she was strong, and regrets and repinings were not indulged in by the young wife. Each had the other and a home, and with her coming to gladden his life with her presence came also the certainty of a competency in time. At her father's death Mrs. Howard inherited a comfortable fortune. The issue of this marriage were three sons, the eldest of whom is Oliver Otis, born on his maternal grandfather's sixty-second birthday, and named for him. The two younger brothers of General Howard were as well educated as he, and both were graduates of Bowdoin College. Rowland Bailey, the second son, became a lawyer, and afterward left the profession to enter the ministry. Charles H., the youngest, who was studying for the ministry when the war broke out, enlisted in the Third Maine Regiment (his brother's) as a private, and was promoted through every grade to be a colonel and brevet brigadier-general. Rev. Rowland B. Howard is at present secretary of the Peace Commission, while Charles Howard has lately been the editor of the Chicago *Advance*, the Congregational organ for the West. He was at one time secretary of the Western branch of the American Missionary Association ; during the existence of the Freedmen's Bureau he was an inspector of a large district, and subsequently inspector of Indian affairs. All of the children of this

exemplary and wise mother have been useful and earnest
Christian men, and the meed of her ambition has been
thrice fulfilled in their careers.

While Oliver (called Otis at home) was yet a little
child his grandfather, Seth Howard, came to live with
his son Rowland, and the fondness of the lad for his
grandfather and of the latter for him was equally strong.
There was no pleasure of his childhood keener than that
experienced when running by the side of the old gentleman, talking to him, as the man, forgetful of the strain
he was putting upon the baby body, strode along at a
gait few grown-up boys cared to accompany, or in sitting
on his knee in the evening listening to his entertaining
stories.   The lad was encouraged to be industrious and
energetic, and he endeavored in many ways to secure his
grandfather's approbation by doing tasks deemed difficult by his elders.   He was healthy and strong, and not
infrequently made trouble for himself by attempts at
feats of endurance to which he was unequal.   His idea
of manliness was to do a man's work, and as he grew up
he was intrusted with many responsibilities at times.   One
of his early boyish duties, commenced when he was
only eight years old, was to go to school at sunrise and
build the fire, and this journey was often made through
deep snow.   The large boys took turns in this work, and
Otis was ambitious to be looked upon as one of them.
They permitted it, and, his mother consenting, he was as
prompt as they in his work.   Active even to restlessness,
he was always doing something, and executiveness and
conscientiousness marked all he attempted.   He was
persistent, too, and determined in his efforts to accomplish anything he undertook.   His lack of mechanical
skill was conspicuous, though he could not be convinced
of the fact.   If he took a fancy that he should like a

box or a sled, he would set about its construction with a
zeal that held out unflaggingly to the end.   Persistently
he would hammer until the nerves of the household
were irritated, and advice would be given him to desist.
It was idle, however, to try to persuade him to stop until
he had completed his work ; he would move his base of
operations, and go on carpentering until his sled was
ready for use.

This want of the mechanical faculty was felt at West
Point, where he had much difficulty with drawing, a
study in which his standing was very low for the first
year.   By hard effort he attained that excellence which
enabled him to lift his standing from thirty-four to nine,
which was his highest rank in that study.

Mrs. Howard was a good musician, and accompanied
her children on Sunday evenings in their singing of
hymns.   This was the one evening of entire leisure for
all the household at the farm, and it was observed in
this pleasantest of ways.   The memory of the hour of
song lives with the man to-day, and he was musing over
them when he wrote :

"It is a sweet picture in the memory to after years.
Possibly, with softer harmonies and more real music, the
same group may occupy and thrill the rooms and hall of
an upper mansion, already preparing, as one after another
is entering the gates. . . .   In the mother's heart these
Sunday evening scenes dwell, though the husband and
father has ceased from his earthly work, and the boys
have grown up and gone forth to bear their part in the
great world's battle."

A circumstance that will partly explain General Howard's unusual interest in colored people, apart from his
convictions on the subject of slavery, was this : When
he was a lad of five years his father, out of compassion,

took charge of a colored boy of seven, who lived for
many years an inmate of the house.   The family had no
race prejudice, and the waif who had come among them
to be sheltered and cared for was a bright, intelligent
child, whose sunny nature and happiness in his new
home made him a favorite with the family.   The
farmers of New England had no servants, and the boy
was never looked upon as a menial.   He was the associate of the sons, and was treated by Mr. Howard with
kindness and consideration.   Young Otis, who was
nearer this boy's age than either of his brothers, was
constantly with him in play and in the work which all
lads perform about a farmhouse.   The example of
benevolence set by his parents in taking this homeless
child, their kind treatment of him, and the responsibility
they felt in his training—all made an impression never to
be effaced on the mind of the little boy whose name in
after years was to become so prominently identified with
the colored race.   Perhaps this accounts for the inability
always shown by General Howard to understand why
the color of a man's skin should be the impassable barrier
to advancement and the cause of ostracism from all association with the dominant race.   During the war, when
race-enmity was at its height, he was perhaps the most
peculiar man in the army in this respect.   He treated
white and black alike, and was able to estimate good qualities at their true value, whether found under the white
or the black skin.   Very recently General Howard, in
replying to a question as to his abolition feelings, said he
did not know in slavery days that he was an extremist ;
he had been taught to respect all who were deserving of
it, and had never heard a reservation made in the case of
the colored people.   He simply acted upon the teachings
of his mother and father, and was surprised sometimes

to see how much more liberal and truly democratic had been his training than that of many of his friends and associates. But he was personally very benevolent, and his freedom from prejudice was due largely to his humanitarian and catholic spirit. His natural tendency toward active benevolence, which is one of his most marked traits, was early exhibited. Though possessed of a quick temper, he was always one of the first to show a friendly spirit, and if any one loved him he returned the feeling tenfold. Kind, tolerant, and sincere as a lad, the child is the father of the man in these his strongest characteristics.

After the death of his father he was a help and comfort to his mother, who for a time remained on the farm, managing it and caring for her children. Young Otis went to a school in the neighborhood until he was old enough to go to the academy at Hallowell. Then he left home to live in the house of his uncle, the Hon. John Otis, a Member of Congress, and a man of liberal culture. Here he earned his board by doing the chores about the place and taking care of the family horse and cow. His aunt was a woman of so much gentleness and sweetness of disposition that he loved her ardently, and her influence over him at this formative period of his life was invaluable. For two years he remained there, and was improved in all ways, by his studies and the associations of his religious life. His aunt and cousins were constant in their attendance at church, and he was their companion at prayer-meetings, church-gatherings, and social entertainments.

The winter months were spent at home with his mother and brothers, and there he attended a country school with his brother. The mother was ever glad to have him with her, for his hands were always willing, so

that he was a helpful member of the family. The
genuine goodness of the boy was constantly attested in
many ways, and wherever he could be doing he was
active.   His energy sometimes tired less restive people,
but he was tractable, and could be controlled by kindness.
The transparent nature was open to all, and, child and
man, he has been easy to read, because there was nothing
to conceal.   His characteristic promptness in any act of
kindness was a lovable trait in him.   Swift to do a good
turn, he did it with such unaffected heartiness that it was
a pleasure to receive a service at his hands.   When he
first went to Hallowell to school, a speaker of the Sabbath-school which he had just joined asked the scholars
for contributions to purchase a Bible for a family in the
neighborhood who had none and were not able to buy.
No sooner had young Howard heard the request than he
ran instantly home, secured his Bible, and hastened back
to the church.   On the way he met the speaker, and
handed his treasure to him to give to the needy family.
The earnest request had, no doubt, made as great an impression upon others who heard it, but no one else had
felt the appeal to be so directly personal.   To have kept
his Bible under the circumstances would have been impossible, and to have delayed in giving it almost as great
a trial as not to have given it at all.

Mrs. Howard, some years after the death of her husband, was married to Colonel John Gilmore, three
of whose children became members of her household.   Colonel Gilmore was a kind husband and step-
father, and was greatly beloved by the fatherless
boys.   The family continued to reside on the Howard
farm, where the youngest son of Colonel Gilmore by the
first wife still abides.   The only child born of this union
was a son, Rodolphus Howard Gilmore, who is now a

prominent lawyer and member of the Legislature in Denver, Col. From Hallowell young Howard went to Monmouth Academy, where he studied a year, and at the age of fourteen he entered Yarmouth Academy, where he was fitted for college. At both of these schools he studied very hard, and in the term intervals attended the district school near his home. He had made such a good record for himself while with his uncle at Hallowell that his mother was entirely confirmed in her purpose of giving him a college education, and his example stimulated his younger brothers to work in the same direction. Otis always looked beyond farm work, though he did much of it when at home in the vacations, up to the time that he began to teach, and his mother, who had never ceased to regret that circumstances had compelled his father to spend his life on a farm, when his education and abilities fitted him to work to better purpose in another pursuit, furthered his wishes in relieving him of this responsibility. After her marriage there was less necessity for him to do so, as Colonel Gilmore took charge of the agricultural labor. The family were well off, but lived economically, so far as mere outlay was concerned. They spent little, and the boys were taught to practise frugality as a Christian virtue and most essential duty. If young Howard owed to his parents no other gratitude, he cannot in this life repay them for the great boon they conferred in teaching him the value of money and how to use it rightly.

Having no expensive habits at any time in his career, neither smoking, drinking, playing cards, nor gambling in any form, his has been a fortunate life in respect to pecuniary matters. He has prayed that prayer which asks " neither poverty nor riches, but food convenient for him," and has lived for the most part untrammelled by debt or monetary anxiety. He lost the savings of years in Washington, from a twofold cause : the depreciation of mortgaged property and the expenses of legal counsel, but was able to live, as before, upon his pay as an army officer and what he earned by his pen, without incurring indebtedness.

While at Yarmouth Academy young Howard, by dint of hard work, completed a two years' course in one, and entered Bowdoin College just before the age of sixteen.

When on his way to college the first term, in company with a fellow-student, they stopped at a wayside inn for refreshments, and while waiting for their food his young companion invited him to the bar, and proposed a drink. Howard declined and kept his seat at the fire. His friend urged him, saying that it would refresh him, and then justified his own conduct in so doing with the excuse that all great men drank. Neither Daniel Webster nor Henry Clay shunned the pleasures of the bottle, he asserted, and he could see no reason why they should. "I prefer, then, not to be a great man," was young Howard's reply, and his friend took his drink alone. It is a sad commentary on the example set by these and other brilliant men then in the height of their great popularity, to add that this young lad died a drunkard.

Howard passed through his first term at Bowdoin, and then tried to get a country school during the winter months. He was refused the position he sought because of his youthful appearance. The winter was passed at home, and it was during this vacation, while on a visit to a classmate residing at Livermore, that he met at a social gathering the young girl—Miss Elizabeth A. Waite—who afterward became his wife. She was a daughter of Alexander B. Waite, a business man of Portland, and

was an only child. Howard was sixteen and she fourteen years of age, her birthday occurring on the 4th and
his on the 8th of November. It was a case of mutual at-
traction, and though the course of true love did not run
perfectly smooth, their affection never abated, and they
were true to their girl and boy fancy for each other.
This absorbing affection was the most fortunate of blessings for the young man, since it settled his mind and in
time influenced and colored his every step. The young
people became engaged while he was at college, where
he studied hard and continued uninterruptedly until the
first term of the senior year, when he remained away in
order to teach in a high school and earn the necessary
means to pay for the final term. His studies were kept
up, and he was graduated well in his class.

While at college he had an experience of a social nature that confirmed him for life in his temperance principles. He was mistaken for another college student who
was seen intoxicated, and his affianced, whose family
were strict temperance people, refused to see him again.
Her relatives had met a young man driving furiously
along the road, in company with a fellow-student, and
were quite positive that it was he, so that there was nothing for the unhappy girl to do but to give him up. The
young man did not know what had caused the change
in the sentiments of the young lady, and for weary
months there was no communication between them.
Howard's room-mate, long after this occurrence,
learned of the great injustice that had been done his
friend, and was instrumental in bringing about a recon-
ciliation.

This was not the only trial that the dissipated habits
of college friends cost him, but it was by far the most
serious, and it made him less lenient to this vice than

before and more zealous in his efforts to save his friends from its soul-destroying and easily-acquired habit.

We have seen that he was an abolitionist by instinct, and from his boyhood expressed himself fearlessly on the subject of slavery. No one at all acquainted with him was left in doubt as to where he stood on the then leading issue of the day. In a graduating oration which he imputed to another,* he had something to say regarding the hated institution, and used these flowery phrases in discussing it :

" As sure, Mr. President, as the fact that the sun rose this morning and will set this evening—as sure as the fact that the moon and the stars are swinging in space and performing their appointed motions—as sure as there is a power behind these motions—the power of the one omnipotent Being who made all things, and who sustains all—so *sure* is God's work among the moral forces in men's souls ! By His silent, mighty working, *Slavery*, the hideous monster, is doomed ! You and I, sir, will live to see the flag of Universal Freedom waving in our clear sky, from the Atlantic to the Pacific."

He was at this time much exercised about what he should do as a present means of livelihood and future employment ; he wavered between the law and medicine. Both presented an almost insurmountable obstacle —that of expense. He could not well ask his mother to devote more of her means to his education. How should he manage to secure professional training ? . About this time in his career he became much interested in religion, though he did not then publicly manifest feeling on the subject. His associations were mainly with people of orthodox views, and all his

* " Donald's School-Days."

real friends were church-goers and Bible-readers. He had noticed that the true Christian life was full of unselfishness ; that the friendship of Christians was a constant absorbing and heart-uplifting interest, and he was in sympathy with their aims and ideals. He says, in one of his early letters : "Christians seem like brothers." But now he would doubtless have studied for and entered the profession of the law, his inclinations leading him in that direction and his respect and admiration for the profession being very strong, had not an opportunity presented itself for an education of a wholly different nature. The ministry in New England, from the earliest times, has been universally honored, and the minister was by far the most important personage in the place in which he lived. He was consulted on all occasions, in sickness and in health. His presence at weddings, feastings, and family gatherings secured for him all the success desired, and his opinion on any subject was authority.

Young Howard, studying and probing his own heart to see what would be his life-work, turned over in his own mind all the advantages for doing good which the ministry presented. He wanted to be useful, to influence men to lead ennobling lives, so that he thought not a little of the Christian ministry. But at this time he was not a member of the church, so he gave the balance weight to the law ; nor had any but his own family any idea of his plans and hopes. The gift from his uncle of a cadetship at West Point decided his career and made him a soldier of the army, as well as subsequently of the Cross.

Hon. John Otis, who, as a member of Congress, had a cadetship appointment, gave it to his own son. The lad failed to pass the medical examination, and the father then offered it to his favorite nephew. It opened the way to a career for young Howard, and he saw in it, if he succeeded, four years of study and a livelihood, if he followed a soldier's calling. It was a great relief to him to be independent of his mother's help. The family property would bear no division, and his younger brothers were yet to be educated. School-teaching offered but a poor inducement to an ambitious young man who was engaged to be married and was anxious to begin work in some permanent pursuit. Self-reliant and physically strong, he felt prepared to enter the military academy, the more especially as he had a talent for mathematics, the crucial study of the institution.

Then, too, the stories of his grandfather, Seth Howard, who had been, as we have seen, a soldier of the Revolution, had fired the imagination of the lad. He now recalled anew the reminiscences of the old man, who had also fought in the later Indian wars, and pictured thrilling scenes of adventure and hairbreadth escapes to the eager listeners about the farmhouse fireside.

The bias in favor of a soldier's life given the youth by his grandfather's evening chats was not fully realized by him until the way was opened to pursue the same calling. He was at his uncle's house when the offer of the appointment was received, and was so overjoyed with his good fortune that he could scarcely wait for his mother's consent before sending his acceptance. This was rather reluctantly given, and he spent the intervening weeks in reviewing his studies and preparing for the examination. His cousin's preliminary trial had taken place in June, and his own was for the fall. He went to West Point the last of August, passed the initial examination, and was enrolled as a cadet in September, 1850. The following November he was twenty years old.

The career he had now entered upon had a marked

effect upon Cadet Howard. He soon learned at the academy system and order practically, as well as theoretically. He encountered rivalry, and measured his abilities with those of other young men who had been trained, as he had been, in the best schools of the land. Among his classmates for four years were G. W. Custis Lee, H. L. Abbott, Thomas H. Ruger, John Pegram, J. E. B. Stuart, and many others whose names are identified with the Civil War.

To a youth of Howard's temperament and religious tendency West Point was not a place where a pleasant time might be expected. The minority among the cadets were church-members, and few were interested in matters outside of their present duties and future prospects as army officers. The subject of slavery was then being agitated in every part of the Union, and the cadets, hailing from the several sections of the country, had much to say on this topic. The larger number of them from the Southern, Middle, and South-western States were hostile to the Northern sentiment on the slavery question, and a New Englander who had very pronounced views either kept his sentiments private or was at once at enmity with the extremists on the other side. Howard almost immediately elicited bitter and persistent hostility, and during his whole course suffered from this cause. His quick temper was a great trial to him, and it was with difficulty that he held himself in check when annoyed by remarks or unjustly treated on parade. None but one who has been a cadet can understand the difficulties of such a position. He was free-spoken and independent, and naturally smarted greatly under the unmerited situation in which, after a time, he found himself. His comrades will remember the spirited and sometimes bloody contests that grew out of these

things ; blows were the frequent results of their dis-
putes, for Howard was always too ready to fight.   Had
blows decided the right of the quarrels he would have
triumphed in the majority of cases, because his lusty
vigor was such that few could overcome in single combat.
In his studies he did well from the start, and had it not
been for an extreme political and religious sentiment
imputed to him, he would have had nothing to mar the
pleasant student life.   He was marked at guard-mount-
ing and parades constantly by the cadets who were his
enemies, and his demerit marks, due to fights, affected
his general standing, as did also absence from the class-
room caused by injuries received.

Once there was a bloody struggle, and the young man
received from another cadet wounds that laid him up for
many days, and have troubled him through life.   Injury
due to another cause also cost him much valuable time.
While practising in the gymnasium one day the hori-
zontal bar turned under his legs, and he came to the
ground, cutting his scalp severely ; erysipelas set in, and
he was dangerously ill.   To the tender care of Dr.
Cuyler, the surgeon, who nursed him through his long
illness, he always attributed his recovery.

Notwithstanding the loss of many weeks from study,
he came out, the first year, at the head of his class.
Mathematics was his forte, and in that study he graduated ahead of all.   His final rank in all studies, conduct
included, was fourth in a class that entered one hundred
and twenty, and graduated thirty-six of the original
members.   George Washington Custis Lee stood at the
head, and in one of General Robert E. Lee's letters to his
sons he makes mention of Howard, and advises his son to
look out for him.   Abbott came second, Ruger gained
the third rank, and Howard, who ranked the three in

the test study at West Point, stood fourth. Chiefly his conduct marks pulled him down to this figure, and it was no fault of his enemies that he was not farther from the head of the list.

Had young Howard's temperance views been as pronounced as his conclusions regarding slavery, he would have fared even worse than he did at the hands of his opponents ; but he did not then hold as extreme opinions as he afterward entertained. However, he passed through his four years' course at West Point, as he had done his college course, without acquiring the habit of tippling. After he entered the army he occasionally drank socially with his brother-officers, but this custom was cut short by an occurrence which led him to see the dangers of even moderate dissipation.

At that time the question of temperance had not grown to be of the importance it is now ; the all-engrossing slavery agitation overshadowed every other, and the Church exhibited a strange lukewarmness on this subject. A few years later it was the reform advocated by a small party, but it was not until about the close of the war that it developed into a live issue in church circles. As yet it is not a political one, though it is undoubtedly destined to be such in the future.

While a cadet Howard was a regular attendant at the chapel and the Bible-class, and was constant in his outward observances of religion. It was second nature to him to keep the Sabbath day, to refrain from profanity, to read his Bible daily, and to try to keep the commandments. His mother had trained him to be punctual in prayer, and he was sincere in his desire to be a good man. Up to this time he had not decided to associate himself with the Church, but his mind was often intent upon the thoughts that grew out of his

position, as a seeker after religion. Had he met with no
opposition, his might have been a merely formal adhesion
to matters relating to the higher life ; but he suffered,
and the conflict made him strong and determined in this
direction. He had aroused some feeling by joining
the Bible-class conducted by Professor Sprole (the professor of English studies, and chaplain), and he had been
accused of selfish motives in so doing. It was said that
he had taken the step in order to curry favor with the
authorities ; but he persisted in his course, and soon his
enemies added to the name of "abolitionist" other
sobriquets. The first time he walked from barracks to
the Bible-class meeting, with his Bible in his hand,
under the eyes of many of his fellow-students, it required an amount of moral courage not always forthcom-
ing in a young man. The habit once established, the
way was easier for him, and the cowardly impulse to
stay away from the class never assailed him after the
first hard step had been taken.

From West Point he went back to the loving household awaiting him at the farm, and the summer months
were spent in pleasure-taking. He was happy in his
success and in the prospect of his early union with the
sweet girl who had been so loyal to him through all the
years of waiting. In September he was ordered to his
first post, and it was understood between them that the
wedding should not be long delayed after he had settled
himself in his new quarters. His mother's happiness
was secured in his, and he enjoyed the satisfaction of
knowing that he was approved' not only by her, but by
all his kindred, and as well by the parents of the young
lady whose future was to be associated with his. Behind
him were the trials he had known at West Point, and if
he thought of them, it was to remember that he had

overcome much of the hostility so freely lavished upon him in the beginning, and had well sustained a part in the drama of cadet life now ended forever, and ended, so far as he was concerned, with credit and honor, and with kindly feelings toward all his classmates.

II.

HOWARD's military career presents a distinct line of cleavage. From the period of his first entrance into military life to the breaking out of the Civil War forms the first part. The second commences when he was appointed to the command of a regiment of volunteers by Governor Washburne, of Maine. The first part, although marked by diligent and useful service, was only a preparation for the new field opened up by the war.

Watervliet, West Troy, N. Y., was the first station to which he was ordered after his graduation at the military academy. After the discipline of the four years' espionage at West Point, the young army officer naturally enjoyed his newly-gained liberties, and in the refined charms of the social life of Troy and Albany, Howard, in common with the young officers of the post, found congenial associates in the family circle of Major Symington, the commanding officer of the Arsenal, which received constant enlivening re-enforcements from social representatives of other cities, to whom the gayeties of an army post afforded many attractions. New interests clustered around his life when, in February, 1855, he brought his bride into these connections. His " brevet" was ended the day after the wedding, so that he was a full second lieutenant when he returned from his twenty days' leave, during which he went to Maine to wed his early love. Howard's marriage made his happiness complete ; he was not then, or at any time in his life, over-fond of social gayeties, and his idea of domestic happiness was fully shared by his wife. The young couple were welcomed to the circle of army people at the post, and were soon fairly settled at the Arsenal. Mrs. Howard was a woman of much personal beauty, and possessed those characteristics which added refinement and expression to her features as time passed away. In temperament she was the counterpart and opposite of her husband. Quiet and reserved, her influence has been a beneficent one in his life, and no man ever was blessed with a friend stancher and steadier than she.

Very soon after their marriage Lieutenant Howard was ordered to Kennebec Arsenal, Me. This independent command, which every ordnance officer looked upon as among the best stations, was a promotion which he did not expect, and the compliment paid him by Colonel Craig, the chief of the Ordnance Department, was a pleasant one to accept. Some of his fellow-officers slyly hinted that he owed it not to his own merits, but to the charming little woman who made his house so delightful to the old gentleman (Colonel Craig) when on his tour of inspection. Doubtless the elderly officer was pleased with the young couple whose hospitality he had enjoyed and very likely thought to make her happy by sending her husband to a higher command. The change of quarters took her nearer home, and that was an added pleasure. The attractions of Kennebec were many, and the station afforded special advantages to Lieutenant Howard, in enabling him to fully master the duties of a quartermaster and commissary. While stationed there

he perseveringly worked in the interests of others, and
made constant representations to the Maine Legislature,
sitting on the opposite side of the river from the Arsenal,
till that body passed a law allowing the soldiers' children
living on United States grounds to have the free benefit
of the public schools within reach.   He became a father
before he left this post, and very naturally took an interest in children and their welfare.   The well-being of
soldiers' children has always concerned him seriously.
At Kennebec were formed many friendships destined to
be permanent.   Here he found the Blaines, the Williams
(General Seth Williams's father's family), the Mullikins,
the Childs, the Wainwrights, the Tappans, the Webbs,
the Lamberts, and other prominent families, with which
he has been more or less connected ever since.   It was
thought at Washington, at the end of the year, that
Lieutenant Howard had long enough exercised, with his
small rank, this command, and he was relieved by Captain Gorgas (who afterward became the chief of ordnance
to the South), and returned to Watervliet, where he
established himself with the expectation of staying for
some time.

    The little home was reorganized at the Arsenal, and the
family circle was enlarged by the addition of the mother
of Mrs. Howard, who in her widowhood had come to
live with her daughter, and Rowland Howard, who was
then studying at the Albany Law School.   With the
expectation of long remaining there the Howards fixed
themselves in comfort, and had every reasonable wish
gratified in their surroundings.   The young couple, in
accordance with an agreement made between them at
the outset, had a Bible-reading every morning, and were
regular in their attendance at church.   They were not
members of the church at this time, but were desir-

able additions to the church society, and were practising if not professing Christians.

Hardly a year had passed when, in December (1856), Lieutenant Howard unexpectedly received an order to report to the then famous General Harney, who was commanding the Department of Florida, in the field against the last remnant of the once powerful Seminoles. These Indians were remarkable for their dexterity in ambush and for their wholesale massacres, as the monument to Major Dade and his companions-in-arms, erected at West Point, attests.

The young wife for the first time realized that she had married a soldier. Her anticipations of home-life were rudely destroyed, and she saw the household articles which she had so leisurely and carefully selected dispersed, the pretty phaeton and pony sold, the home broken up, and the prospect of a long separation from her husband before her. It was decided that she should return with her mother to Maine, while Lieutenant Howard turned his face southward. The wife's unhappiness was not decreased by the thought of the climate and the enemy her husband was to be exposed to, and the day of his departure was saddened by the heavy snow-storm that raged fiercely around. It was his first separation from his wife, and it was a trial severer than he had realized until it had to be met. The contending emotions of a husband and father were traced on his face. He could not bear to go, and when all was ready for the final leave-taking he did not meet it until, for the first time at the Bible-reading, he had dropped on his knees and offered a prayer for strength and resignation. He commended his dear ones to his Heavenly Father, and asked that they might be kept in safety and happiness while he was away. When he had done so he

was more composed, and took his farewell of wife and
mother, child and brother.

Howard had a position well suited to him in Florida ;
he was chief of ordnance, and gained much military experience in preparing volunteers, whom he had to supply
with arms. While stationed at Fort Brooke, near
Tampa Bay, he was thrown in with a circle of young
officers, the majority of whom have attained celebrity in
their country's service. He met his old classmate,
Greble, there, whose untimely death prevented the fulfilment of his early promises ; he was the first regular
officer who fell in the war. There were also Hazzard,
mortally wounded before Richmond ; R. B. Marcy,
whose daughter married General McClellan ; Stephen
D. Lee, subsequently lieutenant-general in the Southern
army ; Pleasanton, afterward the great cavalry officer of
the North ; Dana, Mack, Kilburne, Hancock, and many
others whose names became celebrated in various ways
during the Civil War.

The result of Colonel Loomis's activities was a camp
of Indian captives, poor, forlorn, discouraged, unkempt,
and half clad. In course of these operations a company
of volunteers had chased and brutally treated a number
of Indian women and children, scattering them in the
wilderness, after killing and wounding several. Colonel
Loomis, anxious to avoid further bloodshed, deputed
Lieutenant Howard to take with him a captive Indian
woman and an interpreter, and attempt to get these
to return without any further fighting. Howard gladly
undertook the task assigned to him, and though not
crowned with complete success, the persistent effort gave
satisfaction to his chief. It is an evidence of the confidence he had inspired that he, so young an officer,
should have been chosen for such a mission. Thus early

he began his dual work as soldier and administrator, the latter character best according with his nature. His ideal work is that of a peace mission ; he believes in " nine parts for love to one for force."

How few people remark what great changes come over the course of their lives from circumstances which usually escape notice by their insignificance ! How often do we find one's whole life colored by what would be considered an accident ! But, as Disraeli remarks, with his characteristic shrewdness, " Life itself is made up of accidents." There is no feature in General Howard's later life which is so peculiarly marked as his piety ; tracing back its course, we find its origin, which seems to be strikingly out of proportion with the effects produced. One day the new commandant, who was a Presbyterian of the olden type, handed Lieutenant Howard some religious books, with the remark : " You are of an inquiring mind ; read these ; they will help you." Coupled with these books the lieutenant had another, which his brother had sent to him. He read them all, and was particularly influenced by his brother's gift, which was the life of Captain Hedley Vicars, of the British army.

Previous to this time he had constantly attended the Methodist, the only active church near Fort Brooke, and on one occasion publicly manifested his interest in religion. Several scoffers had annoyed him during the service by their comments upon those who were going up to the altar for special prayers. A small, deformed woman was a source of ill-suppressed amusement to them, and the young lieutenant, as much to rebuke them as for any other reason, rose, and buttoning his military coat about him, walked behind her to the front. He knelt with others at the altar, and as the clergyman

prayed his tears trickled down upon Howard's bowed
head.   No perceptible difference of feeling resulted from
this step, but a stand had been taken before the world.
The radical spiritual change which, under divine leadership, resulted in making him a Christian of a peculiar
type, came to him subsequent to this time, as he sat
alone one day in his little room at the Ordnance Depot.
He was reading that part of Vicars's life wherein he describes his own conversion.   Vicars was persuaded by the
passage of Scripture, " And the blood of Jesus Christ
His Son cleanseth us from all sin." *   Howard, in trying to solve its meaning, found the light through the
realization of the fact that " the cleanseth" was a per-
petual process through which men could always find
Christ.

His heart was filled with peace and his tongue with
praise.   For him it was impossible to keep the joy he
felt to himself ; he talked to his army friends, took
active part in religious work, held meetings for soldiers,
and was constant in visiting the ·sick in the hospitals.
Many were converted through his instrumentality.   He
went to the poor and the sorrowing, and this among
many incidents is related of his strong sympathy for even
strangers in bereavement :

A young volunteer, son of a captain, was accidentally
killed ; his body was taken to his home, where the
mother, totally unprepared for the shock, was overwhelmed with grief.   The tears which relieved the
father came not to her eyes ; the blow seemed to have
completely stunned her.   On the day of the funeral
there stood by the grave a young officer, a stranger, who
wept with her.   He attracted her notice as one about

---

* 1 John 1 : 7.

the age of her lost son ; she spoke to her husband about
him afterward, and Howard was invited by him to visit
them.   He went immediately to the house of mourning,
and talked with the mother of her son until the tears
flowed and the heavy heart found relief.   It has been a
peculiarity of Howard's life that people in trouble instinctively turn to him, and find comfort in his quick
and unobtrusive sympathy.

   It was due to a circumstance which took place during
Howard's stay in Florida that the deepest of impressions
was made upon him by those temperance principles
which he has ever since advocated, both by precept and
unflinching practice.   An officer lower in rank than
himself visited him at his quarters, and was offered a
drink, which probably became the immediate cause of
an attack of *delirium tremens.*   Howard, when he heard
of the condition of the young man, went to his home, and
nursed him through his illness, doing all in his power to
reform the unfortunate officer.   But he resolved then
and there to practise temperance habits and to advocate
them so long as he lived.   Thenceforth the rare indul-
gence in a glass of liquor at the table of friends was dis-
continued, and he was safe from temptation in this direction.   He never at any time in his life had used it in his
family.   The little woman who, as we have seen, had so
nearly parted with him forever because of her belief
that he had been under the influence of strong drink,
was too deeply imbued with temperance principles to
have countenanced such a course.   Fortunately for her,
the companion of her life was early in their married
career convinced of the right of her position, and it became his own.

   As with the use of wine, so with tobacco.   He had occasionally smoked while in Florida and previously, but gave

up the habit from principle.   One day his attention was particularly directed to this verse in the Bible, " Happy is he that condemneth not himself in that thing which he alloweth ;" * and thinking earnestly upon it, he concluded that it applied to the habit of smoking in his case ; therefore he gave it up, and never again indulged in the unnecessary luxury.

During his stay in Florida Lieutenant Howard cultivated a little garden about his quarters, and in the early summer had a fine watermelon patch.   The fruit tempted the soldiers, and they took his melons whenever opportunity offered.   When the crop was sufficiently ripe for a number of melons to be gathered, he greatly shamed the offenders by inviting them to his quarters and treating them to all the fruit that was ripe.   Ever after that feast the lieutenant's melons were his own, to dispose of as he chose.

Lieutenant Howard's work in Florida terminated in September, 1857, when, at the recommendation of Professor Church, he was appointed mathematical instructor at the military academy.   Here Howard was united with his family, which had been enlarged by the birth of a second child.   They lived at first at Roe's Hotel, his rank not allowing him a house.   Subsequently they removed to a little cottage, where a quiet family life was enjoyed for several years.   Within a short time of his arrival at West Point he was advanced to a first-lieutenancy, and before leaving the academy he became Professor Church's first assistant.   Many officers who hold to-day high positions remember Lieutenant Howard's instruction, and speak of him with warm recognition of his helpful interest in them.

---

* Romans 14 : 22.

During the four years he spent at West Point as instructor of mathematics he was active in religious work,
visited the Soldiers' Hospital, and every Wednesday
night lectured to soldiers and their families in the little
church under the hill. These lectures on the different
commandments and on each clause of the Lord's Prayer
were carefully written out, and are kept by him as
souvenirs of those happy days when he was studying
Hebrew, with a view to entering the ministry. With the
families about the mountains and at the Falls below he
was largely acquainted, and was engaged in missionary
work with many of them. He established and conducted a cadets' prayer-meeting, which flourished from
its inception. In his diary, kept during this period of
his life, General Howard has preserved the names of his
class-members, together with some mementoes of the
spiritual work they tried to perform. It was the custom
at each meeting for the class to hand in requests for
prayers, and from among very many in the possession of
their leader a few are copied as indicative of the zeal and
earnestness of the young writer. The names of the class
are also given. They were :

Townsend,	Holgate,	Field,	Hamilton (F.),
Wright,	Ramsey,	Robbins,	Blocker,
Washington,	Drumm,	Burton,	Chapman,
Graves,	Twining,	Nelson,	Adams,
Meigs,	Smith (C.),	Dixon,	Warner,
Butler,	Clark,	Russell,	Dutton,
Phipps,	Buchanan,	Smith (J.),	Farquhar,
Michie,	King (W.),	Murray,	Harris,
Henry (Guy),	Upton,	Hoxton,	Kirby.
Dresser,	Benjamin,	Counselman,	

Cadet Upton, afterward General Upton, was among
the first to attend. He was a devoted Christian, and his

name appears oftenest in connection with petitions.
Here are several of his, which read as follows :

" The prayers of the meeting are requested for a room-mate.
                    (Signed)   " CADET UPTON."

" Prayers are requested for two near relatives.
                              " CADET UPTON."

And again, on June 11th, 1860 :

" The prayers of the meeting are requested for its individual members during the ensuing encampment.
                    (Signed)   " CADET UPTON."

Between Lieutenant Howard and this young cadet there existed the warmest attachment and the heartiest co-operation in their religious work. A letter (dated October, 1860) from Upton to his instructor shows the confidential relations existing between them and the unusual religious fervor of the young man. He is speaking of the death of his brother, and he tells his friend that " he took great interest in religion, and died glorifying God ; after he had told my mother that his hands were cold and that he was dying, he would not relinquish the hand of a neighbor until he had promised to meet him in heaven. His charge to me was that I should delay no longer my preparation for eternity." Speaking of his return from the funeral, he continues : " I read the Bible more attentively, and then resorted to prayer. I continued my efforts until I experienced relief." After attendance at the prayer-meeting he says : " I feel a closer communion with God, and then I enjoy prayer. . . . I look forward to the time when I can show forth my faith more in works. In whatever capacity I may serve, I hope to do good and advance the cause of Christ. . . . I believe in God ; I believe in Christ, and I pray for the time when I shall know no doubt, and when I shall have a steadfast faith in all of God's promises. I ask your prayers that I may continue faithful unto the end, and that I may ever remain a true and humble follower of Christ."

Extracts from Howard's diary will reveal the inner life of the young officer while engaged in his public duties as instructor of mathematics at the academy.

"*Friday, Oct.* 2, 1857.—What is wanting ? More heart, more love, more of the Holy Spirit. I almost listened with pleasure to things said about a lady that will do me no good ; found myself gradually drawn into the man-fearing, praise-loving vortex. How far my spirit gets from my Redeemer ! To-day I went to the Soldiers' Hospital, and visited a young man of the Engineer Company by the name of Haviland, who has the consumption. I talked with him on the subject of his soul's salvation, and tried to draw him to the true Saviour. But I did not read or pray with him. He seemed pleased at my visit, and asked me to come again. I promised to visit him and bring him things to read."

"*October* 7, 1857.—I find the labor of the section-room rather trying to my lungs, but am getting on admirably in my duties. Lizzie and I spent some little time after I returned from recitations in making calls. This afternoon I took little Guy and went to Cold Spring in a small rowboat. Guy enjoyed the row, and particularly enjoyed the sight of hens, dogs, and pigs that he saw in the streets of the town.

" I don't want to do anything else before looking to God for His blessing in the morning. We must try to systematize a little. This evening I went to a prayer-meeting under the hill. We had nine or ten souls only, and a very pleasant season of praying and singing. We must persevere till we get a large audience. God bless our efforts and sanctify our hearts."

"*August* 8, 1857.—A day to be remembered. Saw Haviland ; he, poor fellow ! seems to be failing ; may God bless him ; and may he not have the saving grace ? I read him some of God's promises to him who turns from sin, a letter in the life of Captain Vicars, and prayed in his room by his bedside. This evening Lizzie and I visited Mr. French and his family. Mr. French came to the hotel with us, and talked and prayed with us in the north parlor. Lizzie has resolved to be baptized next Sunday, and his conversation was preparatory. . . . God be near us through this night. May we continue to turn from sin and strengthen our faith at the foot of the throne."

" WEST POINT, N. Y.

"*October* 11.—Lizzie was baptized at the chapel to-day by Mr.
French. The ceremony was very impressive. . . . I had a pretty
full Sunday-school to day. Went to see Haviland, and prayed with
him. He seems low indeed. Attended prayers this afternoon, the
Methodist Church this evening. Heard a sermon from the text, 'He
that will confess me before men, him will I confess before my Father
which is in heaven.' I spoke to the people after the sermon, and appointed a prayer-meeting and lecture for Wednesday night. I have
had a pretty active day and much Christian enjoyment. It is after
half-past ten. Will God bless the ordinances, services, and sermons
of this day to our soul's good? May the Saviour become more precious to Lizzie and myself !"

"*Friday, Oct.* 23.—We seem quite retired here, just after moving
into the little cottage. A little house, a little wife, and two little children constitute a very pleasant family. It is after ten. I am so
happy here I fear I shall not at all times think it gain to depart and be
with Christ. But let me say always, ' Not as I will, but as Thou
wilt.' I did my usual duties to-day ; wrote a letter to Charles this
evening."

"*October* 24.—In the afternoon I went to see Haviland, but he was
asleep, and I did not waken him."

"*Sunday, Oct.* 25, 1857.—I did not visit Haviland. Will the Lord
be gracious and merciful and long-suffering toward him? Lizzie and
I have been searching the Scriptures together. She told me how she
enjoyed communion with God while I was away. She is reading the
life of Hedley Vicars. We are very happy now. Our joys are not all
in the future. We know that God is merciful and gracious. Together
we embrace the privilege of going to Him in prayer. Our children
are all we could wish them, and they are to us not the least of the
bounties of our Heavenly Father's bestowing. May we love them, but
not supremely. May we. enjoy them as precious gifts, but never
idolize. God gives us wisdom and strength."

" WEST POINT, N. Y.

"*November* 1 (*All Saints' Day*), 1857.—I had the happiness of partak-
ing the Lord's Supper for the first time to-day, and with my wife—
this being also her first time. . . . To-day, after the second lesson,
they (the children) were carried forward for baptism. . . . Now we
have all been baptized, and I trust God will give His blessing, that
we may bring up the children in the right way and be able early to
present them to the Church as worthy members. God grant that

they both be made useful in His kingdom! . . . This has been a bright day ; the sun has shone—first communion to Lizzie and me, and the baptism of our children. Thank the Lord, oh my soul !"

"*Sunday, Nov.* 8, 1857.—My birthday has passed—twenty-seven years old to-day. It has been a glorious Sabbath to me. My heart has been much in communion with the Spirit. I had a joyous morning service ; listened to a delightful sermon from Mr. French on faith ; had a very good attendance at Sabbath-school ; visited Haviland at the hospital, and found him more disposed to listen to Christian truth than he seemed to be before ; had a meeting of the Methodists this evening."

"*Friday, Nov.* 20, *Cottage.*—Drum-Major William J. Skinner came in for me to explain the Scriptures. . . . Poor Haviland is gone! He said he died in peace. Thank the Lord for His mercy."

"*Saturday, Nov.* 21, 1857.—Went to Haviland's funeral ; tried to enter into the circumstances of his death with more heart. . . . I have detected myself in many a selfish mood to-day. I desire too much worldly credit. Oh, that I might be more constantly under the influence of my Saviour, and be prepared at any moment to go to meet Him ! I don't like to have doubts as to the work of grace in my heart ; I don't want to be deceiving myself as I do by words. O Lord, help me to gain strength and manliness in the Christian character !"

"*Saturday, Dec.* 19, 1857.—Mr. Greble (lieutenant and classmate) came to visit us. I walked to his room, and we conversed together on the subject of religion. Oh, I would like to have him become a Christian, and may he not? O Lord, show me Thy mercy, and take not Thy Holy Spirit from me !"

"*Sunday, Dec.* 27, 1857.—Christmas was a lovely day. Aunt, Lizzie, and I went to the church ; listened to a beautiful and spiritual sermon from Mr. French. His appeals to the young men are faithful, earnest, and strong. The service, the singing, the trimming of the church—all were excellent. Lizzie and I enjoyed the communion. How delightful to go to the table of our Lord ! To-day I have had the usual exercises. The Sunday-school increases in interest. Mr. Tannatt (afterward General Tannatt, of Massachusetts), a cadet of the first class, came to help us. May God bless him !"

"*Thursday, Jan.* 28, 1858.—I have spent this evening in writing to my friend P., and I pray my Heavenly Father to bless the letter to the awakening of his soul. Give me the power, O my Saviour, to feel more deeply for my friends and companions ! Wilt Thou, I beseech Thee, make me an instrument in Thy hands for the salvation of those with whom I am connected? Help me to walk humbly before

Thee. Cleanse me from all unrighteousness. Oh, deepen the work
of grace that Thou in Thy mercy hast begun !"

"*Friday, Jan.* 29, 1858.—I met my Bible-class to-night at the hospital. We prayed together. Considered the subject of sin, and
branched off into various directions. Oh, I pray that I may be led
to say the truth, and nothing but the truth, at these meetings! I
received great encouragement to persevere. Graham was there. He
kept silent the most of the time. I don't know that he spoke once.
God grant that he may find the light as it is. . . ."

"*Monday, March* 8, 1858.—Lizzie and I have been home ; children
asleep. The girls gone to Buttermilk Falls, and not returned now, at
eleven ; a cold, starry night. Lizzie and I have taken turns at reading 'English Hearts and Hands.' We find much that is pleasant
and much that is encouraging in the book, for these little sketches
show what a field of labor is open to the humblest Christian, and
how very much may be accomplished by persevering effort when one
trusts in God. It shows us how ignorant are the proud and haughty
of a real source of enjoyment in this world."

"*Thursday, March* 16.—On my way home from church Lieutenant
Alexander overtook me, and came home with me. He gave me two
books to be used for doing good in the Christian cause. He also gave
me five dollars to be expended in the way I thought would best pro-
mote the salvation of souls. A. remained with us, and talked a good
deal about religion. He wants to be thought by his men to be on
the Lord's side, that they may come to him for religious sympathy
on the expedition [to the extreme frontier] upon which he is going
with them. Last night I visited Graham, and found him in a good
mood. We talked long together, read the second chapter of Colos-
sians, and united in prayer. He prayed fervently. I tried to direct
him more and more fully to Christ. To-night a young Mr. C., who
has been seeking religion for some time, but don't feel satisfied of
this change of heart, has been talking with us, and Lizzie and I have
been directing him as best we could how to find peace in believing.
O Lord, my Redeemer, show him the way !"

"*Wednesday, April* 21.—Lizzie and I went to walk this evening,
about five o'clock, toward Cro'nest. When we had been gone nearly
an hour the girl, Mary, met us opposite the Cadets' Garden, and said
the baby was sick, very sick. Lizzie and I started to run, and I out-
ran her and almost lost my breath. When I got to the house I found
Mrs. Weir holding the baby. She extended her to me, and said,
' Your dear little lamb.' She was as white as a sheet, froth and r
little blood around her mouth. I put my finger in her mouth, and

instantly removed from her throat one of Guy's marbles, that had remained there for half an hour. Mary had first gone for the doctor to the Cadets' Hospital before she started for us. Grace soon got better, though she looked very pale for some time. The Lord reminds us thus that we must hold His gifts as from Himself, and when He calls and demands His own we should be ready to surrender."

Letter to his Mother.

" WEST POINT, May 23, 1859.

" . . . We have had a nice visit from Rowland (Rev. R. B. Howard). He spoke Sunday evening a week ago at the Camptown Chapel, and made some remarks there on Wednesday evening ; went once to my cadet prayer-meeting, and yesterday, all day, officiated for Rev. Mr. Gray, the Presbyterian minister at the Falls, and preached for him a funeral sermon a mile and a half below the Falls. His discourses were very good, and I trust left a deep impression on many of the hearers. In public Rowland seems possessed of a most excellent spirit, and wins by the kindness and gentleness of his manner. I hope God will continue to bless and prosper him. Before he left this morning I had rheumatism in my knee, but it has all left me now. I got myself damp, and the weather changed suddenly. I am sorry to hear that Charles is not better in health. . ., . It will not be long before we shall be with you. We are talking of going by the way of Niagara and Montreal. The children are pretty well. . . . A few are manifesting an interest in religion, but not many, I fear. You cannot think how delightful West Point now is on a pleasant day, and how rich the scenery, unless your memory is vivid. Goodnight. With much affection,

" Your son,

" O. O. HOWARD."

"*September* 1, 1858.—We had family prayers this morning, and shall have this evening before retiring. I think I enjoy much of the presence of God's Spirit, and feel myself conformed to His will. 'It is the Lord, let Him do what seemeth Him good.' Now I have two new sections in mathematics. I trust I shall struggle harder than ever before to do justice and lead a Christian life before them. . . ."

"*September* 2.—Speaking of an engineer soldier who had just died, the officer's letter before me does not say anything of his religious views and feelings before being launched into eternity ; but it may be that God brought the hours when we met for prayer and the lessons we learned home to his soul. ' He died at the hospital of

the Sixth Infantry, and was buried at the next camping ground.'
I presume by this that it was a moving hospital. . . ."

"*September* 5.—L. and myself had quite a conversation to-night.
She thinks me full of extremes—impulsive and impatient—and I
think she is partially, if not wholly, right. We prayed God for union
of heart and spirit in Christ. I am not close enough in my walk to
Christ. I think too much of myself ; am growing dry, I fear. Oh,
keep me from coldness and lukewarmness !"

"*September* 6, 1858.—The superintendent declined to give me permission to meet the young men in the Dialectic Hall, and said he
must provide me some other place, which he has not yet done. I
thought of meeting them in one of the recitation rooms, but there
being no gas obtained from the fixtures, we postponed our meeting
till Thursday. I hope we will be able to hold our prayer-meeting
again for my benefit, as well as for the cadets."

"*September* 8.—This evening I delivered the address I have been
preparing (in connection with the event of William Slayter's death)
at the little church. There was quite a good attendance. Norris
and his daughter seemed very much affected. Would that they
might give their hearts to Christ !"

"*September* 9.—We opened our cadet prayer-meeting this evening in
one of the rooms in the barracks. I read a portion of Scripture, the
fifty-fourth chapter of Isaiah ; then Mr. Wright led in prayer. After
his prayer, which was a fervent supplication for mercy upon his companions, I read a few passages from a book of sermons, said a few
words, and then we had two prayers. I asked if any one had a word
to say, and a young man who had just come among us arose and
spoke of his peculiar trials and temptations, and asked for our
prayers. He said he was but a young convert. I spoke a few words
of encouragement, telling him we had more for us than against us,
for God is on our side. Again we all united in prayer, as the call of
the bugle blew. Such is a brief sketch of the half hour at the prayer-
meeting. O Lord, have mercy upon us and make our little meeting
for prayer especially beneficial to our souls !"

"*Tuesday, Sept.* 14.— . . . Speaking of Cadet Kingsbury, whom I
visited in hospital ; he is an intelligent young man, and, I should
think, with more than ordinary ability. I would be glad to have his
influence in the cause of Christ."

"*Saturday, Sept.* 18, 1858.—Wednesday evening we had a good
attendance at lecture. Our new choir did admirably, though I neglected to give out the hymns as desired. I lectured on the first of
the ten commandments. I pray that God will bless these lectures

to my benefit, as well as to that of those to whom they are addressed. Thursday evening we had a full prayer-meeting with the cadets. I read them a tract on the ten lepers. We had the pleasure of having two voices new to us. We need the blessing of God upon every effort for promoting the kingdom of Christ. . . ."

"*September* 20.—It is now one year since I came to this post as an instructor. Am I much advanced in the grace and knowledge of Christ ? I find my rebellious heart so ready with its own ways and projects that I tremble. . . ."

"*September* 25.—The week is drawing to a close. I heard early in the week that poor Graham had yielded to the tempter, and begun to drink ; he has succeeded in keeping out of my way. I went to see his poor wife yesterday. She says it is only since he went on a pass, about two weeks since, that he has got in a bad way. He has prayed with her, and she has never been happier than since they have lived here. He has not been seen for two days, and must have deserted. It is all due to liquor. May God have mercy on the poor insane man !"

"*October* 7.—Thursday evening prayer-meeting ; good attendance. Read Bushwell on the confession of Christ. We prayed for the aid of God's Spirit to destroy the profane spirit in the corps ; we continue to pray for the cadets. God will give His blessing at the proper time."

"*Wednesday, Oct.* 6.—Careless in losing proper self-government. Ruled myself pretty well at recitation. Came near getting impatient to-day ; checked myself in time. I fear my policy in procuring quarters is too selfish. I must make sacrifices of comfort for the sake of others."

"*Sunday, Oct.* 17.—I have had a good Sabbath. Mr. French's morning sermon very good ; from the text, ' Love the Lord thy God with all thy heart,' etc.

" This evening I went to Buttermilk Falls ; called at Mr. Gray's ; addressed a roomful at the Methodist chapel on the new life. I hope God will bless the efforts to the good of some. Walked back with Mr. Morrison and Mr. Clark (Edward) ; had religious conversation with them. Mr. C. is with me ; we talked about various things in connection with religion. Oh, my Saviour, that I might be now as true-hearted as the words I write seem to imply ! Help me to be less thoughtful and talkative of self. Mr. C. and I read and prayed together."

"*Monday, Oct.* 18.— . . . On my return I met Lieutenant M. ; we had a long conversation ; asked me about my religion, and talked about the want of it, even in the chaplains on the frontier. The chaplain at Fort Leavenworth makes ' *toddies* ' for the sitters at the gaming-table, etc. In New Mexico they have no religion ; gambling and all manner of corrupt practices a common thing on the Sabbath. . . ."

" *Wednesday, Oct.* 20.—We had the very interesting ceremony of the baptism of a little child, at my little church, by Mr. French this evening. The house was quite full. The little innocent was beautiful, and did not cry, and looked very pretty in Mr. French's arms as he put the water on him and signed him with the cross. After the ceremony Mr. French left. I was sorry, because I wanted him to see what sort of discourses I delivered ; but maybe there is pride in the wish. The Rev. Mr. Parker was present. He made some remarks after the address ; complimented me very highly. I don't need any compliments but to know that souls are being led to God, and ought not to receive any. We can easily get the applause of men ; but how much better is the approbation of our Lord and Saviour ! . . ."

" *Sunday, Oct.* 30.—We had our usual family exercises this morning ; after family prayers I went to the Soldiers' Hospital, talked a little with three sick soldiers (now very sick), and gave them tracts. I got a German youth who used to belong to my Bible-class to come again to Sunday-school. . . . I then started for the Falls ; overtook a large boy and a little one on the road ; little boy had a man's hat on the top of his cap. He looked quite bright, and I began to question him. He was learning the Catholic catechism ; did not know of the Saviour. I chatted with him, pointed to a star, and told him about the star that went before the wise men ; both boys listened quite attentively. I told them how men treated Christ ; how He died, and how He had risen and ascended up to God. The little boy didn't think he could remember all I had told him. He said he swore sometimes. I told him he must not any more. It seemed to be a new thing to the boy to be talked to in this way."

" *November* 7.—Went to evening prayers at chapel ; mind wandering much during service. I conducted the service, and addressed the people at the Methodist chapel under the hill, on the first commandment. The house pretty well filled. Congregation very attentive. My Saviour seemed to draw near to me and bless the lecture—I mean the delivery and subsequent remarks. What a beautiful day is this Sabbath ! How different from those Sabbaths before God called me into His fold !"

" *Saturday, Nov.* 27, 1858.—Another week has drawn to a close. I have been through the same routine duties during tho past week as heretofore. How many thousand words have been spoken ! How much has gone forth never to return till the day of accounts ! O God, cause the words of my mouth and the meditations of my heart to be acceptable in Thy sight ! O Lord, my Strength and my Redeemer !"

"*December* 13.—I obtained the ' Higher Life ' through the Rev. Mr. Gray at the Falls, and Lizzie and I have been reading it attentively, thoughtfully. It has indeed sent a thrill of joy into my heart and been the means of smoothing much rough ground within me. Sunday night, at our evening prayer, after spending a portion of the evening upon the subject of ' a second conversion,' or ' a full salvation,' my heart became full of great gladness ; and the peculiar peace was more than usual. How glorious the Lord is ! How abundant in His bestowments ! I thank Thee, O my God ! that Thou hast blessed, that Thou art blessing, and that Thou wilt continue to bless me ; for such is Thy good pleasure. I will endeavor to bear in mind Thy infinite mercy and loving-kindness, in the imparting to my soul such knowledge of Jesus my Saviour, and Jesus my Sanctifier, so as to render Him all in all. Oh, let me, my insignificant self, be absorbed altogether in the brightness of His image, and fit me for thine own work by helping me to live every moment of my life by faith in the Son of God !"

"*February* 3, 1859.—Last Sunday morning we had a sermon from Rev. Dr. Henry, Episcopal clergyman, a right manly, out-and-out discourse, showing the reason why a man should do right and avoid the wrong—' *because it is right, and not do wrong because it is wrong.*' He attacked that prevalent philosophy with directness and success, which makes a subtle selfishness the procuring cause, the motive of goodness. After church I visited him, and thinking, from his boldness and informal declaration of the truth, a discourse from him might awaken some of the frequenters of the Camptown Chapel, I invited him to go there in the evening. He went, and delivered a most excellent and affectionate discourse on the love, character, goodness of God as exhibited in the gracious invitations set forth in a chapter of the prophet Isaiah that he read. Dr. Henry is eccentric, full of humor, telling anecdotes continually in private, and replete with pointed illustrations in his public discourse. I like him very much, for I believe he has a large heart, and loves his blessed Master. . . . How plainly poor Reed's case shows the necessity of a previous preparation for death ! He says he don't rely much on a

death-bed change ; but I told him he did not know it was his death-
bed. He said, ' True,' and I urged him to give himself to Christ for
life or for death. . . .''

"*February* 8.—Poor Reed died Saturday evening at half-past five,
and was buried yesterday at three P.M. Tuesday night I watched
with him. He grew gradually weaker. I did not see him again
after Wednesday morning. He had the most assiduous attention of his wife, the family, and his friends. His death seemed
to cast a gloom over the corps of cadets. Both brothers were
with him. I wrote Monday, before the funeral, an account of the
conversations I had with him, in the form of a letter, to his
mother. His eldest brother thought it would be a pleasure to
her to have them. His wife bore up wonderfully under the trial.
She went to the chapel and to the grave. The whole service was
completed at the chapel, and the band played there in the gallery,
and did not accompany the remains to the grave. Early, just having
entered upon his career, he was cut off ; but God, who doeth all things
well, will bring the blessing He has in store. Oh, that it be the salvation of the entire family ! Oh, that it be the will of God to bring
those brothers, who have such tender hearts, to the truth as it is in
Jesus ! . . .''

"*Monday, Feb.* 14, 1859.— . . . Good prayer-meeting with cadets ;
nearly all the seats filled. I read a piece on decision of character and
the first chapter of Timothy. I made some remarks on the besetting
sins of the army, particularly drunkenness and gambling. I be-
sought the young men to lay a good, solid foundation in principle,
for they would need it. I got ' Thomas à Kempis' in Latin. Have
read a little of the sketch of his life, a chapter of his sayings, and a
chapter in St. John in Latin this evening. We have had our evening prayer, and now for bed.''

"*Wednesday, Feb.* 23, 1859.— . . . Saturday evening, just before
night, I visited Mrs. Cashman (wife of Sergeant Cashman), who has
the cancer. She can scarcely eat, or sleep, or talk ; is in a terribly
hopeless condition. I talked to her, read a portion of Scripture, and
prayed with her. I had a little talk with Colonel H. this evening.
He is almost persuaded to be a Christian. Miss Maria has some
troublesome doubts of her acceptance ; we have been talking about
them. I trust they will be removed. . . .''.

"*March* 8, 1859.— . . . Mrs. Morrison lies very ill. I have visited
her several times. She can scarcely speak or move, but her trust is
clear and unswerving in Jesus. She says, 'His grace is sufficient
for me ;' 'I put all my trust in Him,' and the like expressions.

She has four little girls ; the eldest does not seem more than eight or nine years."

"*Sunday, March* 20.—In the morning we breakfasted a little after eight. After family prayer I took the 'Lily of the Valley' of à Kempis, given me by Professor Weir for Mrs. Cashman, and went to see her. She was in bed, and did not seem in much pain from the cancer, and I thought appeared more cheerful than when I first visited her. I inquired particularly if she had an interest in Christ ; if she loved Him and trusted Him. She said something about a want of the inward witness of the Spirit. She believes in Jesus, but doubts her own acceptance. I talked to her as best I could, read a portion of Scripture, and prayed. The sergeant came in just before the prayer. He seemed grateful for my attentions to his wife in her suffering. I then went to the Soldiers' Hospital ; sat and talked with Saunders, a soldier. . . .

" To-day, Thursday, the 31st of March (1859), is rather windy weather, and cold. I have done little to-day ; had a good cadets' prayer- and reading-meeting ; one new face. I am reading ' The Shadow of the Cross.' My own religious views perplex me. I find I am certain only on a few points. I think, however, Jesus will take care of me."

" *Wednesday, April* 4, 1859.— . . . After the prayer was said in unison at the cadets' prayer-meeting, Cadet Upton made a short prayer—I expect the first he ever made in public. I was exceedingly rejoiced. He stopped back after the rest had left. Said his brother had died in joy, and invited him to meet him in heaven. Oh, these brothers, whom God has called into His vineyard ! Mr. W. told me he had made a practice of reading two chapters in the Bible every day. God has rewarded him, and will bless him. O'Hearn (sapper) I visited this evening at the Soldiers' Hospital. He bled much last night. He thanked me heartily for my visit, and I saw the tears in his eyes after the prayer when he invited me to come again. . . ."

" *Wednesday, April* 6.—I visited the hospital this evening. O'Hearn, poor fellow ! continues to bleed ; I saw the blood on his lips and in the spittoon. It made me feel badly to see him. He is cheerful and resigned, and I think has his trust in the right place. He asked me if anything should happen and he sent for me if I would come. I told him ' Certainly,' for I saw he meant death might visit him soon. I tried to get ' L.' to do me a great favor. I asked him, as a personal favor to me, not to drink liquor any more—certainly nothing stronger than beer. He said he would not. I lectured this evening on ' The Christian's Hope ;' there were more soldiers out than usual. I said some hard things (to hear), but I hope the truth frankly spoken may do some good. I am still apt to think myself of some considerable importance. Oh, that I might give my whole heart continually to the Lord !''

"*Saturday Night, April 9.*— . . . I am not abstemious enough in the use of food. I fear if God should give me success with my heart as it is now, that I should be puffed with pride, and thus lose the countenance of my blessed Saviour. I am conscious that I do not make a good warfare against the world, the flesh, and the devil. But blessed be God who giveth us the victory through our Lord Jesus Christ! Jesus, will He not bring us off conquerors ?''

"*March* 15, 1861.—Poor Dr. Gray has gone to his reward. He died at Syracuse. . . . I carried the news of his death to his poor feeble wife and his daughter yesterday. . . Two cadets have found Jesus precious to them and been baptized, and I understand that over a hundred souls have been converted here and at the Falls, among those with whom it has been my privilege to work.

". . . I am ever indulging in complacency, thinking of what I am doing, speaking of it. I see and name the failings of others. I find pride, vanity ; don't think I am as kind as I ought to be in recitations, yet I am blessed with much peace of mind, and hate to be brought into subjection by these things. Appetite and passion keep getting the mastery of me; but I love the Lord Jesus Christ, and hope He will keep me from denying Him in the words of my mouth and in the meditations of my heart, and that He will finally help me conquer every wicked thought and resist every temptation of the devil."

"*May* 2, 1859.— . . . Last Wednesday evening I delivered a lecture on the subject of ' Grace,' and last night on the second miracle of Jesus at Cana ; had a fair attendance and good attention. I do hope and pray that the work of grace may show itself among us abundantly, but I don't know as I have the right notions prompting this wish. I have finished the life of Payson, and am reading Cotton Mather's ' History of New England ' aloud to Lizzie. It is very interesting, and I hope will prove useful to me. . . ."

"*October* 6.— . . . Mrs. Cashman (sergeant's wife, who has been sick so long with a cancer) died Sunday ; has gone to sleep in Jesus. Sunday morning she told me she understood the Scripture I read her, and said she was waiting patiently. She put her whole trust and confidence in Jesus, she said, the Friday before. I have visited her regularly every Sunday morning since she has been so very ill, and read and prayed with her, and I think God has made me the humble instrument in leading her to put her trust in Jesus. . . .''

"*November* 8, 1859.—My twenty-ninth birthday is just drawing to its close. God grant that I may be more truly consecrated to His service this year than last. My besetting sin is the love of the praise of men. I am in danger continually of contemplating my own work with complacency. Oh, my Infinite Helper, what is any effort of mine but air without thine assistance !"

"*Sunday, Nov.* 27, 1859.—A shade of gloom has been cast over West Point during the past week. Lieutenant Weitzel, of the Engineers, a short time ago went to Cincinnati and brought back a youthful bride. Last Wednesday, when he was in the hotel office, he heard a scream up-stairs, and immediately ran toward his room. In the hall he met his wife and others, the flames completely enveloping her and rising above her head. As soon as possible the fire was extinguished, but she was so dreadfully burned that she lingered only till the next evening. She was of German extraction, a member of the Lutheran Church, and seemed in her suffering to have a sense of the presence and power of the grace of God. She was perfectly happy, and said she was going to a ' better home.' Her husband seems to look upon her death like a Christian. I hope he may realize the true end of sorrow. Oh, prepare him to meet his wife in heaven !'

"*January* 9, 1860.—Yesterday, about noon, Lieutenant Holabird [now Quartermaster-General] lost his oldest child, a beautiful little girl. To-day we followed her little coffin to the grave, where Mr. French, with his wonted earnest solemnity, pronounced the last solemn words over her mortal remains. The officers were nearly all present, and showed every mark of kind and respectful sympathy with their afflicted brother-in-arms. . . . At the Sunday-school and at the cadets' prayer-meeting this evening prayers were offered for the afflicted parents."

Recording the death of Lieutenant E. H. Day, in Richmond, Va., he says :

"*January* 10, 1860.—Day and I were together in Florida, and had many conversations upon religion before I was fully a Christian. I wrote him once after, telling of what a Saviour I had found. I got one reply. I saw him once afterward, and am hoping he gave his whole heart to the Lord before his removal. Day had a warm heart and noble sentiments. He was a true friend and a modest gentleman."

"*March* 30, 1860.—Brought me a good letter from Lieutenant O. A. Mack [afterward General Mack], now become an earnest helper in

the vineyard of the Lord.   This letter brought to me these first joyful
tidings.''

Lieutenants Mack and Howard were room-mates in
Florida.

"*September* 23, 1860.—Stood as sponsor for little Clara French
Greble, daughter of Lieutenant John T. and Mrs Sallie Greble.   O
Lord, help us to be truly interested for the salvation of this child !
Without Thee, my Saviour, I can do nothing."

Colonel Greble, the classmate and friend of General
Howard, was the first regular officer to fall in the war of
the rebellion, at Big Bethel, Va.

III.

THE darkest days of the nation's history now dawned. The Civil War had come—that period which had been constantly predicted for thirty years by the extremists of both sides. The people were agitated as never before in the history of the United States. The inevitable bitterness between the sections was fast developing into violence, and the opponents were enrolling themselves for the coming strife for supremacy. Army officers were the first to feel the effects of the changed condition of public affairs ; their profession necessarily placed them in the front, and the country looked with no little anxiety to see what course they would pursue in the crisis. Many resigned and hastened to avow their allegiance to their separate States ; others resigned from the regular army to take commands of higher rank, with volunteer organizations, and not a few waited, watching the course of events. These changed so rapidly that men of every class were in doubt as to the effect of any step. Meantime the outlook was gloomy ; army ties were being broken rapidly ; friends were parting, not perhaps to feel personal hostility to each other, but to become public enemies. Those who had been comrades in social life were separating to appear on opposite sides of the conflict, and everywhere men's minds were absorbed in

the troubles of their country. Lieutenant Howard pon-
dered the situation with much concern ; certain religious
convictions (those looking to the ministry) came into
conflict with what he conceived to be his duty to his
country. He reflected much after the first gun had been
fired at Sumter. The government had educated him
at its expense for such an emergency as had now come ;
he had pledged himself to serve his country's flag.
Should he forget his training ? Should he belie his
pledge ? His brothers from the South claimed the right
of secession and adherence to their native States. There
was no such call on Howard. His course thus became
clear ; his heart responded to the voice of duty. He
was prepared to fight for the integrity of the American
Union, and the religion of his soul supported the decision
of his intellect.

Obtaining a temporary leave of absence from West
Point, he answered in person the call of his compatriots
in Maine. Mr. Blaine, then the Speaker of the Maine
House, presented his name for the colonelcy of the first
three years' regiment, the Third Maine, one thousand
strong, and he received his commission from Governor
Washburne, dated the 28th of May, 1861. He had
left West Point on a leave of absence, but before
he received his commission he tendered his resignation as an officer of the regular army, and sent a
friend to West Point to inform his wife and accompany her to New York. Mrs. Howard, in her home
at the Point, heard a gentleman at the door inquiring if Colonel Howard lived there. Instantly the whole
truth flashed upon her : her husband had accepted an appointment in the volunteer army, and would not return
to the academy. Hasty preparations were made, and
soon she was *en route* to meet him, with her three little

children, and to say good-by for an indefinite time. On the 5th of June the regiment left Augusta, and reaching New York the next day, Colonel Howard met his family at the Astor House.

Lord Melville once declared in Parliament that "bad men make the best soldiers." Vicars, in answering a similar argument, made by a fellow-officer who opposed his religious work among the privates, said : "Were I ever, as leader of a forlorn hope, allowed to select my men, it would be most certainly from among the soldiers of Christ ; for who should fight so fearlessly and bravely as those to whom death presents no after terrors ?"

Colonel Howard believed, with Hedley Vicars, the better the man, the better the soldier, and when introduced to his regiment by Mr. Blaine, in front of the Capitol at Augusta, he rather shocked the feelings of some of his hearers by plainly emphasizing his abhorrence of intemperance and profanity. He declared that no man could do his duty under the influence of liquor, and asserted his aversion to profanity, especially in soldiers, who, he believed, needed divine favor above other men. The majority of the newly-enlisted men looked upon a soldier's life as one entirely free from restraint, and many murmured at the Puritanical views of their new colonel. They did not applaud him with the spirit they would have manifested had he shown himself less a disciplinarian and more a maker of fine compliments. But later, when they realized his sterling worth and sincere interest in them, they trusted him, and would have followed him into any danger.

When passing through New York, a silken banner was presented to the regiment, and the officers were entertained at a public dinner given at the Astor House. In his speech accepting the flag, which was presented by

Assistant District-Attorney Stewart L. Woodford, in the old White Street arsenal, Colonel Howard said :

"I was born in the East, but I was educated by my country. I know no section ; I know no party, and I never did. I know only my country to love it, and my God that is over my country. We go forth to battle, and we go in defence of righteousness and liberty, civil and religious. We go strong in muscle, strong in soul, because we are right. I have endeavored to live in all good conscience before God, and I go to battle without flinching, because the same God that has given His Spirit to direct me has shown me that our cause is righteous ; and I could not be better placed than I am now, for He has given me the warm hearts of as noble a regiment as the United States has produced."

At the dinner given to the officers of the regiment Colonel Howard's temperance convictions were characteristically illustrated. The company, consisting of some of New York's best-known citizens, proposed to pledge him in a bumper. All rose. The guest of the evening took up his glass of water, and made this brief response to the toast :

"Gentlemen, our country is in peril ; I go at its call to do my duty. The true beverage of a soldier is cold water , in this I pledge you."

Every wine-glass was put down, and the toast was drunk in water.

He had not intended to influence the actions of others, and was somewhat disconcerted when he saw the effect of his words. Absorbed in the serious duties before him, and solemnly impressed with the responsibility he had undertaken, his intensity of feeling had led him into what he feared his kind hosts would look upon as a breach of etiquette, despite the hearty approval of his course, conveyed through the medium of applause.

Mrs. Howard, with her little children, accompanied her husband to the depot, and while crossing the river she was introduced to the officers of the regiment. Mr. Woodford, who was one of the party, presented the children of their colonel to the regiment, and the men, fresh from their own firesides, gathered about the little boy and girl seated on either of Mr. Woodford's shoulders. War was a new experience awaiting the soldier, and their hearts were easily moved by reminders of family and home, now forsaken for an uncertain fate. The future seemed darkly outlined on the political horizon, and departures of troops were occasions of sadness.

After bidding her husband farewell, Mrs. Howard went to Augusta, Me., to reside, choosing that city because it was the home of the majority of the officers and many of the soldiers of the regiment. She desired to be with the families of the men who had gone with her husband to the war.

The arrival in Washington of Colonel Howard and his gray-clad men was greeted with satisfaction by the anxious Secretary of War, who welcomed the coming of troops commanded by West Point officers. In sympathy with the homesickness of the men, who were enduring for the first time in their lives a soldier's fare, empty barracks, and cheerless meals, he gave the regiment a supper at Willard's Hotel. Army officers laughed at his sentiment, but the people of Maine loved him for his kind heart, and the generous governor had the bill paid by the State, saying that Howard had done enough in devising the thoughtful plan. The regiment was immediately put in training for the task before it, and the hard work of its colonel at once won the confidence of the men. Colonel T. W. Osborne, who was long of his staff, says that he never saw another officer so intensely solicitous for the care and welfare of his men at all times, that they should be clothed, fed, well en-

camped, not over-fatigued ; that they should not be
treated roughly by mounted officers riding along the line
of march, and that their moral and religious wants should
never be neglected.   It is needless to portray the toil
and anxiety he went through in those days of 1861.
Men were commissioned or enlisted fresh from the
fields, the shops, the schools, necessarily without the
knowledge or training of soldiers, and they were to be
physically remodelled and mentally brought under re-
striction and discipline.   This work the colonel had to
do, and shortly after his arrival and the pitching of his
tents on Meridan Hill, near the college, it was not
strange to see crowds witnessing the drills and parades of
this splendid regiment.   But the work and the effects of
a sudden change of climate and diet produced illness,
and in less than forty-eight hours he was at death's door
with camp cholera.   He owed his life to his splendid
physique.   His physician, Surgeon G. S. Palmer, said
of him that he had never found before such recuperative
energy in any system as in his.   In a few days he was
on his feet again and at his work.   Among the observers
of Colonel Howard's diligence in preparing his regiment
for the front was General Irvin McDowell, and one day,
after laughing at the prediction of an army friend that
he would be the first brigadier from Maine, he was the
recipient of a note from General McDowell, through the
War Department, directing him to select three other
regiments besides his own for his command.   He took
three Maine and one Vermont regiments, and this brigade formed a part of the hasty levees which McDowell
hurried into Virginia to meet Beauregard and Johnston
in the first large battle of the great war—that of Bull
Run—fought July 21st, 1861.
      Colonel Howard and his men stood ready that day,

according to orders, the latter burdened with their knapsacks, their ammunition, and their equipments, from half-
past two A.M. till the sun was an hour high. Many grew
faint and became ill, and at last, as the march began,
numbers sat down by the roadside, unable to go farther.
Forward the troops marched toward Sudley Springs,
halting *en route* within hearing of the continuous thunder of the heavy guns and the indescribable rattle of
distant musketry. At one time, as he sat on his horse
waiting for the order to enter the combat, Howard's
heart sank within him and his strength began to fail.
He realized the fact with a momentary feeling of mis-
giving, and then he prayed : " O God, help me and
enable me to do my duty!" The spell at once passed off,
and he was possessed of a cheerful calmness, which did
not leave him during that awful day. Orders came for
him to move his brigade as quickly as he could to the
relief of Heintzelman, and soon his men were hurrying
into their first battle. As they came nearer, the bomb-
shells bursting over their heads attesting the fierce work
going on, some showed signs of fear ; and Colonel Howard, to encourage them, halted at the head of his column,
and had his entire brigade pass by him as if in review.
The men looked up into his face, and reading the resolution and confidence expressed there, gave him an answering smile as they passed on to their places in the battle
line, followed by his silent prayers.

It will be found in the life of General Howard that
his more sterling qualities are brought to light in adver-
sity. When others are sorely troubled, he has his faith
strengthened by prayer ; and when there is really nothing
left but failure, he folds his hands serenely, and wears
that intense expression which indicates to his friends
upon what themes his thoughts are concentrated.

In the encampment, before marching for the battle-field, one who was present says of Howard :

"It was a solemn and impressive scene there on the hill-side, when Colonel Howard, Cromwell-like, assembled his brigade in four lines, facing toward the base of the slope on which they stood, and taking his place in front of them, with his chaplain at his side, in-dicated his wish to have them hear a prayer. Four thousand men uncovered their heads while the chaplain prayed, and when the prayer was ended the colonel addressed to them a few words of hope and counsel, and impressed upon them the necessity now for a com-plete trust in God, before whom they should be ever ready to ap-pear. The majority of the men could not understand one who was always prepared for a battle or a prayer-meeting, and who seemed to have no fear of consequences anywhere."

The Second Vermont Regiment in Howard's Brigade, after the first battle of Bull Run, was much attached to General Howard. After he had been promoted and left them, a deputation of non-commissioned officers, who had just been promoted, came to his headquarters and pre-sented him with a sword, sash, and belt. The sword bears the following inscription : *"Palmam qui meruit ferat. Tuum est."* * This sword has ever been treas-ured by General Howard, and has been used by him on frequent occasions since that day. During his visit to Europe in 1884, he wore this token of his comrades' affec-tion and respect, when representing the American army at the autumn manœuvres of the French forces.

The famous battle of Bull Run was fought on a Sun-day, and it produced a great sensation throughout the country. The outrage on its Christian feelings, because of the violation of the Sabbath, impressed the people with the dreadful horrors of war. The soldiers, once removed from the influences of home and old associa-tions, and other causes arising which need not be

* " Let him bear the palm who merits it ; it is thine."

detailed, went to extremes, and in consequence great demoralization prevailed among them. Subsequently, General McClellan tried to improve matters by issuing the following order :

" The major-general commanding desires and requests that in future there may be a more perfect respect for the Sabbath on the part of his command. We are fighting in a holy cause, and should endeavor to deserve the benign favor of the Creator. . . . One day's rest in seven is necessary to men and animals. More than this, the observance of the holy day of the God of mercy and of battles is our sacred duty."

The state of affairs which this order was intended to rectify was, as could be imagined, very galling to General Howard's feelings, and great was his satisfaction when it was issued by his chief. He has always admired its beautiful spirit, and being the first case of the kind, it made a lasting impression on his mind.

General McDowell, aware of the efforts made after the defeat of Bull Run by many officers to obtain promotion, and anxious to have Colonel Howard receive his star, went to the President, without prompting, and asked that it should be bestowed on him. Senator Fessenden, of Maine, also urged this recognition of merit, and on September 3d, 1861, he became a brigadier-general of volunteers.

General Howard was a constant correspondent, and his home circle retain many letters written from the field. A few excerpts from several penned during the gloomy summer of 1861 are permitted to be used, and are inserted here as giving a glimpse of his interior life.

To his Wife.

" WASHINGTON, D. C., June 11, 1861.
" Poor John Greble's death struck me like a thunderbolt this afternoon. It seems to have been a disastrous fight under incompetent

leaders. His parents, his wife, and the French's—what sorrow for all ! I remember now the relation I have assumed of godfather to little Clara. I recall the walks and talks that Johnny and I have had together, and sorrow fills my heart. '*Be ye also ready*' sounds plainly for you and me, darling. God must comfort them. I shall write Mrs. Greble as soon as I can have heart to do it. I hear also that Warren [afterward General Warren] is slain. I hope it is a mistake. To-night my band came to my tent and played a piece in honor of Lieutenant Greble, and the soldiers crowded around and heard what I said of him in great sorrow. . . ."

To Same.

" ALEXANDRIA, VA., Sunday, July 7, 1861.
" I hope I shall have a chance to go to church, a part of the day at least. Oh L., I should like to be at home to-day, where there is a different aspect of things from what we find here ! The city is gloomy indeed : nearly all the houses shut up ; beautiful residences deserted ; no business transacted, except what an army carries with it.

" Soldiers at the best are like locusts : fences and trees are consumed, and private property generally is much infringed upon. . . ."

To Same.

" SANGSTERS, July 18, 1861.
(Just before first Bull Run.)
"I wish we had men who had more regard for the Lord. We might then expect His blessing. . . ."

To Same.

" CENTREVILLE, VA., July 20, 1861.
" We haven't yet been in battle. The Lord will take care of us ; (but) if we were not so wicked He would not bring such disaster upon us as Tyler's defeat. . . . Above all, remember me constantly at the throne of grace. . . ."

To his Little Boy.

" BUSH HILL, VA., July 25, 1861.
(Just after Bull Run.)
" Mrs. Scott lives here with four little children. She asked your papa to conduct prayers this morning. The little ones repeated the Lord's Prayer after me, as you and Grace do, and it makes papa cry to think of it. Oh, my son, do love God and serve Him ! . . . May God bless and keep you all, for Christ's sake !"

To his Wife.

" August 1, 1861.

" Mr. M. wonders how I can be so completely engrossed with my official duties and say so little about my family, particularly when I have so interesting a family. I told him it was because I exercised faith in God, who is able to protect and care for them, and is willing to do so. I do pray to Him constantly for you, and Guy, and Grace, and little Jamie. I do regard you all as sacred treasures that will be kept in store for me, while I am trying to do my duty for my country. There are untold trials after a defeat. Everybody is sick in body or in heart. . . . Grumbling, fault finding, and charges against my officers come to me from every quarter ; but thus far my heart has been light. I try to do my duty as I have done heretofore, and don't worry. I think of Mrs. Greble and her dear little children often, and try to remember them in prayer. . . . There seems to be a want of principle and true patriotism among our friends. I don't know what we will come to."

To Same.

" August 8, 1861.

" There are over one hundred sick in each regiment. . . . They are quite well cared for, though it is rather sickening to go through that Clermont House, where there are so many poor fellows together. . . . I visited nearly every room last Sunday morning, and tried to say a word for my Saviour to them. Charles thinks we fall far short of living such lives as Vicars and Havelock did."

To Same.

" August 15, 1861

". . . I couldn't think of going home, as delightful as it would be, even if I could get a leave, after having refused so many poor soldiers. . . . Lieutenant M. thinks I have sweet little children, and so do I. God bless them and help them to grow up to do His will."

To a lady who wrote General Howard, with bitter complaints, after the Bull Run confusion, he says :

" August 24, 1861.

" I thank you for writing me just as you believed and felt. . . . Permit me to say that you have been entirely misinformed with regard to me by some one. [Then follows a full explanation of the causes of the destitution and other evils complained of.] I shall, dear madam, take the greatest pains to do my duty, and, as you say, ' God is my Judge.' I ask no better. I have worked for my command early and late. 1 have been without proper food and sleep, and sometimes I am weary—weary ; and then I am misrepresented and misunderstood ! Still, I believe the soldiers love me, and know that I have left no stone unturned to get them their dues.

" I am truly sorry for the unpopularity that awaits me in your section, but I have been unpopular before ; the thing that I want is to see the men provided for, contented and happy, and ready for duty. . . . My religion consists in striving to do my duty."

Referring to the plundering of the soldiers, in a letter to his wife dated August 25th, 1861, he says :

" You ask about robbing Clermont. The Hospital Department of my regiment, without my knowledge or consent, took all the bedding, some divans, and, I think, crockery and cooking utensils, and I learn that plate has been taken, and that the house has been completely ruined. The defence is that it belongs to secessionists ; this is true, but we do not allow people to steal even secession property. I have had to fight this propensity to steal ever since I have been here. Nothing will be safe in Maine when we get home."

Extract from Letter to Mrs. Howard.

" HEADQUARTERS THIRD MAINE VOLUNTEERS, }
September 15, 1861. }

" MY DEAREST WIFE : I haven't yet left my regiment, as you see by the heading (Monday morning). After I wrote the above line I was employed all day without intermission. The men are bringing me their money to send by express to their friends, and it has made me a good deal of extra work. I am going to Washington this morning to send the money and make other arrangements. I am disappointed in Major Staples not returning before this. It will make me behind everybody in the choice of my brigade. I should not have gone to West Point if you had been there now, darling [she was in Maine], for I shall not show myself at the North under reverse if I can help it. It is no time to leave one's command now. Political generals may do it, but army generals had better keep the field and keep their eyes open, not for credit, but for the salvation of the country. We have had glory enough ; now is the time for work."

While awaiting assignment to a command General Howard remained in Washington, and from there, under date of October 22d, 1861, he wrote a letter to his wife, in which is a reference to General Baker. He says :

"This morning we have the sad news of General Baker's death and the fear that we have met with a defeat again in the vicinity of Leesburg (Ball's Bluff). The enemy manage in every encounter to outnumber us. God has not yet seen fit to withhold His hand from humbling us, neither will He, I fear, till we have to acknowledge Him. 'The battle is not always to the strong.' General Baker is the Senator from Oregon. . . . I am glad you took [step] father's bond, for father's sake. I do not mind taking an interest in the Government loan. I think the very debt that is accumulating will cement us, unless there comes a general break-up, which nobody can account for. . . . I met the Prince de Joinville, and exchanged a word with him about General Baker's death. He says 'he died a soldier's death, fighting for his country.' I think he must have been a little rash in exposing himself, and I feel especially the regret that one of our first men should be sacrificed to so little purpose."

To his Wife. His first Letter after Promotion to Brigadier-General.
"September 4, 1861.
"I have been appointed brigadier-general. I hesitate now whether it is better for the country, for the cause of Christ, and for my poor self to take or decline the position. . . . May God direct us all in the way He would have us walk !"

Howard spent the fall and winter of 1861, after the disasters of Bull Run, in camp near Alexandria, Va. Here he occupied his time in industriously drilling his men and in teaching them every requirement pertaining to their calling. He made them practise firing, with himself in front of them, and instructed them that they must be cool enough in action not to hit him or any other officer he put there to lead them. This brigade, which was a new one assigned him after his promotion as brigadier-general, became a strong one, passing through the most desperate battles, but never failing to honor General Howard, who gave it its first lessons in discipline and organization. General Sumner, whom he names as the "strict, straightforward, brave general,"

commended General Howard highly for his scrupulous
fidelity during this period of preparation.

In the spring of 1862 the Confederates, under General
Joseph E. Johnston, withdrew from Centreville too soon
for General McClellan's plans ; the latter, however, hurried forward Sumner's division and some cavalry and
other troops to follow up his retreat, while he himself
took his army down the Potomac to Yorktown.   Sumner,
in command of the Second Corps, hastened the pursuit
of Johnston, with French's, Howard's, Blenker's, and
Meagher's troops, and made his first halt at Warrenton
Junction.   Then the corps went to the Peninsula, land-
ing at Shipping Point.   General Howard was intrusted
with the dangerous exploit of a reconnoissance forward
to the Rappahannock from Warrenton Junction, and
drove the enemy across it.   In this short expedition he
met the troops of his Confederate classmate and former
intimate, General J. E. B. Stuart, who in his retreat
across the river burned the bridge behind him.   While
Howard's troops camped for the night at the river's
side, the enterprising Stuart is said to have visited the
neighborhood of the camp during the darkness, and re-
connoitred the position of his old friend.   Finding him
altogether too well prepared against a surprise, he withdrew to the opposite side of the stream.   The booming
of the guns next morning could be heard by the troops
at Warrenton, and General Sumner was anxious for the
safety of the command until he received a message from
Howard to the effect that Stuart's cavalry, which had
slowly retired from point to point, disputing every mile
of the way, was now out of the way of the army's progress.   General Sumner was much pleased with the young
general, who accomplished his hazardous undertaking
with so little loss of men or time.

While on the march to the Peninsula, as in camp at Alexandria, General Howard, while attending to his military duties, almost constantly devoted some time to religious observances. He kept the Sabbath day holy, and induced others to do so ; held meetings in his tent, and encouraged the officers who attended to a greater faith and more willing service in the Master's work. Happily for those who loved him he kept well and was always cheerful, hopeful, and busy. His recreation was in visiting the hospital, lending religious books, reading the Bible, and praying with the sick. Disagreeable days, when it rained and time hung heavily on the hands of those around him, he would invite all who would come to his tent to hold a religious meeting and talk over the things that concerned their mental and spiritual development. He was so happy in his faith, that he could not realize the entire absence of such a feeling on the part of any one, and he knew no greater delight than in sharing his spiritual peace and contentment with others. He never wanted to be alone or apart from those who were, like himself, Christians ; they were his kinsmen, and he made his tent a meeting-place and a quiet retreat always for men wishing to chat with him or read and pray together. In the bloody battle of Williamsburg, fought the 4th and 5th of May (1862), it was not permitted General Howard to take part ; he could not get his troops forward in time, though they marched all night through the deep mud and rain. In the morning, when he reached the battle-ground, the conflict, "fought," says General Webb, "without a plan, with inadequate numbers, and at a serious sacrifice, without compensating result," was over. General Howard went over the field where the dead lay in numbers, and in one of his letters home he speaks of the prayer he is "constantly making, that God will hasten the end of this horrible war." From the time of his conversion in Florida he had been in the regular habit of visiting hospitals, for the purpose of talking and praying with the sufferers always there. And now, as soon as he had viewed the field of battle, he went into the hospitals, and sympathized with the wounded of both armies, who lay writhing in pain. The least kindness he could show the occupants of the cots—a glass of water here, a word or a look of interest there—he gave unstintedly, and wherever he went men felt happier for his presence and his earnest " God bless you !"

His brigade was, a little later, ordered back to York-town, and from there to West Point, Va. At the Chickahominy, near which occurred so many hard contests on and after the last day of May, General Johnston was waiting, his army drawn up in order and ready for the advancing foe. General McClellan divided his army, Heintzelman's and Key's corps facing Johnston on the Richmond side of the river, and the main body on the other side, and much dispersed. While the river was low it was everywhere passable, and this separation was of no account ; but there came on a fearful storm ; the rain poured in torrents ; the waters rose rapidly, and the bridges began to give way. Johnston, taking advantage of the favoring circumstances, began, the morning of the 30th, a most vigorous attack, first attacking and displacing Casey's division. Before the day was over and the battle entirely lost to McClellan, Sumner, whom McClellan's orders had kept back, finally worked his way over the trembling bridges nearest the Fair Oaks Station, waded through the water and mud, and with Sedgwick's division and the troops he found on the ground, waged battle upon Johnston's exposed flank. Johnston's troops, hitherto victorious, were suddenly checked by a force supposed to have been on the other side of the swollen river. Johnston himself was severely wounded, and carried from the field. Yet the battle was not over. General Howard, now belonging to Richardson's division, bore his part in the second day's battle, and his name is imperishably associated with Fair Oaks. He showed extraordinary bravery among brave men, and fought with a courage as dauntless as it was abiding. Headley says of his conduct at Fair Oaks :

"Howard exposed himself like the commonest soldier, until at last he was struck by a ball, which shattered his arm. Instantly waving the mutilated member aloft as a pennon, he cheered on his men to the charge, and was then borne from the field."

He was first wounded in his sword arm, and his brother, near at hand, tying a bandage about it, he held it high in the air, and called for the men of his command to charge. He is represented, incorrectly, as having had the arm severed by a shell.

Shortly before receiving this wound his horse was badly wounded in the shoulder. Waiting a few moments for another horse, he caused his men to lie down and creep under the shelter of the railway embankment. As soon as a fresh horse was brought up he mounted and rode in front of his troops in line, and the men obeying his command with a shout, passed up through the woods and across the enemy's outer lines, taking prisoners.

General Webb says of the fighting, which followed in front of General Casey's old camp :

"The fire soon became the heaviest yet experienced, the enemy putting in fresh regiments five times to allow their men to replenish ammunition. This lasted for an hour and a half, when the enemy, unable any longer to bear the fire, fell back, but in the course of half an hour renewed the contest with re-enforcements, when an action of about an hour's duration ensued."

During this action General Howard was wounded for a second time in his right arm, this time by a large minie-ball, which tore through and broke the bones of the elbow. He was helped from the saddle by Lieutenant McIntyre, of the Sixty-fourth New York, aided by one or two private soldiers. Soon after he turned his command over to Colonel Barlow, and started for the rear. On the way, meeting his friend Colonel Brooke, he requested him to send Barlow re-enforcements. The loss of blood caused great faintness, and he was moving painfully along when a private, who was also wounded in the arm, though not so severely, put his well one around General Howard, and sustained his failing strength.

The surgeons examined the disabled arm, and declared that it must come off; and gaining his ready consent, the sufferer was carried to the hospital and put upon the operating-table. From the nature of the wounds the suffering was intense until the amputation was completed. Then General Howard appeared to recover his usual vitality, which continued to sustain him.

General Howard's brother Charles, who rose gradually from a private to brevet brigadier-general, was severely wounded in the same battle. The two brothers started from the field in the same train, and on reaching Fortress Monroe their wounds were dressed by the venerable Surgeon Cuyler, who had nursed Cadet Howard at West Point through his long illness.

An incident occurred at Fair Oaks Station between Generals Kearny and Howard which has been reported in so many ways that it is perhaps well to give the true details here. General Kearny was at the station to bid farewell to General Howard, and he jocularly remarked to him that he would be consoled during his absence from the army by the sympathy of the ladies when he reached home. This officer's left arm had been sacrificed to his country's service, and General Howard calling attention to the fact, said " they might buy their gloves together in future." " Sure enough," he replied, and then they parted, to meet no more in life.*

At Baltimore, New York, Boston, and Portland the attentions shown General Howard convinced him that his services were known and appreciated by the country. At Lewiston, Me., the destination of the wounded heroes, a large crowd greeted them, a speech of welcome was made, and the tired and suffering general summoned strength enough to make a fitting reply. He was then permitted to seek his wife and children, who, after the long and anxious separation, awaited his coming at their home on the other side of the river.

At home once more, the careworn man, upon whose face were signs of the great anxieties he had experienced, sat down at his own table, with his loved ones about him, and but for the empty sleeve hanging loose at his side they would have been wholly happy. This empty sleeve, which touched many hearts by its silent elo-quence, moved the poet, David Barker, to dedicate to it the following poem. The circumstances were as follows : In one of General Howard's addresses at Bangor, Me., while speaking one night from the steps of the Bangor House to a large throng of citizens in the street, Barker, the poet, stood within the hallway watching the scene and listening to the speaker's words. Suddenly the picture outlined itself on the poet's brain, and placing his paper against the wall, he wrote the verses substan-tially as they now stand.

---

* General Kearny was killed at the battle of Chantilly.

" By the moon's pale light to a gazing throng,
   Let me tell one tale, let me sing one song ;
   'Tis a tale devoid of an aim or plan,
   'Tis a simple song of a one-arm man.
   Till this very hour I could ne'er believe
   What a tell-tale thing is an empty sleeve—
   What a weird, queer thing is an empty sleeve.

" It tells in a silent tone to all,
   Of a country's need and a country's call,
   Of a kiss and a tear for a child and wife,
   And a hurried march for a nation's life.
   Till this very hour who could e'er believe
   What a tell-tale thing is an empty sleeve—
   What a weird, queer thing is an empty sleeve ?

" It tells of a battle-field of gore,
   Of the sabre's clash, of the cannon's roar,
   Of the deadly charge, of the bugle's note,
   Of a gurgling sound in a foeman's throat,
   Of the whizzing grape, of the fiery shell,
   Of a scene which mimics the scenes of hell.
   Till this very hour would you e'er believe
   What a tell-tale thing is an empty sleeve—
   What a weird, queer thing is an empty sleeve ?

" Though it points to a myriad wounds and scars,
   Yet it tells that a flag with the stripes and stars,
   In God's own chosen time will take
   Each place of the rag with the rattlesnake,
   And it points to a time when that flag shall wave
   O'er a land where there breathes no cowering slave.
   To the top of the skies let us all then heave
   One proud huzza for the empty sleeve—
   For the one-arm man with the empty sleeve."

IV.

AFTER a few days of rest and recuperation General Howard left his bed, and commenced active religious and patriotic work. Within ten days he made two public addresses before a large religious convention ; spoke to political gatherings in favor of McClellan ; pleaded for volunteers, and promised to return with them to the field. On the Fourth of July he addressed an audience of several thousand men for a full hour. On this occasion a touching incident occurred. As he stood upon the platform after the meeting, a lady apparelled in mourning approached him, unattended, and putting her hand in his, said : " Oh, general, my husband, whom you helped to a commission after he and I treated you so badly, is dead. He was killed in battle !" The bystanders, who heard the hysterical exclamation of the poor woman, saw the quick, kindly response of the general, as he offered her his left hand, and spoke words of comfort and resignation. The past was forgiven, and both were glad of the meeting.

The husband had written home grievous complaints after the first battle of Bull Run ; the wife had, in response to these, sent an anonymous letter to General Howard, full of reproaches and accusations of selfish conduct on his part. The latter had divined the source,

made a careful reply, and, for subsequent good conduct, recommended the husband for advancement to a
lieutenancy.   General Howard never met her husband
again or knew of his fate until the heart-broken widow
described his death upon the field of battle while doing
the duty he had given up family, home, and friends to
perform.   No man living would have been more prompt
than General Howard to relieve the sufferings of another
under the circumstances, and the public interview between the two was not lost upon the observant multitude,
many in it knowing the facts of the case.

At Brunswick he spoke to a great throng, among
whom were many of his old teachers of Bowdoin College.   His reference to his lost arm created great enthusiasm.   Calling upon men to enlist for the service of
their country, he added that he wanted them to go with
him and help him recover the ground where it was
buried—ground which, as all present knew, McClellan
had lost in his retreat after Howard's departure.*

The endeavors of General Howard, with Senator Lot
Morrill, Barker, and others, to raise the assigned quota
of volunteers in his native State were crowned with success.   He canvassed the State, and his brief and serious
appeals   for   volunteers   were   wonderfully   effective.
Great crowds greeted him with a hearty welcome, and
wherever he appeared his utterances were received with
respect and approval.   His earnestness touched all men.
They would look at his pale face and empty sleeve as he
pleaded with them to go to the rescue of their country,
and weep like children.   Even those opposed to the

---

* While in Rome, in 1884, General Howard met the distinguished
artist, Mr. Simmons, who recalled the words of this address.   He
was a young lad at the time, but they made an impression which the
lapse of years has not effaced.

party in power and the measures being adopted to put
down the rebellion yielded ready assent to his persua-
sions, and many enlisted solely from his version of the
public need and from a trust in the results he predicted.
Extremists, such as were known in France as " Red
Republicans," were ever disappointed in Howard ; they
expected a partisan, one who would denounce and cast
imprecations upon his enemies ; but he was never heard
to speak either harshly or depreciatingly of the Confederates. He would say, in his moderate, thoughtful way,
" They are undoubtedly wrong ; they are mistaken ;
how happy we shall be when the struggle is over, and
the Union restored !" Beyond utterances like these he
would not go. There was no hate in his heart—no hostility toward any man. He was a soldier, not a partisan.
His motives were pure, and his desire was to be an instrument for good in the sad work in which the Government was engaged. His aid was invaluable in raising
troops, and Governor Washburne gave him the credit of
filling the State's quota of men in that darkest period of
the war. His earnestness was the irresistible weapon
which none could resist. He was better than an enthusiast for the task he was trying to accomplish, for he was
able to arouse enthusiasm in others.

After an absence of two months and twenty days from
the army, nearly the whole of which he spent in travelling about and making speeches, he rejoined General
McClellan's army as it came back from the Peninsula.
Here he was assigned to the command of a new brigade,
which Senator Baker, who was killed at Ball's Bluff, had
organized and named the " Californian Brigade." It was
composed of Pennsylvania soldiers, and General Burns
had just been wounded and retired from its head. The
first battle in which he was engaged with these troops

was the closing reconnoissance of General Pope, as Generals Lee and Jackson threw him back upon Washington after the second battle of Manassas. In the depressing retreat that followed, when General McClellan came back to take command, he inquired regarding the disposition of the troops. He observed, after hearing that General Howard was in command of the rear-guard of the Chain Bridge column, " There could not be a better selection."

At Antietam General Howard succeeded General Sedgwick in command of his division (Second Division, Second Corps) when the latter was wounded in charging the enemy's troops, which occupied a formidable position in a thick wood.

Regarding the battle of Antietam—a battle in which victory was claimed by both sides, and concerning which recrimination and fault-finding were widely indulged in at Washington—General Howard, in a letter, described it as a triumph for Lee. The plans of the Union generals were good, but their execution was bad. Howard believed that if Burnside had been an hour earlier on the field Lee's army would have suffered a great defeat. Lee's generalship he considered superb, and Burnside's movements vigorous, but not successfully supported.

General Sedgwick's grand division had received a severe check, and lost some ground before General Howard came to the command. He helped to gather the men and put them into line. The troops after that did not accomplish much, but kept their ground, and contributed to the general result, which was a victory for the Union army, though not a very decisive one. Howard's division stayed to bury the dead —a dreadfully offensive task, there being many horses on the field as well as men. The thick atmosphere, full of the smoke of the burning animals, made General Howard quite sick for several days, but he went with his command to Harper's Ferry, and then left the field for a few days. When he returned to that point the army was on the march southward toward General Lee, and was already below the Rappahannock. General Howard took a conveyance and followed the army through an unguarded part of Virginia, till he overtook it near Rectortown. The day after he arrived (November 7th, 1862) orders came for the relief of McClellan and the appointment of Burnside. Lee withdrew and crossed the Potomac, and Porter's command, which followed him, suffered severely.

Howard heard of the change of commanders with surprise and sincere regret, and wrote in his letters home most touchingly regarding the subject. An apology is hardly needed for quoting General Howard's opinion about the two principal characters who figured in this army. Opinions form the integral part of a man's nature ; the world of thought is perhaps as real as the world of facts. Incidents but exhibit one side of a man's character, whereas thoughts reveal another and more important side. For instance, the publication of Carlyle's opinions about his contemporaries has shown to the world most forcibly its mistaken estimate of that profound thinker.

Speaking of McClellan's conduct on receipt of the news of his removal, General Howard says :

" Burnside betrayed more feeling than McClellan ; the latter, after reading the dispatch, passed it to Burnside, and said, simply : ' You command the army.' . . . The next morning I turned out my troops and drew them up beside the road to give a parting salute to General McClellan. He rode along the line ; the tattered colors were lowered ; the drums beat, and the men cheered him. Burnside rode quietly by his side. At my last interview he said to me : ' Burnside is a pure man and a man of integrity of purpose, and such a man can't go far astray.'

"One other remark I have preserved : 'I have been long enough in command of a large army to learn the utter insignificance of any man unless he depend on a Power above.'

"It is easy to see from the details which I have given why the officers and soldiers were so much attached to McClellan.

"Soon after this interview I met Burnside, who appeared sad and weary. He had been for two nights almost without sleep. He remarked in my presence that he had concluded to take the command of the army, but did not regard it as a fit subject for congratulation."

There was widespread opposition toward Burnside on the part of many officers, whose affection for McClellan outweighed every other feeling. This the new commander knew, and calling together a number of officers, he addressed them on the subject. General Howard was one of many who listened to his manly protest against their hostility toward himself, and he was one of those who gave him loyal support from first to last, as he did every officer who ranked him.

His note-books are full of references to his fellow-officers, and from first to last there is not a harsh expression. General Reno fell at the battle of "South Mountain"—a battle which preluded Antietam, and General Howard finds time to record his appreciation of this man. "True and strong" he styled Reno, and then he writes of him and of other officers whose eyes were there closed in death : "When they awake, may it be in the likeness of the Man of Peace and clad in the garments of the redeemed !"

Into battered and deserted Fredericksburg General Howard accompanied his brigade on the evening of December 12th, 1862. On the morning of the 13th, as he sat with his officers at breakfast, a charming old lady who lived near by accosted him with an assurance that though they had taken Fredericksburg, the South would yet win the day. She was firm in her faith, and though the general predicted a different ending of the war, she smilingly asserted that her foes would have a " Stonewall " to encounter, " Hills" to climb, and a " Longstreet" to wander through before they had finished their task. She watched the officers as they listened to the usual morning reading of the Scriptures by the general, and heard their cheerful words as they separated to attend to their respective duties. The old lady was struck with their actions, and said to General Howard, as he bade her good-morning : " Now I fear you more than ever, for I had understood that all Lincoln's men were bad." She wondered, she said, at his cheerfulness on the eve of battle, and was surprised that there were Christians among the Yankees.

The next day was almost fatal to the Union cause. General Howard came into action again with his division, and took part in the hopeless fight, which proved a slaughter for the Federal troops, in front of General Lee's prepared defensive works on Marye's Heights. The loss in his division, which remained in close proximity to the foe till far into the night, was sixty-four officers and eight hundred and thirteen men. The poor fellows lay in clusters all over the hill-side, and far into the night the living fought over the ground and struggled against the fate that was irrevocable. General Burnside retired to the north side of the river on the night of the 15th inst., and the weary army rested after its fierce and almost fruitless effort.

The letters which General Howard constantly wrote to his wife from the front gives us an insight into the real character of the man. The winter following his return from his forced furlough at home was one of the most depressing periods of the war. The outlook was gloomy, and not even the most cheerful could foresee any hope of a termination of the terrible struggle now at its fiercest point. He writes :

" Men are getting discontented, restless, complaining—their hearts are failing, money is growing scarcer, business is paralyzed. Now is the time for all men of true patriotism and courage to stand fast ; we must as a people see hard times ; we must be humbled before the Lord will exalt us."

He was constantly visiting the sick in hospitals and holding meetings in his tent for Bible-reading and prayers. In a letter written to his mother just before the battle of Fredericksburg, dated Falmouth, Va., December 2d, 1862, he says :

". . . We are still in the same place. I heard that we were to have re-enforcements—General Couch said some sixteen thousand to the right grand division. We shall then probably halt till these troops come up. The enemy have much heavy artillery across the river in position, and mean to contest our passage, and unless our crossing is managed very carefully we shall suffer a very heavy loss, if not defeat. It is the most difficult of military operations to cross a river in the face of an enemy of equal strength. We could easily have done it the day we arrived, but General Halleck had withheld the pontoon-bridge, and it was impracticable to move over without it, and folly to throw over a small force for the enemy to crush, as at Ball's Bluff. We had to wait, and while waiting the enemy brought a hundred thousand men to our front, and Jackson brought some thirty thousand to threaten our base of supplies. So goes war, a game that both armies can play at, and one that the small item of a bridge may disconcert if the bridge is not at the right place at the right time. However we may get impatient, God's ways are not always our ways, and He will doubtless regulate us to His own praise. I feel that I am too little dependent on Him, too disposed to be ambitious. You must pray for me that I be kept in the right path."

After the battle he wrote his wife from the Knox House, Fredericksburg, December 13th, saying :

" . . . On Thursday we left camp at half-past six A.M., and moved down near the railroad and near the place of crossing the river. . . . We got as far as Third Street, parallel with the river, and I ordered firing to cease as soon as it could be done. Pickets were placed. Our men were in the houses, and pillaging and destroying went on to some extent. Women and men who had spent the day in cellars came for protection ; some mothers brought little children for permission to cross the river. A few men got into wine-cellars and became pretty drunk, but no instance of abuse occurred that I heard of. I took headquarters in a little old house knocked to pieces somewhat by our shot ; did not sleep much, and went out frequently to quiet the men. Another brigade came over the bridge, built half a mile below, commanded by Colonel Hawkins, Dexter's brother. This bridge was built like ours, by throwing over men in boats, after they heard what we had done. Colonel H. reported to me, and took post on my left. At three A.M. I went around the outlying pickets, and found all quiet, no enemy near. At daylight I threw forward General Sully and Colonel Owens, took the whole town, and picketed the front range of heights near by. During the day we have had a little skirmishing. The enemy have shelled us from their hills, but the army has been crossing. General Franklin is over, so is General Sumner. To-day the heights will be attempted. By God's blessing we shall be successful. Burnside says he puts his trust in God. He made some remarks to a roomful of generals on Wednesday evening. He heard they had murmured ; he rebuked them, and told them he lacked, but his trust was in God. Solemn, noble, and manly were his remarks, and God will bless him. We are now in a house abandoned by Mr. Knox and near the front line. One or two shells have passed clear through it, but my room is in pretty good shape. Charles joined me the day before the battle ; is well and sleeping ; so is Mr. Stinson, Captain Whittlesey, and Mr. Atwood. Mr. Steel is sleeping on the floor near me. I am sitting on the floor by a fireplace which is like that of Professor Church's, writing on my lap, having inkstand, candlestick, and paper on a large portfolio, with Tom, a little colored boy, holding up the outer edge. Tom drops asleep now and then, when my candle, etc., with its light, and inkstand with its ink, slip down. But I wake Tom, and it is soon all righted. Tom also acts as paper-clamp at the bottom of the pages. Tom works for Captain W. and Charles, and, as you see, everybody works for me, darling, but rebels. Guy and Grace will be much interested in papa's letter, and Jamie can be told that papa found a little white pussy here, and a big, big dog, big as Lion. Much love to my precious children, and a prayer to God in their and your behalf, that He will bless you and keep you all as His faithful children. By the military committee I learn that I am unanimously recommended for a major-general. It seems less strange, now that I have become accustomed to a larger command. Oh, that I may increase in love to God, who so abundantly blesses me! Much regard to Mrs. Stinson. Harry [Stinson] is a man, a brave and true one. He is among my blessings. . . . We may be in battle to-day. We trust in God to do for us.

"Affectionately, your own

"OTIS."

To his Wife.

"NEAR FALMOUTH, VA., December 26, 1862.

"General Sedgwick has now returned and assumed command of the corps, and I have only my own division to attend to. The weather is rather warm, and I do not feel as strong as I wish I did, though I am well, and endure a great deal of fatigue. I am nervous, and feel, like Dr. Wiggin [one of the surgeons], as though a few days' rest would not hurt me. When I think of you, my patient little wife, suffering so much without complaint, I don't feel that I have a right to say 'I am tired.' Dr. Wiggin spent two days with me for rest and recuperation, and went back evidently refreshed. His eye was dead [dull], his flesh thin, and he looked worn. . . . You can hardly think how pleasant my tent is. John has got me a white table-cloth and a tall brass candlestick from some place. My ground floor is now nearly covered with boards, and my fireplace and hearth very cheerful. John puts on big logs which last all night. . . . General Sedgwick, who dined with us to-day, exclaimed, as he came in, 'What a beautiful tent! I would as leave have it as a house.' General French has gone, and General Sully has been assigned to his division. There has been a reduction of generals of late. In this corps, the Second, there is not one commanding a brigade. All are wounded, dead, or on the shelf.

"I did hope for success in the last battle [Fredericksburg]. I prayed for it when Hooker's men were giving way, but it was not the will of God. Oh, we must wait on Him, and learn His will, and then do it! Would that He would give me the wisdom! I omitted to tell you that our noble General Couch was taken sick and obliged to leave. He expected to return, but I fear will not be able. I like General Sedgwick. I believe I always have good commanding officers; at least, I have had the good fortune to get along with them."

During the winter of 1862 the favorite son of President Lincoln died, and the public heart saddened in sympathy with the grief of the head of the struggling nation. General Howard, in a letter to his wife, refers to the event in these characteristic words :

"You will have read of the death of Willie Lincoln before this reaches you, and perhaps think how the Lord tempers prosperity with sorrow. I hope He, in infinite wisdom, may make President Lincoln a Christian like George Washington. My trust is not in princes, but in God ; but no auspices are more satisfactory and promising than the work of the Lord in raising up men after His own heart to hold the rule. The inauguration of Jefferson Davis, encroaching upon the anniversary of Washington's birthday, is not by any means in joy or hope. Washington City and Richmond are shadowed in sorrow, and I am hoping that good will come to us from both events. How calm, how firm, how constant a man can be if he has a *real* trust in his divine Master ! He knows, he feels that events are in good hands, and that all will be well—Jehovah Jireh."

The defeat of Burnside, the withdrawal of his army, the few other futile attempts to renew the campaign, followed each other in quick succession. In January, 1863, Burnside was superseded by Hooker. It must be remarked here that on the 29th of November preceding Howard had received promotion to the rank of major-general.

The 2d of April (1863) General Howard went to Stafford Court-House, and assumed command of the Eleventh Corps. Of this time he thus writes :

"As soon as General Sickles, who was my junior in rank, was assigned to the Third Corps, feeling that I had been overlooked, I wrote a brief letter to General Hooker, asking to be assigned according to my rank. Immediately I was ordered to take command of the Eleventh Army Corps, which General Sigel had just left in some dissatisfaction. . . . The corps was then, in round numbers, thirteen thousand strong. It had about five thousand Germans and eight thousand men of American birth. . . . Outwardly I met a cordial reception, but I soon found that my past record was not known here ; that there was much complaint in the German language at the removal of Sigel, who merely wanted to have his command properly increased, and that I was not at first getting the earnest and loyal support of the entire command. But for me there was no turning back. I was soon permanently assigned, and did my best."

A month after his assignment to the Eleventh Army Corps General Howard led it in the Chancellorsville campaign. He, with General Slocum, received much credit for the long and successful preliminary march around Lee's flank ; but after Hooker had begun his attack, on Friday, May 1st, he (Hooker) suddenly changed his mind, and drew back his troops to the ground first occupied, an indefensible position. The Eleventh Corps was on his right flank. Stonewall Jackson was detached from Lee's corps on Saturday, with twenty-five thousand men, and under cover of the forest succeeded in getting around General Hooker's extreme right. While Jackson's march was progressing, General Hooker and others, thinking Lee's whole force was retreating, sent forward the Third and Twelfth corps from Howard's immediate left. These, it must be observed, were Sickles' and Slocum's corps ; and finally Howard's principal reserve was sent also.

Howard was left with about eight thousand men, the nearest help being some two miles or more away, and then engaged in battle. Jackson, at about six o'clock in the evening, came speedily through the thick wood with his twenty-five thousand men, well organized and full of ardor. An attack was made, and the right brigade of the Union forces soon gave way, and not long after the other brigades followed, and a panic ensued. General Howard and many of his officers endeavored to change front ; he filled his cross intrenchments with his retreating men, but nothing could keep them long standing firm. Steinwehr's division, occupying his left, faced about and held on for an hour, and some of the batteries were well served. After falling back more than a mile General Howard met his friend, General Hiram Berry, of Maine, commanding a division. The two generals grasped hands, and General Howard said : " Berry, you take the right, and I will take the left of this road, and make a stand." A firm stand was accordingly made, and many cannon were brought forward and located on a neighboring hill. General Pleasanton's troops, with others, had checked Jackson farther to the left, while General Howard was at this hill, working with all his might to rally men and place regiments in support of batteries. Berry's men did their part, but their gallant commander fell at the head of his column. The Confederates, however, came no farther.

The Eleventh Corps had the worst of it in this battle, and afterward and for a time was in disgrace, and Generals Howard and Sedgwick have fared alike in the criticisms passed upon their generalship on that field. This was the only occasion where General Howard's reputation suffered. He was charged with having located his command in an indefensible position ; but he went precisely to the place he was ordered to occupy, and made good disposition of his men, intrenchments, and covers for his artillery. He believed and asserted that had Barlow's command, his main reserve, not been carried away by Captain Moore, an aide of Hooker's, that the panic of his right would have been checked in time and the main field saved till re-enforcements from Chancellorsville could arrive. Under precisely the same circumstances in subsequent battles, he was able to stop more than one fierce assault, by the means he then adopted, long enough for help to come.

Colonel G. C. Kniffin, of Kentucky, who was on General Stanley's staff during the war, gives this account of the conduct of General Howard at Chancellorsville, which was furnished him by a Southern gentleman who lived near the field of battle, and from whose family name that of the battle-field is derived :

" Fortunately we have, to substantiate the narration of the day's operations as given by General Howard, the testimony of Rev. Mr. Chancellor, who lived at the Dowdall House, where General Howard had his headquarters.

" Meeting Mr. Chancellor during the excursion, while returning from Spottsylvania, the writer asked him if he remembered the events of the day on which Jackson's forces charged the Eleventh Corps, and, if so, to be kind enough to give them to him in detail. He replied that every event of the day was ineffaceably impressed upon his memory, and made substantially the following statement : ' I was living at the Dowdall House then, and General O. O. Howard made his headquarters there. The day before that on which the charge was made by Jackson General Hooker came out from Chancellorsville and rode with General Howard and several other officers along the line of General Howard's troops, and on his return I heard him say to General Howard and quite a number of officers who were assembled in the yard in front of the house : " You have a very strong position here, and if you do your duty you can hold it against anything." The next day everything was quiet ; the farm in front of the house was alive with men and animals, and the woods, extending from the road beyond the junction of the Orange Road, around beyond the Hawkins's House, were full of men. Just as General Howard and his staff-officers sat down to dinner they jumped up and ran to the door. We all went out, and there seemed to be a good deal of commotion along the edge of the woods and a good deal of firing. General Howard called for his horse, and rode rapidly down the road toward the front. In a few minutes the field was swarming with men, running for dear life, throwing away their guns and knapsacks and everything that could impede their flight. Looking down the road, I saw that thousands of men were pressing toward Chancellorsville, and I saw General Howard and his officers trying to stop them. When they reached the Dowdall House I could hear him plainly. He turned his horse around, rose in his stirrups, and shouted : " Here, men ; form a line here !" but they paid no attention to him—neither officers nor men—but ran on as fast as they could. As far as I could see him, he was begging them to stop, but to no effect. Yes, sir ; if there were any brave men on that field that day, General Howard was one of them. If they had obeyed him they would not have run away without fighting, even if they had been whipped.'

" A year later General McPherson, the splendid commander of the Army of the Tennessee, was killed at Atlanta. General Sherman chose General Howard to succeed him, and the inevitable conclusion is that the astute general of the army, during the hundred days of battle in the Atlanta campaign, had discovered qualities in the commander of the Fourth Corps that eminently fitted him to assume command of an army and department."

General Howard was, of course, mortified at the reputation given the corps, and he begged, at Hooker's council, to be allowed to recover the *esprit* of his command by leading an attack. Napoleon would have permitted it, but Hooker, lacking his insight, refused. That General Howard disobeyed his orders or shrunk from his personal duty nobody who knows him believes. Certainly at the time General Hooker would have brought him to trial if he himself had believed it. The charge of disobedience came years after, and was groundless.

Concerning Chancellorsville, General Howard once remarked to the writer : " I think this battle perhaps the weakest link in my military record, but no military critics who have represented the facts just as they were have found any flaws in the dispositions within the limits allowed me."

It has been said that Howard answered certain Germans who criticised his position that day by saying : " Trust in God." That is not like him ; he is a man not given to disrespect, even toward the humblest. He did say, substantially, " Let us obey our orders ; do the best we can, and trust the results with God." Such a rejoinder would be most like one who trusts all issues beyond conscientious effort to the great Ruler of events.

Some one once asked General Howard how he and " Stonewall " could both be answered by the God of heaven. Howard replied, thoughtfully, " We *were* both answered. He won the battle and gave his life. I was put into the deepest valley of humiliation for that time, but was never sent there again. The cause for which I prayed was finally won, and my life was spared."

Mr. Lincoln, when requested by an army delegation to remove General Howard, replied : " No, let him alone ; he is a good man. Give him time with his command, and he will come out all right."

V.

Gettysburg—The three days' fight—Honors to General Howard—Congress and the Maine Legislature thank him—Hastened West—In command of the Army of the Tennessee.

WE next meet, in the history of the war, with the name of General Howard at Gettysburg, and the story of his work on that battle-field appears in different lights as presented by different writers, though all agree to certain undoubted statements. He had clung to his Eleventh Corps, reorganizing it in some measure, and at this time Generals Barlow, Von Steinwehr, and Carl Schurz commanded his three divisions. The 1st day of July (1863) Howard set in motion his corps, under instructions from his wing commander, General John F. Reynolds, who was bivouacked six miles nearer the field. Leaving the little town of Emmettsburg in two columns, he sent one column, under Barlow, to follow the direct route behind Reynolds ; the other, with Schurz at its head, moved eastward by Horner's Mill, and reached the famous Gettysburg Cemetery by the Taneytown Road. As soon as his men were well in motion General Howard, accompanied by his staff and a small escort, hurried on through the fields, avoiding the crowded thoroughfares, with a view to join Reynolds and ascertain his plans and wishes, for the instructions were for the Eleventh Corps to keep within supporting distance. On approaching the town he met a staff-officer of Reynolds after the firing on the Oak Ridge had begun. This officer reported that his general wished the Eleventh

Corps to come quite up to Gettysburg. "Supporting distance" for the corps while in campaign had been five or six miles off. An enemy of unknown strength was in front, and with all haste General Howard moved forward to the highest point of Cemetery Hill, where he expressed to his adjutant, Colonel Meysenburg, his appreciation of that point and the neighboring ridge as the best defensive position in that region. Meysenburg responded that it was "the only position." At eleven o'clock General Howard went to the top of Fahnestock's Observatory in the town, and was there with two maps spread out before him studying the field, while the roar of the battle beyond Oak Ridge reached his ears, and while Captain Hall, of his staff, and several orderlies were searching for Reynolds that he (General Howard) might join him if Reynolds so desired. His own corps was yet far back, obstructed on the shorter route by dreadful roads and by the trains of the other corps. The other route, by Horner's Mill, was thirteen miles, so that the two divisions there could not be expected till between twelve and one o'clock. It was at this critical time, while putting his leading troops into position, that the wing commander fell. A staff-officer appeared below, in the street, and said, "General Howard, General Reynolds is wounded !" "I am sorry," was the quick response ; and then, expressing the wish that he might be able to keep the field, General Howard turned to attend to a messenger, when another officer hurried in with the news, "General Reynolds is dead, and you are the senior officer here." The battle had begun ; prisoners taken indicated the presence of a large force ; Meade's main body was far away, and the Union force at hand, inclusive of Buford's cavalry, did not exceed thirteen thousand !

A strong sense of responsibility came upon the young
general, but he met it promptly, and planned and acted
without delay.   Aides and orderlies were quickly
despatched to Schurz, to Barlow, to Sickles at Emmettsburg, to Slocum toward Baltimore, and away to Meade
at Taneytown.   General Doubleday took the First
Corps, Schurz the Eleventh, and Howard commanded
the whole.   On the cemetery crest General Howard had
his own position.   Steinwehr's division and the reserve
corps of artillery were near by, and the remainder of the
Eleventh Corps were moved through the town, with
Schurz at the head, and placed on to the right of
the First Corps, already engaged.   Then leaving his
officers, orderlies, and escort there, with the exception
of two aides-de-camp, General Howard rode quietly
down to the Emmettsburg Road, where, meeting General
Barlow at the head of his column, he accompanied him
through the principal streets of Gettysburg.   The can-
non-balls from the left were crashing chimneys and striking houses, and shells were bursting in the air above.
The inhabitants had nearly all fled, and the streets were
given over to the troops.   One young woman, alone and
seemingly undaunted, stood on a porchway waving her
handkerchief as the corps passed by.   The soldiers responded with a shout as they moved by the home-remind-
ing vision.

General Howard inspected his lines from right to
left ; all told his men did not exceed twenty-four thousand, while General Lee had, more quickly than Meade,
concentrated at least fifty thousand effective troops.   As
soon as word of the situation reached General Meade he
sent General Hancock forward, and he reached the
cemetery just as General Lee was pressing back the
forces of Doubleday, Schurz, and Buford from the line

beyond the town. General Howard had previously ordered the retreat, and had covered it by a brigade from Von Steinwehr in the outer edge of the village, and arranged batteries to do effective work against all who should approach his right. Under the terrific fire and rapid advance of Lee, his troops, however, except those at the cemetery, became much entangled and broken. It was then that Hancock arrived. The troops were rallied and well posted, stragglers were stopped and brought back, and everything made ready for the next attack, which Lee then but faintly attempted. Meeting with increased obstinacy, he withdrew and postponed further attack until the next day.

For this first day's work General Howard's name was associated with that of General Meade in the thanks of Congress, and he received also a beautiful recognition from the Legislature of his own State.* Whenever rivalry assails his record, the general's friends point to the report of General Meade, which commended him for having selected the field for the great and decisive struggle of the contending armies ; to the eloquent words of

---

* *Resolution extending the thanks of the State of Maine to Major-General O. O. Howard.*

Whereas, In times of national trial and war, the security and happiness of the people, the fame of the nation, and the permanence and progress of the country's institutions are committed to the courage, fidelity, and ability of patriotic soldiers, it becomes the duty, as it is the pleasure of an intelligent people, publicly and gratefully to honor those who have served them well, and particularly to acknowledge splendid individual achievement, even where all have done gloriously ; therefore,

Resolved, That the State of Maine has watched with deepest satisfaction the brilliant and successful military career of Major-General O. O. Howard, and particularly his distinguished conduct on the Peninsula, at Gettysburg, and throughout the Georgia campaign, and

Senator Grimes concerning that day on the floor of the Senate, and to the unanimous and unsolicited approval, by formal vote, of the two distinguished legislative bodies referred to, as well as also to the press records of the time. In sending him the resolution, Mr. Blaine wrote him the following letter :

" WASHINGTON, D. C., 28 January, 1864.

" MY DEAR GENERAL : I enclose you a copy of the joint resolution, whose adoption by a unanimous vote in both branches of Congress you have doubtless already noticed.

" The effect of the resolution is to recognize you, and to permanently record you in the annals of the country as the hero of the great battle of Gettysburg.

" I congratulate you on a result at once so just and generous on the part of the national Congress, and so honorable and auspicious to yourself.

" I remain, very heartily, your friend,

(Signed)   " J. G. BLAINE."

MAJOR-GENERAL HOWARD, etc.

The joint resolution expressive of the thanks of Congress to Major-General Joseph Hooker, Major-General George G. Meade, Major-General Oliver O. Howard, and the officers and men of the Army of the Potomac, read thus :

Resolved by the Senate and House of Representatives of the United States of America in Congress assembled, That the gratitude of the

---

offers him the public thanks for the honor he has conferred on his native State.

Resolved, That the Governor be requested to cause a copy of these resolutions to be transmitted to General Howard.

In the House of Representatives, February 23d, 1865. Read and passed.

W. A. P. DILLINGHAM, Speaker.

In Senate, February 24th, 1865. Read and passed.

DAVID D. STEWART, President.

February 24th, 1865. Approved.

SAMUEL CONY.

American people and the thanks of their representatives in Congress are due, and are hereby tendered, to Major-General Joseph Hooker and the officers and soldiers of the Army of the Potomac, for the skill, energy, and endurance which first covered Washington and Baltimore from the meditated blow of the advancing and powerful army of rebels led by General Robert E. Lee ; and to Major-General George G. Meade and Major-General Oliver O. Howard, and the officers and soldiers of that army, for the skill and heroic valor which at Gettysburg repulsed, defeated, and drove back, broken and dispirited, beyond the Rappahannock, the veteran army of the rebellion.

Senator Grimes, of Iowa, said on this occasion : " As I read the history of that campaign, the man who selected the position where the battle of Gettysburg was fought, and who, indeed, fought it on the first day, was General Howard ; and to him the country is indebted as much for the credit of securing that victory as to any other person."

It was intimated afterward that General Howard was ambitious for the command of the army. Hearing this on many sides, General Howard wrote the following characteristic letter to Mr. Lincoln :

" HEADQUARTERS ELEVENTH CORPS,
ARMY OF THE POTOMAC, NEAR BERLIN,
July 18, 1863.

" *To the President of the United States :*

" SIR : Having noticed in the newspapers certain statements bearing upon the battle of Gettysburg and subsequent operations which I deem calculated to convey a wrong impression to your mind, I wish to submit a few statements. The successful issue of the battle of Gettysburg was due mainly to the energetic operations of our present commanding general prior to the engagement, and to the manner in which he handled his troops on the field. The reserves have never before, during this war, been thrown in at just the right moment ; in many cases when points were just being carried by the enemy, a regiment or brigade appeared, to stop his progress and hurl him back.

" Moreover, I have never seen a more hearty co-operation on the part of general officers than since General Meade took command. As to not attacking the enemy prior to leaving his stronghold beyond the Antietam, it is by no means certain that the repulse of Gettysburg might not have been turned upon us. At any rate, the commanding general was in favor of an immediate attack ; but with the evident difficulties in our way, the uncertainty of a success, and the strong conviction of our best military minds against the risks, I must say that I think the general acted wisely. As to my request to make a reconnoissance on the morning of the 14th, which the papers state was refused, the facts are that the general had required me to reconnoitre the evening before, and give my opinion as to the practicability of making a lodgment on the enemy's left ; and his answer to my subsequent request was that the movements he had already ordered would subserve the same purpose. We have, if I may be allowed to say it, a commanding general in whom all the officers with whom I have come in contact express complete confidence. I have said thus much because of the censure and of the misrepresentations which have grown out of the escape of Lee's army.

"Very respectfully your obedient servant,

"O. O. HOWARD, Major-General."

Mr. Lincoln's reply was as follows :

"EXECUTIVE MANSION, }
WASHINGTON, July 21, 1863. }

"MY DEAR GENERAL HOWARD : Your letter of the 18th is received. I was deeply mortified by the escape of Lee across the Potomac, because the substantial destruction of his army would have ended the war, and because I believed such destruction was perfectly easy ; believed that General Meade and his noble army had expended all the skill, and toil, and blood up to the ripe harvest, and then let the crop go to waste. Perhaps my mortification was heightened because I had always believed—making my belief a hobby, possibly—that the main rebel army, going north of the Potomac, could never return if well attended to, and because I was so greatly flattered in this belief by the operations at Gettysburg. A few days having passed, I am now profoundly grateful for what *was* done, without criticism for what *was not* done. General Meade has my confidence as a brave and skilful officer and true man.

"Yours very truly,

" A. LINCOLN."

General Howard, in an article in the *Atlantic Monthly* on the " Campaign and Battle of Gettysburg," publishes these two letters, and says of the battle :

" The main hindrance to our concentrating at Gettysburg as rapidly as Lee was a strategic one. Meade threw forward the left flank
of his general line, so that Lee was able to strike it. Had Gettysburg, and not Taneytown or Pipe Clay Creek, been Meade's objective
point, his general line on the 30th of June would have been more
nearly parallel to that of Lee. But a kind Providence overruled
even this mistake to our advantage, inducing, as it did, undue confidence on the part of General Lee.

" For myself, I am content with the work accomplished at Gettysburg, and avoid aiming any bitter criticism whatever at those true-
hearted officers and men, in any corps or division of our army, who
there acted to the best of their ability."

Mr. Lossing, in his history of the war, speaks in these
words of General Howard's plan of the battle of Gettysburg :

" Howard, who had arrived in advance of his corps, had left Steinwehr's division on *Cemetery Hill*, placed General Schurz, whose division was intrusted to General Schimmelpfennig, in temporary charge
of the corps, and, ranking Doubleday, took the chief command of all
the troops on the field of action. He placed the divisions of Barlow
and Schurz to the right of the First Corps to confront Early, and so,
from the necessity of meeting, an expected simultaneous attack from
the north and west of the national line was lengthened and attenu-
ated along a curve of about three miles. This was an unfortunate
necessity that could not be avoided, for Howard had perceived the
value of *a position for the* [whole] *army* on the series of ridges of
which Cemetery Hill forms the apex of a redan, and had determined
to secure it, at all hazards, if his inferior numbers should be pressed
back from the battle-line on the north and west of the town, which
now seemed probable."

The statements of eye-witnesses are always interesting,
and the following, bearing directly upon the Gettysburg
battle, published in a Washington journal, is additional
evidence of the historical truth outlined in these pages
in regard to that battle and the events immediately preceding it. The author is W. A. Bentley, U. S. Signal
Corps, and his statement is as follows :

" In 1863, and at the time of the battle of Gettysburg, I was a resident of the town of Gettysburg. At that time I was about seventeen years of age, and subsequently I enlisted in the Signal Corps, U. S. A. Some five or six hours after the battle had been in progress, myself and a companion, Daniel Skelly, together with Mrs. E. G. Fahnestock, were together, and had ascended to the upper floor of Fahnestock's Observatory. We were looking anxiously to the north and west of the town where the battle was raging, and of which we had from our elevated position a good view. This observatory was on the south-west corner of Baltimore and Middle streets. While we three were watching the movements of the troops a general with only one arm (Howard), with his staff and an escort of cavalry, came dashing down Baltimore Street and halted in front of the observatory. A staff-officer directed the general's attention to us, and we were asked how to reach our position. Young Skelly went at once to the side entrance on Middle Street and admitted General Howard and a staff-officer, who seemed to be a captain and a German ; I cannot say who he was. This officer had a large field-glass. General Howard took the glass and swept the field long and anxiously. Just at this time an officer came dashing up on horseback, and shouted : ' General Reynolds is killed.' General Howard, I recollect, seemed profoundly agitated, but at once turned, and in these exact words said : ' Captain, go immediately to General Steinwehr and tell him to stop his division on Cemetery Hill and put his men in position for defence.' The captain went down at once. As General Howard gave this order, Mrs. Fahnestock said : ' Oh, sir, you are not going to let the rebels come into town, are you ?' To this General Howard said : ' Madam, no one can tell what may happen in war.' Soon after this shells began passing near, and we all went down. As I came down I inquired of a wounded officer who that general was, and he replied that it was Howard, this being the first time I had ever seen him. As to the exact time when Reynolds's death was announced, I can only give my best judgment ; I think it was between twelve and two o'clock. The general speaks of being in the observatory, and I am confident he will recall these facts. Of course I know nothing of what orders he may have had, but as he had no general command until Reynolds's death, it is impossible that he could have been directed to fortify Cemetery Hill, and I do know that information of Reynolds's death came to him at the observatory, and that he gave the orders in the above language. The other parties who were with me this eventful July 1st, 1863, are still living, and will verify these details. That General Howard is entitled to the credit of selecting the battle-field of Gettysburg, I am quite certain."

Returning to his corps, Howard bore his part in the subsequent battle. The evening of the 2d of July (1863) the Confederates broke through Von Steinwehr's lines ; it was after dark, and the struggle for a time became hand-to-hand. General Howard, who was present, called upon Schurz for re-enforcements, and as the struggle grew fiercer and fiercer, and one of his brigades gave way, General Carroll, sent by Hancock, who heard the terrific firing, deployed his brigade, and the men charged with a shout, and cleared the breach. Howard's lines now being safe and strong, he sent troops to aid Generals Green and Wadsworth, who were meeting an attack from an overwhelming force.

There are many incidents related of General Howard in connection with this battle. Lossing * introduces two characteristics of him. The first, referring to his batteries, is as follows :

" The batteries of Bancroft, Dilger, Eakin, Wheeler, Hill, Taft, under Major Osborne (General Howard's chief of artillery), were placed in the cemetery, where the kind and thoughtful General Howard had caused the tombstones, and such monuments as could possibly be moved, to be laid flat on the ground, to prevent their being injured by shot or shell."

Of the other he says : " There is one incident related by Professor Stoever, of the Gettysburg, Pa., College, as coming under his own observation, which so vividly illustrates the character of a true man and Christian soldier, that it should not be unrecorded, and is here given :

" When orders were issued for the army to pursue Lee, General O. O. Howard, commanding the Eleventh Corps, hastened to the bedside of Captain Griffith, one of his beloved staff-officers, who had received a mortal wound. After a few words the general opened his

---

* " Sherman and his Campaigns."

New Testament, read part of the fourteenth chapter of John, and then, kneeling, commended his dying friend to God. An embrace and a hurried farewell followed, and so the friends parted, never to meet again on earth. That night Captain Griffith died, and Howard, in pursuit of Lee, bivouacked in a drenching rain near the base of South Mountain range."

At the end of the battle, July 5th, he wrote to his wife :

"We are through another terrible conflict of three days. The enemy has been baffled and is gone. God grant us a complete victory ! Charles and I are well ; love to the children, and the blessing of our Father be yours."

Soon after Gettysburg one of General Howard's divisions was detached from his corps and sent to South Carolina, yet for the fall and winter of 1863 the corps organization was preserved with two divisions—those of Schurz and Von Steinwehr. These, under Howard, with the Twelfth Corps (Slocum's), after Rosecrans's defeat at Chickamauga, he being penned up at Chattanooga, were hastened West, Hooker leading the two for Rosecrans's relief. When they arrived at Lookout Valley that grand soldier, General George H. Thomas, had succeeded Rosecrans in command of the Army of the Cumberland, holding Chattanooga. Thomas had despatched troops twice crossing the Tennessee to the mouth of Lookout Valley to meet Hooker's force coming up from Bridgeport. Howard's troops had gone along in the valley under fire from Lookout Mountain, and succeeded in forming a junction with those sent by Thomas ; but Hooker left what he had there of the Twelfth, commanded by General Geary, back at a junction of roads called "Wauhatchie." Geary had with him quite a train of wagons. The Confederate commander on the top of Lookout Mountain thought he saw a grand opportunity for a night surprise and capture.

The terrible attack came after midnight. Geary repulsed the direct assault, and Howard's divisions cleared the intervening foot-hills, where reserves and supporting Confederates were posted. It was a hard battle, though on a small scale. General Howard in person, with a small body of cavalry, managed to make his way to Geary just after the latter had hurled back the night attack, and at the moment when he was standing near the body of his own son, an officer of artillery, who had been killed but a few moments before. In his depressing grief General Howard was a strength and a solace, and General Geary never forgot the strong sympathy he exhibited toward him on that night of gloom and carnage. General Thomas's published letter gave to General Howard's troops, as well as to Geary's, the highest commendation for their gallantry during that fearful night. So the Eastern and Western soldiers began their acquaintance in battle, while the taking of Lookout Valley gave food to Chattanooga, already nearly starved out.

" General Thomas remarked," says Colonel Dodge, in congratulating Hooker on his victory at Lookout Mountain, that " the bayonet-charge of Howard's troops, made up the side of a steep and difficult hill, over two hundred feet high, completely routing and driving the enemy from his barricades on its top, . . . will rank with the most distinguished feats of arms of this war."

The battles about this stronghold, including Lookout Mountain and Missionary Ridge, were momentous to both North and South. General Grant came to combine Sherman's and Thomas's troops against General Bragg, who, trusting to the immense natural strength of his positions on the heights of Lookout Mountain and Missionary Ridge, had recently sent away Longstreet's corps to operate against Burnside, then holding Knoxville,

East Tennessee. The battle need not be described. As it was beginning, General Howard, taking Bushbeck's brigade, his corps being massed as a reserve near Fort Wood, with his usual fearlessness when duty called, worked his way up the Tennessee on the Confederate side of that river, skirmishing as he went. It was done so rapidly, under cover of ravines and trees, that the brigade met with no disaster, and the general was in time to walk out upon Sherman's pontoon-bridge and meet him as the last boat was being brought in. Sherman sprang over the remaining unplanked chasm, and the two generals met, not absolutely for the first time—for Howard had seen Sherman before—but this was the first real recognition between them, an acquaintance which ripened into a lasting friendship. Sherman took Howard's hand, looking pleasantly into his face, and thanked him warmly for his resolute and prompt co-operation. He asked for the brigade that Howard had brought, and it did gallant work in his severe flank attacks upon Bragg's position near the railroad tunnel. Under its distinguished German colonel, Bushbeck, it had much fighting to do, and many of its officers and men met death on the hill-sides in that bloody and discouraging part of the conflict. Soon General Howard marched the remainder of his corps to the extreme left to support and help General Sherman, while General Thomas, at the centre, was breaking over the Confederate lines and crowning the heights of Missionary Ridge, which the confident Bragg had deemed impregnable.

As soon as the battle was over Howard joined Sherman in the pursuit, and made a flank march through Parker's Gap of Taylor's Ridge so speedily that the Confederate rear guard, which had done so much damage to the pursuing Union troops farther south, was obliged to let go and withdraw.   Taking a strong liking to General Howard as a soldier, Sherman asked for him for the immediate Knoxville march.   The troops of Sherman and Howard stopped for neither tents nor supplies; they crossed numerous rivers, making their own bridges, and succeeded in relieving Burnside and forcing off Longstreet toward Virginia before he could complete his siege.   General Sherman was delighted ; he found Howard always wide awake, cheerful, sanguine, and indefatigable.   Here is what Sherman said of him after this memorable campaign :

" In General Howard throughout I found a polished and Christian gentleman, exhibiting the highest and most chivalrous traits of the soldier." *

General Thomas, who was for eight months his army commander, never ceased to trust General Howard.   He had been his instructor in artillery at the military academy, and there was a mutual affection existing between them, which is often enthusiastically expressed in General Howard's letters and writings.   It resulted from this confidence reposed in him by these commanders that, after General Sherman had replaced Grant in the West in the chieftainship of the three armies, and a partial reorganization had taken place, the Fourth Corps in the army of Thomas fell to Howard.   It was in the spring of 1864 about twenty thousand strong, and composed mainly of Western men.   Generals T. J. Wood, Stanley, and Newton were its division commanders.   Sherman,

---

* A less formal though as gratifying a tribute was paid General Howard by this distinguished officer, in a good-natured rebuke which he gave General Wood.   The latter was urging General Howard to take a drink with his friends, as the others were doing, when General Sherman, who was standing near by, said, " Let Howard alone, Wood ; I want one officer who does not drink."

with his four helpers—Thomas, McPherson, Schofield, and Stoneman—made his beginning against General Joseph E. Johnston at or near Dalton, Ga., about May 1st, 1864.

Howard's corps, forming a third of Thomas's force, for a hundred days, almost in succession, took what one may call the brunt of the battles. It mounted to the crest of Taylor's Ridge, defended by an intrenched foe ; it followed on the heels of Johnston, retreating through Dalton to Reseca, and joined McPherson's flanking force, which had the day before hurried on through Snake Creek Gap. It fought in the centre at Adairsville and Cassville. It came up beside Hooker, who had the new Twentieth Corps (a consolidation of the Eleventh and Twelfth), at the intrenchments and tangled thickets near Dallas, Ga., and helped fight the bloody battle of "New Hope Church." One of its divisions made that strong left flank movement together with the Fourteenth, under R. W. Johnson, and at sundown of May 27th made the almost hopeless assaults at Pickett's Mill, and afterward worked the whole night through to intrench and "log up." The Confederate General Johnston, who had with a larger force anticipated that movement ordered by Sherman, said, after the war, that he never in his life saw better conduct than that exhibited by Howard's men in that spirited engagement. He mentions a case where six non-commissioned officers, successively disabled by wounds or killed, had in turn held up the flag and kept it flying. Howard's two divisions, though repulsed in their assault, still held the ground, and forced the Confederate commander to change his front and fall back. His corps bore its part as ordered at the desperate ascent of the Kenesaw Ridge ; they were compelled to attack unapproachable abatis and to leave many bodies close up to strongly-manned intrenchments. All the way to Atlanta they were fighting, and digging, and marching close to resolute, obstinate foes commanded by able generals. Through the battles of Smyrna Camp-ground, Chattahoochee River, Peachtree Creek, and Atlanta this command fought to the entire satisfaction of General Thomas, and met the warm approval of General Sherman.

One instance among the many that could be gathered will serve as an illustration of General Howard's conduct in battle. At Bald Hill, a place which was reached after passing the fields of Dallas and Good Hope, the Fourth Corps found a Confederate force in strong possession. The Confederates held the hill by infantry, and covered it by batteries not far off, bringing to bear a fearful artillery cross-fire. The men of Howard's leading division had tried to take the hill by storm, and had been more than once driven back. Hearing of the repulse, General Howard made his preparations with care, and when all was ready he took a position in plain sight of his men, quietly waiting the advance of his infantry on the crest of a parapet behind which was a battery in full play. It was firing to clear the way for an infantry charge. The general did not move while the replies of the Confederate batteries caused shells to strike the parapet beneath his feet, the trees over his head, and filled the air with smoke, roar, and fragments. His staff and others begged him to dismount and go under cover. "Not this time, gentlemen," he replied ; "we must take that hill." Soon his men, who knew that he was watching them, cleared the crest and gained the height. It was a hot place, full of peril, and the general was anxious lest his men be again dislodged. He meant that they should stay and intrench the hill,

and the instant he saw the skirmishers pass the crest he
sprang into the saddle and, followed by one or two
officers and orderlies, galloped to the very top of the
height.   His soldiers welcomed him with a shout.   The
position was soon strongly intrenched by the willing men,
and made secure against attack.

It is related that two soldiers of Howard's command,
who were watching him while he sat motionless on his
horse as the enemy's guns were discharging, remarked
upon his attitude :

"He don't seem to hear the thunder," one said, mo-
tioning toward their commander.

"Oh, he's praying," was the quick reply ; "wait till
he's through, and then he'll go in."

Several letters, which give us glimpses of the individual life of General Howard during this busy time, are in
place here.

To his Wife.

"LOOKOUT VALLEY, March 8, 1864.

". . . This morning Mr. Reynolds, a young man, you will remember, who came to me while I was wounded, and whose father gave me
the *Herald* to read, arrived by cars to take the place of clerk to Colonel Hayes.   He rode with Charles and I over Raccoon Mountain
to the rough, stony valley beyond.   We visited the people living
there.   One family, consisting of an old man by the name of Scott, a
second wife, and little daughter, presented a picture of wretched des-
olation very painful indeed.   As I entered his log hut, just opposite
the door lay what looked to me like a corpse, the head bound up, the
arms thin, the eyes closed, the face deadly pale, and no breathing
perceptible.   I asked Mr. Scott if his wife was sick, and he said
' Yes.'   The little child was dirty and pale, as nearly all the poor
children are here.   I still thought the woman must be dead, but suddenly a coughing fit came on.   She opened her black eyes and looked,
if anything, more miserable than before.   She said she couldn't
cough many more times like that.   When I spoke of the *better land*, at
first neither understood me ; but when I said *beyond* the *grave* the old
man brightened up, and said it was a good thing if he were only prepared.   He had a hope in Christ, but didn't think he was holy

enough. I asked, 'How is it with you, madam?' She said she had
had a 'hope' for many years, and then wanted to know if I was a
'professor.' 'Yes.' 'What do you belong to?' 'A branch of the
Presbyterian Church.' Her friends were Presbyterians, and my reply
seemed to please her. As soon as they found my name was Howard
they seemed like new people. Brother Charles had been there before, had spoken kindly, and protected their corn when we first came
to the valley. But oh, the poverty, the misery of these poor people !
No clothes but rags, no bedding but filthy old coverlids, no sheets,
no cleanliness, living on meat and hard bread. 'Oh, I can't eat that !'
she said. He has money, but nothing else, and cannot buy. The
old man was quite familiar with Scripture. Thousands will die from
want of vegetable diet. All the people look thin and haggard, with a
sort of chopfallen expression of countenance. We have to feed
every family within five miles of us out of the common crib. . . ."

To Same.

"NEAR DALLAS, GA., May 29, 1864.
" DEAREST : This is a little the longest and most fatiguing of any
campaign we have had. For twenty-five days, with the exception of
two, we have been more or less under fire. Thus far a kind Providence has protected us all except poor Stinson. The doctor thinks
this morning that he will get entirely well. He was close by me, ex-
amining the enemy's works with a glass, when the ball struck him.
He stooped forward and said he was hit, but he thought by a spent
ball. He lay back, and we found the wound. The ball had struck
his breast, and passed quite through him. We carried him back a
little way into a safer place. He began to fail, growing cold. I
asked him if he was trusting in Christ, or something like it, when he
said, 'Yes ; tell them all at home that I expect to meet them in
heaven.' After he was given a little stimulant he rallied and looked
bright. The surgeons came to him. Our own beloved medical direct-
or, Dr. Head, is attending him. How much I wish he was at home !
Stinson is a perfect man. As I review his life and think of his personal character, I find no fault in him. Always ready for duty,
always cheerful, night and day, always brave, I never thought how
much I loved him till I thought I was bidding him a final good-by.
I had seen General Wood cry over a beautiful young officer who was
mortally wounded earlier in the day. Now my turn came. The Lord
can come very nigh us all in these terrible blows. I had my foot hit
by a piece of shell the same day (Friday, May 27th), but my boot-sole
was so thick that my foot was saved with only a contusion. The

shock was enough to make my foot black and blue across the instep and toes, but I am able to wear my boot and walk to-day. Yesterday I rode and walked in a slipper. At the time I was wounded I was commanding two divisions—General Wood's and General Johnson's—attempting, under cover of the woods, to turn the enemy's flank ; but they were prepared, and we had a severe engagement. We succeeded in gaining a position two miles nearer the railroad, but did not dislodge the rebels. They were behind well-constructed intrenchments, as usual. The army opposed to us is large and in good condition, and we have no easy task before us ; but under the Divine blessing, and with a cause as sacred as ours, we shall succeed. As soon as Harry Stinson is able to take the ride, we will send him North. At present he is better here, with good medical care." *

Extract from next Letter.

"June 2.

"We have at last really got into the sunny South. We are encamped in a wood. My tent was our only one, and that we gave to Stinson. Charles and I put our robes on the ground under a tent-fly, and when the rebels will let us we sleep very well. Give my love and sympathy to Mrs. Stinson" [the mother of Captain Stinson].

To Same.

"   HEADQUARTERS FOURTH CORPS,
    ACROSS CHATTAHOOCHEE, NEAR POWER'S FERRY,
        July 16, 1864.

" . . . We are still in same camp as when I last wrote. General Schofield often visits me, and I him. He has proven himself a very fine officer, good to manage men, and of excellent judgment in other military matters. . . ."

To Same.

"NEAR ATLANTA, GA. (two miles), July 23, 1864.

"DEAREST : We were all made sad yesterday by the death of McPherson, so young, so noble, so promising, already commanding a department. I believe you saw him at Watervliet. . . . We are now within two miles of Atlanta, and the matter will soon be decided. Hood, now in command of Confederate army, was a classmate of McPherson. He is a stupid fellow, but a hard fighter ; does very unexpected things. . . ."

---

* Captain Stinson died in Florida just after the war from the effect of his wound. General Howard has a son named after him.

To Same.

"HEADQUARTERS DEPARTMENT OF TENNESSEE, }
July 29, 1864. }

"DEAREST : You will see by the papers that I have been assigned to the command of this department and army. It is indeed a very high compliment to me, as I am junior to Generals Hooker and Slocum ; but as a matter of fact it is an assignment to new duties and new responsibilities. The first day, the 27th, I received the army in motion from our extreme left, and was obliged to displace the enemy to put it in position on the extreme right. We did not have time to get into position at night, so that early yesterday morning the movement was continued. We had hardly got into position before the enemy attacked me all along General Logan's corps (Fifteenth) and a little beyond the flank. My flank gave back probably thirty paces. The enemy was repulsed at every point, and even on the flank every inch of ground was recovered. I was about two hundred paces in rear of the centre, and I assure you for four hours the engagement was terrific, on one point and another, and sometimes all along ; there was a continuous roll of musketry from half past eleven A.M. till half past three P.M. Our men had covered themselves with rails and old logs, hastily thrown together. We had about six hundred in killed, wounded, and missing, but the dead lay in great numbers in our front. All night the enemy's ambulances were carrying off their wounded. Poor fellows ! they were rushed into the fight without mercy. They lost a thousand where we lost a hundred. My first engagement in command of the Army of the Tennessee has proven a success. I take the place of a commander very much beloved and very accomplished. It remains to be seen whether I shall be able to fill his place. . . . Captain Stinson has got back ; came yesterday. I shall have him keep a journal till he gets strong enough for hard knocks. He says he is well, but he is a shade or two whiter than his fellow-soldiers. . . ."

To his Wife (after Arrival at Savannah).

"SAVANNAH, December 26, 1864.

" . . . I want to see the loving faces—yours and the children's—so much that I am really homesick. I went to General Sherman and told him, ' Now let me off. I don't ask but two days at home.' He said, ' General, I would give a million of dollars, if I had it, to be with my children ; would you do more than that ? ' I told him I should say nothing more, and I have given up for the present. . . . I brought in a flock of little children last night—some little girls and boys—and had a nice time with them. Carrie Emstein, an accomplished little girl, ten years old, promised to come and play for me on *my* piano some time. Carrie was very sweet, but couldn't give me a kiss. 'Not allowed to kiss people,' so I must go home to get sweet kisses."

General Howard thus describes his first meeting with General Grant, in one of his letters to his wife (dated Bridgeport, Tenn., October 24th) :

" General Rosecrans called to see me as he came through, and I accompanied him to Stevenson. There I met General Grant, who had telegraphed that he would be at this place that night. The telegram came after I had left. I returned immediately in his train. He, General Meigs, and Mr. Charles A. Dana, Assistant Secretary of War, took tea with me. General Grant was on crutches still. I gave him up my bed and tent, because he was lame, and not wholly because he was General U. S. Grant. I liked his appearance better than that of any major-general I have seen. He is modest, quiet, and thoughtful. He looks the picture of firmness. He does not drink liquor, and never swears. A member of his staff told me he never had used a profane word. How different from what we had imagined, when those stories of Shiloh were being circulated ! I rode with him Thursday morning as far as Jasper, a ride of about twenty-four miles. . . . I expect some change of organization will take place soon, as General Grant has taken hold. . . ."

" November 4.

" . . . I am very much pleased with General Grant. He doesn't play the great man at all, but goes straightforward about his business. General Grant's headquarters are also at Chattanooga. The rebels still occupy Lookout Mountain, and occasionally throw a shell down into this valley. . . ."

" LOOKOUT VALLEY, November 20.

" . . . Some rebel letters were thrown across the lines to-night, open. One is from a captain to his lady-love, and the other from a soldier to his mother. As there was no harm in them, I sealed them and sent them on. Poor fellows ! how many of them long for the war to be over and for home. Many have come in lately and given themselves up. May God bless and protect you and the children ! Pray for me that I may rise above all temptations to evil. I hope you are well. Lovingly, OTIS."

After the death of the gallant McPherson, near
Atlanta, July 22d, 1864, Generals Thomas and Sherman
recommended General Howard to the President for this
vacancy—the command of the Army and Department of
the Tennessee. The President promptly made the
assignment as requested. It now appears that General
Howard, for the sake of harmony, urged General Sherman to give the place to General Hooker, as Hooker was
Howard's senior in commission and much desired the
special promotion. Logan, too, having fallen to the
command in the battle of the 22d of July, because of
his relative rank there, naturally desired to continue as
an army commander. Much feeling arose in consequence of Sherman's ultimate decision and recommendation—a feeling which had some immediate and serious
results. General Hooker resigned his corps, the Second,
and left the front ; General Logan remained with his
troops, and commanded the Fifteenth Corps under General Howard, but he and his friends greatly blamed
General Sherman. It will be of interest to insert here
General Sherman's own explanation of his reasons,
given in his Memoirs, which are so honorable to General
Howard. He says :

" . . . It was all-important that there should exist a perfect under-
standing among the army commanders, and at a conference with
General George H. Thomas at the headquarters of General Thomas
J. Wood, commanding a division of the Fourth Corps, he [General
Thomas] remonstrated warmly against my recommending that General Logan should be regularly assigned to the command of the Army
of the Tennessee by reason of his accidental seniority. We discussed
fully the merits and qualities of every officer of high rank in the
army, and finally settled on Major-General O. O. Howard as the best
officer who was present and available for the purpose. On the 24th
of July I telegraphed to General Halleck this preference, and it was
promptly ratified by the President. . . . I wanted to succeed in
taking Atlanta, and needed commanders who were purely and techni-

cally soldiers, men who would obey orders and execute them promptly and on time ; for I knew that we would have to execute some
most delicate manœuvres, requiring the utmost skill, nicety, and
precision.   I believed that General Howard would do all these faithfully and well, and I think the result has justified my choice. . . ." *

General J. D. Cox, in his " Atlanta," † in speaking
of the reorganization of the Army of the Tennessee after
McPherson's death, says :

" Hooker was the senior officer available, if the whole
army were considered, and Logan, if the Army of the
Tennessee should furnish the commandant.   A doubt
whether other corps commanders of the army would
cheerfully serve under Logan, owing to some existing
jealousies, was one of the reasons for making a selection
outside of that organization.

" Hooker was the senior of both Sherman and Thomas,
and looked upon the appointment to the vacancy as his
right.   Since the incident of June 22d Sherman had
found the differences between them increasing, and
honestly doubted whether he could have the cordial
co-operation from him which was so essential in his
principal subordinates, and he put Hooker out of the list
of those eligible for assignment.   After consulting with
Thomas, Sherman recommended Howard for the position.   In Howard Sherman found most of the same
traits which made his association with Thomas and
Schofield a satisfactory one.   Conscientiously true and
loyal to their superior, all three of them asked only how
they might most thoroughly carry out his plans, without
caption, hesitation, or complaint.   Their abilities and
experience made them at ease in the handling of large
bodies of men, and it is rare that a large army has had

---

* Sherman's Memoirs, vol. ii.   † Campaigns of the Civil War Series.

its principal generals so cordial in co-operation, so free
from jealousies or intrigues, and so able to relieve the
general-in-chief from the details of administration and of
the tactical handling of troops."

General Bowman says of Howard in similar connection :

" General Sherman seems greatly to have admired the Christian
character of Howard, making frequent mention of him in his correspondence in terms similar to those above quoted ; and not only as a
Christian, but as a soldier, preferring him and promoting him to the
command of one of his armies."

Mr. Blaine wrote General Howard from his home in
Augusta, Me., when he heard of his promotion, these
words :

" August 13, 1864.

" MY DEAR GENERAL : Your promotion to the command of the
Department and the Army of the Tennessee has been hailed by your
friends and the public with profound satisfaction.   Enviable as was
your record before, you have added to it immensely by your masterly
conduct in the trying and splendid campaign from Chattanooga to
Atlanta.   Not to detract from others, I should say to-day that in
popular esteem Grant, Sherman, Howard, and Hancock stand a niche
higher than any other generals in our service. . . .

" Most truly yours,

(Signed)   " J. G. BLAINE."

General Howard was put to an immediate test.   The
next day, after he took command of his army, it fought
unaided the hard battle of Ezra Chapel against the Confederate General Hood, who had but recently replaced
General J. E. Johnston at Atlanta.   Howard had moved
his command from the left, where McPherson fell, by
the rear of Thomas and Schofield, to the extreme right ;
and just as he had deployed his force Hood attacked
him with great suddenness and fury.   But the assault
had been carefully prepared for by General Howard,

who had ordered his right front to be covered with piles of fence rails. The attack of Hood was most successfully met. Three times did General Hood try his utmost, and once drove back Logan's right, but General Howard sent two regiments from Blair, who were armed with repeating rifles, and took from Blair and Dodge enough cannon to be so massed in *échelon* with his right flank that the enemy could not stand against its fire. General Hood was at last forced to retire within the works at Atlanta, and General Howard had the honor of gaining a battle with his new command. Howard and Hood were three years together as cadets.

General Howard, in an article in the *Atlantic Monthly* (October, 1876) remarks about the closing scenes of this combat :

"I heard, I think it was through Colonel Howard on his return from Sherman, that the men who had given away at the first onset had fled as far as Sherman's headquarters, and that an officer had headed them in the retreat and had said to the general, 'Everything is lost ; the troops are missing McPherson ; if you don't at once take care of that flank you will be defeated !' Sherman simply asked, 'Is General Howard there?' 'Yes.' 'Then I shall wait for his report.'"

General Howard remarks further :

" It is difficult to fight any battle without suffering from at least a few stragglers and croakers. Approaching the battle line during the progress of an engagement, the nearer you come to the actual front the cooler and steadier you find the men. This was my first trial with those men, and I was delighted with their conduct."

The confidence was mutual ; the front line had seen Howard with them when the danger was at its height ; and at the close of the eventful day, as he rode along by the piles of rails, they gave him cheer after cheer. In the next movement General Howard by night drew his

command out from fronting Atlanta with so much care
and quietness that his march was undiscovered by Hood.
He swung off southward twenty-five miles to strike
Jonesborough, Ga.   Here he obtained great credit from
Sherman for taking in the situation, anticipating all
orders, moving six miles farther than prescribed ; for
forcing the abandonment of the Flint River Bridge ; for
stopping the flames already lighted and intrenching the
heights of Jonesborough all night, close up to the ranks
of the Confederate General Hardee, who had, with a good
portion of the Atlanta garrison, hurriedly come hither by
rail to meet him.   The battle of Jonesborough, August
31st, 1864, was joined the next day by an assault from the
Confederates, and General Howard was again successful.
Other troops of Sherman came to complete the battle,
and Hood was thus forced to abandon Atlanta, which
had been so long and so ably defended.

General Sherman, in his reports, commended General
Howard for his independent and vigorous action, and indeed the results due to his ability and energy were certainly confirmatory of the wisdom of his choice.

VI.

THE indomitable Hood did not close his operations after the loss of Atlanta. The last scene of the first act was at Lovejoy Station, below Jonesborough, where he again, after the evacuation of Atlanta, brought together his separated forces. The battle at Lovejoy was but a brief combat ; then Sherman withdrew and moved back to East Point, the first railway station south of Atlanta. General Howard went into camp near this place for the purpose of resting and re-supplying his army. He had, however, sent one division, under General Corse, back to the north of the Etowah, to guard Sherman's communications with Chattanooga and the North. Meanwhile, after but a brief respite, Hood turned his face northward, turning Sherman's right flank and towing back all Sherman's army except the Twentieth Corps, which Sherman obstinately kept at Atlanta during his blind chase after the appearing and disappearing Confederates. As Hood neared the Etowah, he sent one division, ten thousand strong, to take the sub-depot at Altoona Pass, near where the railroad crosses the Etowah. Corse hastened thither from Rome, Ga., and with fifteen hundred men successfully defended the pass and depot.

General Howard, with the remainder of his three corps, made forced marches night and day, first reliev-

ing Altoona and then following up Hood closely toward
Chattanooga. So fast did he come that Hood tried to
get away from him by turning to the left through the
famous Snake Creek Gap, which for a space of five miles
in length, though narrow in width, the Confederates had
filled with bushes and felled trees. Howard, almost
upon his heels, with staff, orderlies, engineers, pioneers,
and a division of infantry, quickly cleared the crooked
canyon of its obstructions, and he and his antagonist
slept the night following Hood's passage on the same
side of Taylor's Ridge. General Hood now took a
south-west course with great speed, passed to Graysville,
Ala., and threatened another turn—namely, to cross the
Tennessee and move toward Nashville. Sherman, at
Graysville, seeing this threat, really desired to favor the
movement ; so he slowly brought his forces back to the
line of the Chattanooga and Atlanta Railroad, and rested
them, while he matured and perfected his plans. These
were to send the troops of Schofield and Stanley, the
Fourth Corps, and what could be spared from the Mississippi and elsewhere to Nashville, with as much despatch
as possible. The new army thus formed was to be
under the command of General Thomas, to stand warily
on the defensive, but to be strong enough to meet and
defeat Hood if he came north ; while the remainder, the
Army of the Tennessee, under General Howard, the
Army of Georgia, consisting of the Fourteenth and
Twentieth Corps, under General Slocum, and Kilpatrick's cavalry, in all sixty-eight thousand men, should,
under Sherman's command, make a march to the sea and
form a junction with the naval fleet then in Southern
waters. The movements began, Howard having the
right wing, and also, for a few days, Kilpatrick's
cavalry. He set out from Atlanta November 16th,

1864, toward Macon, Ga.; Slocum and Sherman accompanying him moved directly toward Augusta. General Howard had a battle near Macon, that of Griswoldville, where he engaged G. W. Smith, who had been his engineering teacher at West Point. One division only was much involved ; General Smith's troops were principally raw recruits, and were badly beaten, so that General Howard was now able to cross the Ocmulgee River and draw off in safety his long trains and those of Kilpatrick, which Smith had threatened to destroy. He parted them and bivouacked his men at Gordon, coming up abreast of Sherman, then at Milledgeville, the two wings being now well forward and but ten miles apart. The cavalry passing to the left, all the divisions moved on, sweeping both sides of the Macon and Savannah Railroad. General Howard marched habitually in three columns, Slocum in two, the whole force making a swathe of forty miles in breadth.

At the Oconee River, General Hardee, the Confederate commander, had troops to dispute its passage. The river-crossing was a narrow place, with high bluffs on either side, well defended by Confederate artillery and infantry. General Osterhaus, who commanded for Logan during his absence at home, was puzzled how to proceed. He said at first, " I can go no farther." General Howard advised him to deploy skirmishers under the nearest trees and keep extending his line up and down until he could get no reply from the other bank. It was done, and then farther up the river, beyond danger, a brigade was sent over. The Confederates, fewer in number, fled when the movement was discovered by them. The bridge was rebuilt, and soon the command was quietly marching along, chatting and smoking as if nothing had happened. Some dead re-

mained there, but numerous wounded were borne along
the hard corduroy roads to Savannah, watched over by
their commander, who took the deepest interest in the
comfort of his men, especially of the sick and wounded.
Wherever he saw an ambulance train his attention was
attracted to it, and the poor men always had a cheery
word or a kind assurance of sympathy from their leader.
To the dying he went with sincere prayers and earnest
faith, and soothed their sufferings as their eyelids closed
in death, far from home and loved ones.   It was a duty
he never ignored, and one that he was peculiarly fitted
to perform.   Gifted with a hopeful, religious nature,
he saw the cheerful side of every affliction and misfortune, and where the case admitted of no hope, he pointed
the way to the rest that remaineth for the weary.   To a
man of his temperament war had no triumphs.   Only
a stern, impelling sense of duty, joined with great ability
and discipline, made him a soldier and kept him to his
profession.

There were many things he did not like in the life
he was compelled to lead.   He could not bear to inflict
pain or cause suffering upon the meanest of God's
creatures.   His heart ached for the poor people, who,
powerless to protect themselves, were often left destitute
by the foraging parties which gathered supplies for the
army.   In one of his letters home he says, on this point :

"We do so many things that are wrong in this living off the country, in the way we do, that I do not like it, and I am afraid of retribu-
tion.   I hope, indeed, some wonderful thing will soon happen, so as
to let us return to peace and prosperity."

The march to the sea continued, and its story is full of
interest.   The accounts of the last fight, at McAllister,
vary.   The fort at the mouth of the Ogeechee River
was to be taken, and Sherman ordered Kilpatrick to

attack it, while he, with the army, should try more
directly to get into Savannah and expel General Hardee
from that city.   Kilpatrick tried, but failed to take the
fort, for cavalry could not traverse the swamps, ditches,
and abatis.   General Howard went to Sherman, and ,
asked the privilege of sending Hazen's Division.   It was
granted, and immediately Howard ordered Chief-Engi-
neer Reese to rebuild the burnt bridge over the Ogeechee,
by having the piers, only partially destroyed, sawed off
to near the water's edge, and then replanked, using the
sheds, barns, and buildings near at hand for this purpose.   The work was quickly done.   As soon as Hazen
had set out, Sherman, taking General Howard with him,
went to the Rice Mill, and there they witnessed the
battle.   The field of encounter was several miles away,
but plainly in sight, the signal-officers communicating
back and forth, giving Hazen's report and Sherman's
orders.

General Sherman says of this engagement :

" The signal-officer had built a platform on the ridge-pole of the
rice-mill.   Leaving our horses behind the stacks of rice-straw, we all
got on the roof of a shed attached to the mill, wherefrom I could
communicate with the signal-officer above, and at the same time look
out toward Ossabaw Sound, and across the Ogeechee River at Fort
McAllister. . . .   The sun was rapidly declining, and I was dreadfully impatient. . . .   Almost at that instant of time we saw Hazen's
troops come out of the dark fringe of woods that encompassed the
fort, the lines dressed as on parade, with colors flying, and moving
forward with a quick, steady pace.   Fort McAllister was then all
alive, its big guns belching forth dense clouds of smoke, which soon
enveloped our assaulting lines.   One color went down, but was up in
a moment.   On the lines advanced, faintly seen in the white, sul-
phurous smoke ; there was a pause, a cessation of fire ; the smoke
cleared away, and the parapets were blue with our men, who fired
their muskets in the air, and shouted so that we actually heard them,
or felt that we did. . . .   During the progress of the assault our little
group on Cheves's Mill hardly breathed ; but no sooner did we see our

flags on the parapet than I exclaimed, in the language of the poor negro
at Cobb's plantation, ' This nigger will have no sleep this night ! ' "

During the northward march across by sea to Beaufort,
to Pocotaligo, across River's Bridge where General
Wager Swayne lost his leg ; at the Battle of Congaree
Creek, crossing two bridges—Saluda and Broad rivers—
in the face of Wade Hampton, the burning of Columbia, the skirmishes and losses at Cheraw, the battle of
Averysborough and of Bentonville (the last engagement of Johnston and Sherman), General Howard nobly
performed his part.   Not one of his seven grand divisions was ever known to be fifteen minutes behind
time.   His men became strong and hardy, and were
equal to great strains of endurance.   After the surrender
of Lee to Grant, and of Johnston to Sherman, the army
which General Howard commanded was marched from
Raleigh to Richmond at the rate of twenty-five miles a
day.   No depredations were now committed.   Howard
was the disciplinarian of the right wing, and his orders
were of the sternest character.   On the march and while
at fight property was stolen ; but as soon as peace was
secured General Howard invited the co-operation of
residents to report any soldier who violated his strict
commands.   He respected the sufferings of the sad and
dispirited people of the South, who were meeting the
double calamity of defeat and poverty.   Many are the
incidents of his kindness at this time, and not one individual during or after the war heard from his lips a word
of hostility or animosity toward the Southern people.
Where he met individuals who were moody or resentful,
and maintained that the North had overwhelmed them
with numbers, he always admitted the fact, and in tones
of conciliation advised them to resume their avocations
and try to restore their material prosperity.

When Howard and Sherman reached Columbia, S. C., the brigade of Stone (Charles R. Wood's Division), having halted and stacked arms, cheered Sherman lustily. Howard noticed that some men among them were unusually wild in demonstration, and at once sent an officer to see if they had obtained liquor. The latter reported that obsequious dealers in goods had sent buckets filled with whiskey along the lines ; that the men, having been skirmishing and marching since daylight, had had no breakfast, and several were already drunk. General Howard ordered them to be put under guard, and until late in the night intoxicated men were being picked up and put in places of safety. Some poor fellows, incapable of taking care of themselves, wandered off through the city, and were burned to death during the conflagration.

General Sherman had given orders that all arsenals and public property not required for the use of the army should be destroyed, but private property and schools were to be protected. General Wade Hampton, who commanded the Confederate rear guard of cavalry, before he abandoned the city ordered all cotton stored there to be burned. Accordingly, bales upon bales were rolled into the streets, the bagging cut, and the contents fired. The wind was very high, and flying bits of cotton were blown about, kindling all kinds of combustibles in various parts of the city. It was not necessary to execute General Sherman's order as to the destruction of the public buildings, for they were soon all on fire, and the Union generals were taxed to their utmost to save the people, whose lives were endangered as much by the unruly element as by the flames. As the fire progressed the prisons were opened, and the wildest excitement prevailed. It was in vain that the commanders issued

orders regarding liquor. General Howard, whose instinctive hatred of intemperance made him hostile to any
insubordination in this direction, tried in vain to stop
numerous soldiers in their debauch, but it was impossible. White men and black, citizens and some soldiers,
steeped themselves in liquor, while the flames, raging
and hissing, wrapped themselves over the houses, licking
up everything that was touched. Frightened women
and children hurried through the streets, while the better
soldiers, under command of energetic officers, worked
hard to save some buildings by tearing down others, or
to carry water to roofs still unharmed. The picture of
grief, horror, and wickedness that the two generals witnessed as they rode about the city they can never forget.
The unselfish effort of those who labored through the
night General Howard tried to supplement ; he sent for
Wood's Division ; for men free from the influence of
liquor, and detailed organized bodies to work with them
and protect the lives and property of citizens. The
officers under Howard executed his orders with enthusiasm, and did humanitarian work that night which
greatly benefited the suffering people. General Howard himself remained all night on duty, directing and
watching the scenes about him, and the morning after
the carnage was thoroughly sick at heart over the misery
all around, and which he was almost powerless to relieve.

From Columbia General Howard marched northward,
and at Raleigh, N. C., under date of April 17th, 1865,
he wrote to his mother regarding the national calamity
which had occurred a few days before, on the 14th inst. :

"MY DEAR MOTHER : You have probably seen by the papers before
this time that we are in Raleigh. I would give you a little description of our campaign, and dwell upon our bright prospects of peace,
were it not that my whole mind and heart keeps returning to the

terrible news that has just reached us. I cannot realize it, yet it comes so straight I cannot doubt it. President Lincoln has been everything to the nation, and the nation will never cease to do him honor. But to me, personally, he has been a friend ; though dealing with thousands, he never forgot me after our first interview. When at Savannah the Secretary of War took my hand in both his and assured me in the kindest manner of the President's sincere regard and appreciation of my service, I anticipated a real pleasure in serving under his administration after the war was over, cherishing the same complete confidence in Mr. Lincoln that I would in my own father, and knowing that he would sustain me in every right course. The prospect of peace and home had filled all hearts with enthusiasm, and everybody was generous ; but the revulsion will be sudden and overwhelming. I am afraid of the spirit it may awaken when it is known that men have been set on foot to murder those so much beloved and trusted as Lincoln, Seward, Grant, Sherman, and others. I can only say of these blind fools, ' God forgive them, for they know not what they do.' Give my love to all around you. It will not be many days before I shall be with you. . . .''

On reaching Richmond General Howard received a telegram from Mr. Stanton, Secretary of War, to cause his army to march overland, but to come himself by water as quickly as.possible to Washington.

The 6th of May he arrived, and reported himself at the War Department, where he was informed by the Secretary that it was Mr. Lincoln's wish that he should become the Freedmen's commissioner, as contemplated in the law of Congress, as soon as his services could be spared from the field. And thereupon he put into General Howard's hands the act establishing the Freedmen's Bureau. " Will you accept ? Think it over, and give me your answer as quickly as you can," said the Secretary. General Howard looked upon the request as a legacy from the martyred President, and was inclined to yield a ready assent. At the same time he wanted to remain in command of the army with which he had fought so many battles until after the grand review.

General Sherman advised him to accept the trust, and deprecated his refusal for any such reason, saying, "Howard, you are a Christian ; what do you care for that day's display ? It will be everything to Logan to have the command ; why not let him have it ?"

"If you put it in that ground, General," replied Howard, " I yield at once."

He was disappointed, but quietly conquered his feeling, and asked permission to ride with Sherman's staff. General Sherman generously replied, " Ride by my side, Howard." And so, on the day of the great review, when this great commander at the head of the troops saluted President Johnson in front of the White House, General Howard was at his side, and with his bridle-reins in his mouth and his sword in his left hand, saluted the chief of the nation, and was a noticeable figure in the assembled multitude. Wherever he went he was quickly recognized, and hundreds cheered him as they looked at his empty sleeve.

*   *   *   *   .   *   *

But a brief account has been given of General Howard's military career during the great war of secession ; and as it was a personal strife among our own people, it is difficult to divorce one's self sufficiently from the influences, causes, and effects of the civil struggle to behold the ability and worth of a great actor, without bias to one side or the other.

General Howard had conceived that his duty to man was of an ethical nature, and had meditated, even planned, to leave the military service. He had studied the Scriptures in Greek and Hebrew ; had read extensively in connection with this study ; had even gone so far as to arrange for a course of study at one of the theological seminaries of New England. When the war broke out, he, being a soldier who had been trained for the work at his country's expense, like Jackson, Farragut, and Bishop Polk, followed what he declared were the " limitations and the leadings of Providence." He had always written and spoken much to those who were glad to meet with him in public at Sunday and Wednesday evening meetings ; and in his tent, as at home, he never omitted a brief supplication aloud at his table, whether that table happened to be a mess-chest or a canvas spread on the ground. On the Sabbaths, when the necessities of war permitted, he gathered together all he could, and read or spoke to them of what pertained to their highest interests, calling on them to exercise filial fear and love, and to obey the commandments of their Heavenly Father.   In all dark days he not only kept up heart, but encouraged all who came near, from the highest officer to the humblest orderly.   His faith was strong in the Lord, and he felt that in His keeping were all the issues of life.

It is well to note the views of his fellow-officers regarding General Howard's military career, and of civilians who knew him in his higher character as a Christian man.   Of Fair Oaks, Colonel Bowman thus speaks :

" General Howard was with the Army of the Potomac on the Peninsula until the battle of Fair Oaks, where he lost his right arm while leading his brigade in a charge against the enemy.   Two bullets entered the arm, one near the wrist and the other near the elbow ; but he did not leave the field until, on being wounded the second time, his strength gave out, and he was obliged to go to the rear and submit [six hours afterward] to amputation.   After an absence of two months and twenty days, he returned in season to be with his corps at the second battle of Bull Run, and on the retreat from Centreville he commanded the rear guard."

This historian adds :

" General Howard, it is well known, has been pious and exemplary from his boyhood, was ever faithful and devoted in the discharge of his religious duties, and this even while a student at West Point."

" He carried his religious principles with him into the army, and was guided and governed by them in all his relations with his officers and men. No matter who was permitted to share his mess or partake of his repast, whether the lowest subaltern of his command or General Sherman himself, no one thought to partake, if Howard were present, without first the invocation of the Divine blessing, himself usually leading, like the head of a family."

And in "Sherman and His Campaigns" is given this estimate of Howard's work and military character :

" Thoroughly educated, an accomplished scholar, a true gentleman, and a brave soldier, General Howard is eminently calculated to inspire the confidence of his superiors, the respect and obedience of his followers, the affection and esteem of all with whom he may be associated. Quiet and unassuming in his deportment ; a fervent and devoted Christian, not only in his belief, but in his daily life ; conscientious to a degree in the performance of the smallest duty ; careless of exposing his person in battle, to an extent that would be attributable to rashness or fatalism if it were not known to spring from religion ; strictly honorable in all things ; warm in his sympathies and cordial in his friendships, Howard presents a rare combination of qualities no less grand than simple, equally to be imitated for their virtue and loved for their humanity."

From General Sherman we have always the uniform testimonials, like the following, written at the close of the great campaign through the heart of the Southern country, in which he gives his estimate of a Christian soldier.

" At my last interview with Mr. Lincoln [he wrote to Mr. James E. Yeatman, of the U. S. Sanitary Commission, May 21st, 1865, on his boat anchored in James River, in the midst of the army], your name came up as one spoken of to fill the office of commissioner of refugees, freedmen, etc., and I volunteered my assertion that if you would accept office, which I doubted, the bureau would not go into more kind and charitable hands ; but since that time the office has, properly enough, been given to General Howard, who has held high command under me for more than a year ; and I am sure you will be pleased to know that he is as pure a man as ever lived, a strict Christian, and a model soldier, the loss of an arm attesting his services. He will do all that one man can do, if not forced to undertake impossibilities. . . ."

General Howard's life has been marked by wide usefulness in serving individuals whose needs he has helped and whose shortcomings he has tried to remove. Numberless instances might be related, and one or two are, in justice to this phase of his character, given.

E. C., a resident of Oregon, a man with a large family, had been for many years a notorious gambler and a rough. Through the prayers and influence of a few good women and the Lord's help, he had been converted.

General distrust of the man led people to leave him and his family to shift for themselves. General Howard was his constant and never-failing friend, often lending him money, sometimes as high as two or three hundred dollars at a time.

From being one of the worst of men he became one of the best, and has now for years led a most exemplary Christian life, and though poor in this world's goods has repaid every cent of those early loans.

Mr. M., for years an infidel, had an infidel book to peruse. When his heart was smitten for his infidelity he brought his book to General Howard, and begged him to read it.

General Howard said, " No ; it might weaken my faith. That author is an able man."

" But, General," said he, " read it for my sake." General Howard read the book, making marginal notes. One was, " What is needed here is the Holy Spirit of the living God."

The general then gave him back his book, and one evening Mr. M. was among the seekers for divine guidance in the Young Men's Christian Association rooms. His voice shook with emotion while telling the incident and his eyes filled with tears. He became a changed man, and his Christian family were made happy by his conversion.

One who had been a soldier with General Howard went to him, one night, and said :

" General, I am a gambler ; I hope soon to be a better man, but I must wait God's time."

" Oh, no," was the impetuous reply ; " *now* is the time."

The two, General Howard and this veteran, walked and talked together for two hours. Soon he stood up in a meeting and made a public confession of religious belief. He became a Christian, surrendering his gambling implements, and has for years led a good life.

An instance illustrative of the occupations of General Howard in the intervals of his public duties is as follows :

"W.'s father was taken suddenly insane, at his home near Richmond, Va. In trying to restrain his father he was sadly hurt. He was poor, and misfortune had followed him closely, for when but a lad he had, in a moment of exasperation, struck a man with a knife, and in consequence had spent years in prison at Richmond.

"Some time after the war he went to General Howard in Washington, and frankly told his history. He must have employment to support his poor father's family. The general, touched by his forlorn condition, gave him employment himself, and, when he could no longer do this, secured him a place in the Interior Department. But W. was pursued by those who wanted his place, and who knew his unfortunate early history. His special foe laid his life all bare, and threw up to him his boyish misfortune, and thus drew him into a personal difficulty. Under the terrible provocation he struck his enemy, and was arrested and put in confinement. Then followed the loss of his position. General Howard visited him, paid his fine, and started him in life again, and gave him an honorable place. He stood by him in more trying ordeals than the one mentioned, and finally obtained for him the official position he now holds, and which he is filling with credit. To-day, in consequence, this young man and his family are happy and respected.

" On one occasion W., nearly heart-broken and in deadly pallor, gave up all hope. General Howard stood by him until he had breathed faith into his heart, took him by the hand, and promised to be to him a brother—a promise which he has always kept."

The following is one of many letters of a similar import received by General Howard during the war, illustrating the wide faith reposed in his Christian helpfulness :

"CANANDAIGUA, N. Y., September 14, 1864.

" DEAR GENERAL : The accompanying letters will inform you of the fate of our dear son Albert. Mrs. Murray, having made your acquaintance at West Point, and you having spoken favorably of our dear boy, she intended to write and thank you for your Christian example, and the interest you expressed and exercised in his spiritual welfare ; but as she has not been able to do so, she desired me to give utterance to the gratitude and great obligation we feel toward you for the part you have taken in preparing our child for that rest to which he has been called. Although it is hard for us to part with him, we are comforted with the belief that for him to die is gain, and we bow in submission to the wise providence of God. It would be a great comfort to us to procure his remains. Lieutenant Breckenridge has been very precise in his letter in describing his grave, and it may be possible that an opportunity may present itself for its removal, which, I feel assured, you would approve and have it done, or advise me if it could be done, and the manner of doing it. We may be unreasonable to feel so anxious, but it is a long time since we have seen our dear child, and we have not a relic as a memento, as everything belonging to him was taken with his battery. . . . I congratulate you upon the brilliant success of your army. It has imparted hope to the country and encouraged recruiting, so that our depleted armies will soon be strongly re-enforced, and the rebellion subdued. I ask pardon for this trespassing on your valuable time.

" Very respectfully yours,

" A. G. MURRAY."

All Christian workers turned to him in time of trouble, and always in the confident belief that he would help the cause that lacked assistance. One letter of this character is as follows :

" U. S. CHRISTIAN COMMISSION,
BRANCH OFFICE,
NASHVILLE, TENN., April 13, 1864.

O. O. Howard, Major-General, Commanding Fourth Army Corps.

" MY DEAR SIR : Your own kindness is my apology for troubling you with a statement of a new difficulty into which we have fallen.

" General Sherman has never met the Christian Commission as an organized effort in the army, and consequently holds our request for so much passing and transportation as a presumption to be denied and rebuked. He says that nearly every regiment at the front has a champion. This, of course, will make a speedy end of all our present plans of working in this military division. These plans require the passage, on an average, of one delegate per day from Nashville

front. Perhaps for an army so encompassed with difficulties of transportation, some change of plan will be best, that shall lessen the
number of delegates to be passed, by increasing their term of service.
But there are great advantages in these frequent reliefs. Each man
brings a full, *fresh* invoice of home feeling and religion, and carries
back reliable information of the need and encouragement for benevolent and religious work in the army. If, however, the public service
is more hindered than helped by this frequent passing, then there
must be a change.

" Will you not give us your views on this matter as relates to this
army ?

" I am waiting a suitable opportunity to lay before the general
commanding a statement of the object and plan of the commission,
and ask his permission to go on.

" A note of introduction and your indorsement of the twofold purpose of the commission—bodily relief and moral re-enforcement—
would be of great weight in our favor.

" My full conviction after a year's experience is, that an average
delegate, in his volunteer service, re-enforces the fighting ability of
the army by as much as one able-bodied veteran.

" Your love for the Master and solicitude for the welfare of men in
service, and your well-known appreciation of the endeavor of the
Christian Commission, lead me to ask this favor at your hand. So
that, if in my ignorance of the delicate nature of military relations, I
have asked what you cannot grant, I shall have no difficulty in appreciating the ground of your refusal.

    " With gratitude and unfeigned respect,
        " I am, General, your obedient servant,
                " EDWARD P. SMITH,
            " General Field Agent, U. S. C. C."

General Howard promptly aided in securing the
presence of these workers.

*   *   *   *   *   *

And now the war was over, and he was called upon to
take charge of another army, greater than any he had
commanded, and to assume a responsibility the magnitude of which would have appalled any man whose
courage was unfortified by religious conviction and trust
in a Higher Power. Of this position to which he was

destined by the martyred President, one of his fellow-officers wrote subsequently these truthful words :

"At the close of the war General Howard was made chief of the Freedmen's Bureau, headquarters at Washington. His duties were ' to correct that in which the law, by reason of its universality, was deficient.' He was placed at the head of a species of poor-law board, with vague powers, to define justice and execute loving-kindness between four millions of emancipated slaves and all the rest of mankind. He was to be not exactly a military commander, nor yet a judge of a court of chancery, but a sort of combination of the religious missionary and school commissioner, with power to feed and instruct, and this for an empire half as large as Europe. But few officers of the army would have had the moral courage to accept such an appointment, and few men are so well fitted to fill it, and discharge one half its complicated and multifarious duties."

As soon as General Howard concluded to accept his new appointment, he apprised his old commander of the fact by a friendly letter, and received the following in answer :

"IN THE FIELD, DUMFRIES, VA., }
May 17, 1865, 9 P.M. }

"DEAR GENERAL : Your letter of May 12th, inclosing General Orders, War Department, No. 91, of May 12th, reached me here, on arrival at camp, about dark. . . . I hardly know whether to congratulate you or not, but of one thing you may rest assured, that you possess my entire confidence, and I cannot imagine that matters that may involve the future of four millions of souls could be put in more charitable and more conscientious hands. So far as man can do, I believe you will, but I fear you have Hercules' task. God has limited the power of man, and though, in the kindness of your heart, you would alleviate all the ills of humanity, it is not possible, nor is it in your power to fulfil one tenth part of the expectations of those who framed the bureau for the freedmen, refugees, and abandoned estates. It is simply impracticable. Yet you can and will do all the good one man may, and that is all you are called on as a man and a Christian to do ; and to that extent count on me as a friend and fellow-soldier for counsel and assistance. . . ."

After giving his views of the negroes and whites in

their new and trying relations, Sherman closes with
these words :

"I am not familiar with the laws of Congress which originated
your bureau, but repeat my entire confidence in your pure and ex-
alted character, and your ability to do, in the premises, all that any
one man can do."

VII.

GENERAL HOWARD in his northward march passed the island of Beaufort, S. C. Here he visited the schools for colored children then in existence under the charge of Northern people, who had gone there to begin the work of educating the race. At this time, while on a visit to a Sunday-school, he relates this incident : He asked the smaller boys, " Who was the Saviour of the world ?" A little stammerer quickly answered, " I ken tell gen'l, sah : Ab'am Lincoln, sah—Ab'am Lincoln."

He had, at the time Sherman issued his orders sending negroes to the Sea Islands, sent away from his wing of the army eighty-five hundred blacks—men, women, and children—who had made an exodus from the Carolinas. They had followed the troops day by day, and had been a source of anxious care to General Howard, who had treated them with marked kindness, bestowing covering and food, and supplying them with wagons and escort to their new homes. The care of these helpless people was a serious problem to all the generals, and to General Howard especially, because of the numbers who were gathered about him. The young men and women were hilarious and happy in their new freedom ; the old were sad and burdensome, but all had to be cared for alike. General Howard was their hero ; he could not

go among them without the greatest demonstrations of
affection on their part. He asked an old auntie, who
had marked her fourscore and ten years, when she joined
the number and commenced to trudge along beside the
marching men, " Where are you going, auntie ?"
" Along with you !" " What for," he asked ; " can
you not fare better here ?" " No, sah," was her reply ;
" I'se want to be wid you !" and she continued her
journey from day to day, with a bundle in one hand and
a long staff in the other.

General Howard was kept busy on the march caring
also for the whites who were in great distress and whose
pitiable condition touched the stoutest hearts. It was no
unusual sight to see people sitting in their doorways,
after the foraging wagons had passed by, in utter despair.
He was constantly trying to prevent injustice, and
while the army had to draw its subsistence from the
country, he supplied the needy and re-issued rations to
the poor whites, whose condition was hardly better than
that of the blacks. General Sherman, when appealed to
in all such cases, would say, good-humoredly, " Go to
Howard ; he will be better to you than your own generals ;" or, " Go to Howard ; he runs the religion of
this army, and is feeding the poor."

General Howard never turned away 'the poor ; he
never lost patience nor grew tired of hearing their griev-
ances. With the better class he was sterner, but it is
said that he has but one instance in all his experience to
regret. At Orange, S. C., a woman worried him greatly
by her demands for a guard, which at this time he could
not spare from his working party. He reminded her
that she had no claim upon the Union army. She went
to General Sherman, who laughed at her complaint
against General Howard ; but the latter, when told of it,

said that she was right, and that he was very sorry he allowed himself to be impatient.

About the time that the operations of the war were closing General Howard wrote to a friend, from New-bern, N. C., to whom he said, after speaking of the news, just received, of the taking of Richmond, and of seeing unexpectedly in the papers a notice of his promo-tion to brigadier-general in the regular army : "I believe I detect some little ill-feeling on the part of old army friends. They probably suspect me of manœuvring to get the place, and cannot easily forgive me for ranking them." And, after noticing the vote of thanks of his State, he said, speaking of his brother Charles, who had just become the colonel of the One Hundred and Twenty-eighth Colored Regiment, and had gone to the Sea Islands :

"I have rather stood in his way than assisted him, and he is obliged to be directed so much by me when we are together that he is not fully himself. Where he is now going good men are needed— men of principle and men who are interested in doing good to their fellows, whether white or black. I expect during my life to have a great deal to do with the negroes, especially because I have so high rank in the regular service ; for, both on account of the increased demand of the Government for soldiers, and that the Government will be obliged to support and govern a large portion of these people, so suddenly set free, general officers will be obliged to organize and superintend this new department of the service."

While at Newbern he thought much of the condition of the negroes and what their future would be, and in reflecting on this subject the old desire to enter the min-istry returned. He believed that God had a plan in his life, and he had about concluded, for the second time, that he ought to leave the military service so as to work more directly in keeping with his heart. About this time General Grant's telegram (May 7th, 1865), ordering him to report to the Secretary of War without delay, reached him.

His decision in regard to the Freedmen's Bureau being made, and Secretary Stanton being notified of his acceptance of the task, he went to the War Department for instruction. Mr. Stanton handed him a copy of the act of Congress and a large wooden tray filled with huge bundles of papers relating to the refugees, saying, as he did so, " There's your bureau, General," at the same time adding that he could have his army officers and existing agents from whom to choose his helpers. A building had been secured for the work at the north-east corner of Nineteenth and I streets, and the Secretary advised him to do what was necessary to organize, and he would give him what assistance he could. " Remember," said Mr. Stanton, " there is not one dollar of appropriation !" Thus was begun the work of the Bureau, and the first great trouble to General Howard that ensued was due to lack of funds. Had there been money enough to organize it properly, the work would have been accomplished with half the.worry and humiliation to its chief, and the Government would have escaped much of the trouble caused by its alleged failure to meet the requirements of the case.

General Howard took his tray to the National Hotel, and while waiting for his building to be made ready, he set at work to find out the needs of the freedmen, who were, in Washington and other cities, clamoring for assistance. Meanwhile he submitted a list of proposed assistants to Mr. Stanton. To some the latter objected. For example, General Howard selected General E. J. Hartzuff for Virginia, and Mr. Stanton favored the retention of Colonel Brown, who was already working as an agent at Norfolk ; also Mr. Stanton favored the continuance of

Rev. Mr. Conway (chaplain) for Louisiana, who had very soon to be replaced by General Absalom Baird. General Howard did not know either of these men. The assistant commissioners who had the States, and were to be responsible for all sub-assistants and agents in those States, were : Colonel Orlando Brown (Virginia), General Eliphalet Whittlesey (North Carolina), afterward General N. A. Miles ; General Rufus Saxton (South Carolina, Georgia, and Florida). Afterward General Davis Tillson had Georgia and Colonel T. R. Osborne Florida, leaving General Saxton in charge of South Carolina only ; General Wager Swayne (Alabama), General John Eaton (Mississippi), Rev. Thomas Conway (Louisiana), and General Gregory (Texas). Soon General Gregory was transferred to Maryland, and General Griffin was given Texas. The latter held the position until his death, and was succeeded by General J. J. Reynolds. General J. W. Sprague was given Arkansas, General Fiske Tennessee and Kentucky ; later General Davis was given the latter State. Colonel Seeley was sent to Missouri, and General S. C. Thomas took General Eaton's position, while the latter was transferred to supervise the District of Columbia and a part of Virginia. When the work grew so as to require more force, General Eaton was called to assist in the office at Washington, and General C. H. Howard finally had Maryland, Delaware, a part of Virginia, and the District of Columbia. The latter officer had been previous to this appointment an inspector at large. Finally General Eaton left Washington to become superintendent of education for the State of Tennessee, under the reorganized State government.

All these appointments were considered good, and not one of the original assistant commissioners recommended

by General Howard has to-day aught against him.
Their subsequent careers were all remarkable. General
J. W. Sprague was for years the superintendent of the
western half of the North Pacific Railroad. General
Swayne, an eminent and successful lawyer, was, like his
father, Justice Swayne, of the Supreme Court of the
United States, a high-minded and upright man. General Tillson in Maine and General Thomas in Ohio were
at the heads of great business enterprises, and General
Whittlesey, a college professor, afterward filled a like
position in Howard University, and was the secretary of
the Board of Indian Commissioners.

The appointments were conferred on military men
(1) because Congress had failed to make an appropriation
directly for the Bureau, and (2) because of the wording
of the act, which was to the effect that the officers of the
Bureau might be detailed from the officers of the army.
There was much feeling about this at the time ; civilians
claimed that they were better suited to effect the exercise
of the benevolent functions of the Government than
army officers, and complaints were made to General
Howard on the subject. He always made the reply that
the gentlemen whom he proposed as assistant commissioners had, with very few exceptions, gone from civil
life into the army at the beginning of the war ; that they
were lawyers, merchants, civil engineers, and teachers,
and well suited to do the work because of their experience with the negroes during the war. President Johnson much desired, and finally, on General Howard's
recommendation, so ordered, that under the primary instruction the military commander of each State should
be also the assistant commissioner of that State. The
only trouble that General Howard anticipated was that
each officer so situated would be obliged to have two

heads at Washington—one General Grant and the other Howard himself. However, the harmony existing between Generals Grant and Howard was such that the work was never impeded from this cause.

General Howard organized the Washington office gradually. The divisions became six in number, as follows : The (1) adjutant-generals, (2) quartermaster and commissary, (3) disbursing, (4) educational, (5) medical, (6) abandoned lands. Later on the payment of bounties was added by an act of Congress, making seven separate departments.

The large wooden tray which Secretary Stanton had given into General Howard's hands held evidence of upward of one hundred and forty thousand poor people, white and black, who were receiving rations in Washington, Richmond, Atlanta, Nashville, and other Southern cities. He had at once a large army transferred to his care. Army rations were allowed to these people for a time ; but when the famine came on, at General Howard's solicitation, special appropriations from Congress were made for the purchase of food to supply the necessaries. Before the appropriation was made, and while the suffering was greatest along the Southern coast, General Howard bought a ship-load of provisions and sent them at once to be distributed in the destitute districts. Congress subsequently relieved him from his personal risk. While the work of feeding these people was under way, a sensational report that " General Howard was feeding niggers in idleness" arose, and the newspapers spread it over the whole country.

The work of securing employment for the able-bodied, and transferring them to places where their services were wanted and would be compensated for, was begun as soon as the dangers of starvation were overcome, and in time from Washington alone ten thousand were sent away to different parts of the North. The word " refugee" was broadly interpreted by the colored people in those days, and the department very likely furnished homes for many who had no claim whatever for help. Complaints of this nature were made, to which General Howard replied that he could not prove the genuineness of every case, but at least the colored population of Washington was reduced by the removal of those who, in spite of his efforts, secured the advantage of being ranked as refugees.

The educational division of the Freedmen's Bureau, enlarging as other divisions diminished, was the one which did the greatest work, and with it General Howard accomplished the best results. He called to his co-operation twenty-seven different Northern benevolent organizations which were sending teachers into the Southern field. Some were Freedmen's branches *per se*, and some were societies of churches. The Methodists, Episcopalians, Catholics, Congregationalists, Presbyterians, Baptists, Friends, Unitarians, etc., had their respective societies and associations under different names. Nearly all these General Howard succeeded in consolidating into a Union Agency for a time, with its headquarters in New York, and known as the Freedmen's Aid Union, with a national executive committee at its head. Some bodies, like the American Missionary Association, which disbursed much money, and already had many schools, deemed it best not to enter into that Union. This fact, together with some obstacles that the Union met with, divided it, and the plan was after some months abandoned.

To facilitate the educational work General Howard adopted the simple arrangement of giving a dollar for every dollar that a society would invest in the work. This dollar-for-dollar plan worked well, and the funds for it he raised by the sale of abandoned property. Much money was secured in this way, and structures were erected for schools, and teachers transported from their homes to their new scenes of labor. The different church societies paid the salaries of these teachers, who did such excellent work. As the Government could not lawfully buy land, General Howard welcomed the appointment of trustees from the different societies, who made the purchases and held the titles to the school lands. In many instances the buildings used for schools were rented, and thus, in one way and another, the ignorant classes were put at school.

Much public objection was made to General Howard's educational projects. It was said that it would lead to voting and other ills, and many school-houses were burned in the South. In the North the opposition was to colleges and universities for the colored people. The common schools were enough, and the argument was that the race designed to be benefited could not appreciate or profit by anything higher than these. In the South the greatest bitterness was expressed toward the project of universities for negroes, for the whites themselves could hardly afford to support the public-school system.

General Howard, in his writings, speeches, and orders, insisted that the common schools brought into existence by the general government could not be permanent; and, further, that to keep up the lower grades the higher must be provided as an incentive, and to give a supply of the needed teachers. His enemies denied his assertions, and maintained that " Howard never would see that niggers are not white men." And he, enthusiast and Christian as he was, demonstrated in reply that the color

of the skin did not necessarily paralyze the intellect.
His favorite method of persuading people to his own way
of thinking was to take a visitor from the South or
North into one of the best schools in Washington and
show him its actual results.   Thoughtful and reasonable
people in great numbers were converted to his view, and
early came to his aid ; and in time there sprang up many
seats of learning which have become permanent, such as
Howard University (at Washington), Hampton (Virginia), Atlanta (Georgia), Fiske (Nashville), Straight
(New Orleans), and others.   Some, like Lincoln University (Pennsylvania) and Berea College (Kentucky), were
simply "aided into larger proportions."   In time the
common schools passed to the control of the States ; but
the higher graded schools have remained, with their
good organizations and with increased constituencies.
Their pupils to-day furnish the greater proportion of the
teachers of the descendants of the emancipated race, and
Southern and Northern leaders of political parties vie
with one another in commendation of their good work.
A few years ago a one-armed Governor of Virginia,
while visiting Hampton Institute, took the remaining
hand of Howard, and with great emotion thanked him,
before a great audience, for what he had done there for
the colored people of Virginia.   He, like thousands of
his countrymen, was surprised at the results obtained by
educating the freedmen.

Not so with General Howard.   He was too firm in
two cardinal principles to be surprised at the fullest frui-
tion of his work.   He had always maintained that there
should be no distinction on account of color, and none
on account of sex.   He applied these two principles not
only to the schools, but to the church in Washington
(the First Congregational), where he was an influential

member. He clung to the idea that Christ died for all men, and that rights and privileges, in His temples, were not to be given to some and withheld from others. To love God and one's neighbor, he insisted, took in all humanity, and he could not exclude a person because of sex or color from any civil or religious liberty. This liberal position was deemed fanatical by narrow minds, but upon a less generous and noble platform General Howard would not have succeeded as he did. It is still alleged that he favored his own Congregational denomination, and much criticism was passed upon him. Before the Congressional Committee and the Court of Inquiry he denied all this. It came before these bodies in the form of a charge, made in a vile letter forged at the War Department under General Belknap's administration. It is almost needless to say that it was fully disproved. Acting on the proposal he had made, of giving dollar for dollar, some organizations received more money than others. But if the American Missionary Association received much help, it was because it had put many dollars into its work.* If the Friends had large aid, it was for the reason that this sect gave liberally. What mattered it to a true friend of humanity who engineered the educational work, so long as it was effectively done ? General Howard was not the man to favor a society because he belonged to it, but if it did well he heartily commended that work. He had too much enthusiasm to show favoritism to one section of his workers.

The adjutant-general's division had charge of the labor question, and to it General Howard gave much thought.

---

* The American Missionary Society alone, from 1862 to 1869, expended $1,650,000 in the education of colored children in the South.

He influenced the organization of joint-stock companies to raise money for farming the abandoned lands, and with the transportation funds which Congress placed at his disposal he gave employment to thousands of idlers. He visited the South in the autumn of 1865, and set up those "Bureau Courts," in which contracts were settled between the freedmen and their employers. These courts were composed of three men : one, the agent of the Bureau ; another, the black man's agent, and the third that of the white man. In all the workings of the Bureau he tried to introduce the simplest details, in order that the most ignorant of its beneficiaries might understand its workings. From town to town General Howard journeyed, addressing all, white and black, and explaining the aims and objects of the Freedmen's Bureau. He visited Richmond, Raleigh, Wilmington, Charleston, Hilton Head, Savannah, Tallahassee, and other places in Florida, Mobile, and Atlanta, and returned to Washington by Tennessee and Kentucky. It was while on this trip and in Atlanta that the incident related by the poet Whittier occurred. It is as follows :

HOWARD AT ATLANTA.

" Right in the track where Sherman
    Ploughed his red furrow,
Out of the narrow cabin,
    Up from the cellar's burrow,
Gathered the little black people,
    With freedom newly dowered,
Where, beside their Northern teacher,
    Stood the soldier, Howard.

" He listened and heard the children
    Of the poor and long-enslavéd
Reading the words of Jesus,
    Singing the songs of David.

Behold the dumb lips speaking,
   The blind eyes seeing !
Bones of the Prophet's vision
   Warmed into being !

" Transformed he saw them passing
   Their new life's portal !
Almost it seemed the mortal
   Put on the immortal.
No more with the beasts of burden,
   No more with stone and clod,
But crowned with glory and honor
   In the image of God !

" There was the human chattel
   Its manhood taking ;
There, in each dark, brown statue,
   A soul was waking !
The man of many battles,
   With tears his eyelids pressing,
Stretched over those dusky foreheads
   His one-armed blessing.

" And he said : ' Who hears can never
   Fear for or doubt you ;
What shall I tell the children
   Up North about you ? '
Then ran round a whisper, a murmur
   Some answer devising ;
And a little boy stood up : ' Massa,
   Tell 'em we're rising ! '

" Oh, black boy of Atlanta !
   But half was spoken ;
The slave's chain and the master's
   Alike are broken.
The one curse of the races
   Held both in tether ;
They are rising—all are rising,
   The black and white together !

" Oh, brave men and fair women !
   Ill comes of hate and scorning ;

> Shall the dark faces only
> Be turned to morning?
> Make time your sole avenger,
> All-healing, all-redressing ;
> Meet Fate half way, and make it
> A joy and blessing."

After President Johnson had decided upon returning the abandoned lands to their former owners, upon certain conditions, General Howard went to the Sea Islands, and met the negroes there, addressing them in all the towns he passed through. He urged them to see things as freemen saw them, and impressed upon them the necessity for industry and uprightness for the grown people ; right training in schools for the young, and the fear of the Lord for all. The burden of his appeals were the resistance to vice and fidelity to God, and he inculcated the lesson of kindness by making the most careful effort to bring about good feeling between the whites and the blacks. Mutual toleration and friendliness he aimed to secure by his presence, and he succeeded in inspiring his assistants with a large share of his own spirit. Perfect results he never expected, but he approximated them as nearly as possible. His work was that of preparing the foundation for the enfranchised race, to begin their work of education and higher development ; he realized that it was a task never to be understood by those for whom he was immediately concerned. The difficulties constantly before him would have discouraged any but a temperament like his own. He is simply incapable, by reason of his all-abounding trust in the Higher Power, of being wholly subdued by disappointments or failures. His career from boyhood abundantly proves this fact.

The task of reasoning with the negroes of the Sea

Islands regarding the decision of the President was most difficult and delicate. They were dreadfully chagrined at losing their recent possessions of land, and charged him with robbing them to help their enemies, the original owners. In one church where he was to speak he met with much excitement and anger on the part of the audience, an immense one, which had assembled to hear his explanation. The decision of the government, as they understood it, was cruel, and their great rage was blind and fanatical. General Howard talked to them quietly until he had aroused their interest ; then he explained the nature of a title, how it rested in the owner or landholder, and declared that neither the President nor Congress had the right to wrest the land from the real owners and give it to them. The Government gave them tax-titles, he told them, and where the people owning the islands had paid up their taxes the Government could not lawfully prevent their claiming the soil they originally possessed. The promise made in General Sherman's orders could not be fully kept, now that the owners were pardoned and reinstated in their full rights. It was hard to control the storm. His hearers insisted that a distinction should be made between loyalty and disloyalty, and maintained that they had lived on the lands when the whites abandoned them, and finally that the great general (Sherman) had given to them and to the refugees whom he sent there these lands, which they were now called upon to leave. General Howard expressed his strong sympathy for them, and touched their hearts by talking of their trusted leader, Abraham Lincoln, who had appointed him to the freedmen's work, because he was their friend. Then he asked them to trust him with the settlement of the matter, promising faithfully to do the best he could for the poor black settlers. All over the building voices cried out, "We'll trust you ; we'll trust you !"

He had promised very much, as he knew, but he carried out the policy of the government in this case, and settled the troubles without any serious difficulties.

A problem which perplexed General Howard in another direction was the following. The valuable lands on Meridan Hill and in the environs of Washington were overrun by refugees, former slaves of Maryland and Virginia, who were living in temporary huts and old war buildings. They could pay no rent, and the owner of the land wanted to be rid of them. He called upon General Howard, and asked for their removal. The latter went with him in his buggy to see the black settlers. They were miserably poor and ragged, and it pained him to be the bearer of such ill tidings as he had to. convey. He assembled them, however, and explained carefully the situation ; the land they were on would soon be sold and divided into building lots, and they must go. They answered, Where can we go? He looked into their distressed faces, and instantly devised a plan for them. Then he asked how many men about him were willing to work ? Nearly all replied, "We do work." "How many will help to get farms of their own ?" he asked. "How can we ?" was the hopeless response. "Suppose," said he, "I get the money for a house and farm near the city, how many of you will work together and pay me for your section of it ?" Nearly all excitedly exclaimed, "I will, Gen'l ; I will !" He then promised to go and see what could be done.

It was this emergency which led him to secure from the appropriation for schools, etc., a fund which, upon taking legal advice, he transferred to trustees, and the "Barry Farm," near the Hospital for the Insane, was purchased. Little plots of an acre each were made, the lumber for a building was quickly purchased, and the accommodations for these homeless people obtained. The needed relief was secured by this plan, and, be it said to the honor of these people, the proceeds of the sales of the little farms enlarged the school fund, which was distributed to certain institutions. This became the best colony of negroes near the capital. Men of character and standing among them influenced those weaker than themselves ; school-houses and churches were erected, and General Howard took great pride in their prosperity.

Good people in England, watching his work, sent him funds to further its prosecution. This money he used in similar projects. He saw the best results follow the plan of making the blacks land-owners, and he helped hundreds to purchase small tracts convenient to schools. The main problem was to employ the people, and he resorted to every practical expedient to obtain work for this purpose. He was constantly warning himself that he must not make paupers. A favorite remark of his was, " Give a staff to a lame man, but if you would cure him he must not use it too long !"

The hospitals and children's asylums from the Delaware to the Rio Grande took all army structures, Confederate and Union. General Howard's medical men conducted them, wherein great humanitarian work was done. Gradually they were transferred to the local authorities, who were reimbursed for so doing with the buildings and other property belonging to the Government. In these different institutions, when the transfers were made, were between five and six hundred of old and decrepit people for whom nobody would care. These General Howard had taken to Washington, where they became inmates of the Freedmen's General Hospi-

tal, which still exists in connection with the Medical Department of Howard University. Here these aged people were made as comfortable as possible, and the Government gave them appropriations.

The next duty General Howard undertook in connection with the freedmen was to abolish the Bureau
Courts, which had fulfilled their purpose. After some
correspondence with the Governor of Alabama, he, accompanied by General Swayne, who had advised the
change, had a consultation with the governor, and the
plan of turning over the Bureau cares to the local magistrates was discussed and approved. The governor guar-
anteed the freedmen full right to testify in local courts,
and the transfer was thereupon made. Immediately the
people of the North cried out against the step. The
newspapers, in many instances, said that General Howard was giving lambs into the care of wolves, and pro-
tested against the course he had pursued. He replied
that the policy of the Government was to close the
Bureau work as soon as practicable, and that justice
would work itself clear in this instance if the right to
testify was not restricted. And this was the beginning
of the negro's testimony in the courts of the South. It
soon extended to other States.

Little by little the work of the Bureau was narrowed
in a similar way, by encouraging local or outside help,
and every department, excepting the educational, was
gradually restricted, until, at the end of two years, the
business was practically finished.

Unfortunately for the completion for which he was
always ardently hoping, Congress imposed upon him and
his Bureau a yet heavier task. An act was passed, as
before stated, by which devolved upon him as commissioner the payment of bounties and dues to those col-

ored soldiers who had served in the war, or to their legal representatives. There were about two hundred thousand of these. They were to be paid by Bureau agents without checks, the law requiring the money, in greenbacks, to be placed in the hands of each soldier. These men were scattered throughout the United States, and many of them to regions outside its limits. The task was the heaviest imposed upon General Howard, but he organized the work, and as good a system as could be devised was adopted and put into active operation. The disbursing of so much money attracted dishonest people, who looked upon it as an opportunity not to be lost. Claim agents were corrupted and bought up, false claims were put in, and the money obtained was too often divided between the agents and the claimants. But, after the most thorough investigation, it was proven that *" the entire loss of the Government from all sources in the disbursement of vast sums by General Howard's Bureau came within one eighth of one per cent of the money expended."*

It was not possible that an officer carrying on such a work as the Freedmen's Bureau should escape calumny. In its prosecution he was brought into contact with selfishness, self-seeking, rivalry, party spirit, deep-seated race prejudices. Against him were also made charges of misappropriation of funds belonging to the Government. He was accused, and asked for a trial. The country rang with the foul aspersions cast upon his name, and his usefulness was well-nigh paralyzed before the truth was established.

It is not necessary to enter into the details of the origin of the scandals circulated against him, or name the persons who were instrumental in bringing them. His ardent advocacy of the rights of the negro was the primary cause of these attacks, and the ignorance of the public regarding the Bureau and its workings led to many erroneous and exaggerated stories gratuitously circulated throughout the country. He, as its chief, was held responsible not only for the faithful performance of his work, but for that lack of hearty co-operation which the public withheld from him. He was at the head of the most unpopular work which the Government had on its hands—a work which, in view of race prejudice and political opposition, seriously threatened the long military record and national reputation of General Howard.

The freedmen were difficult wards to care for, and the legitimate work given the commissioner to do was sufficient to engross his time and thought. Helpless as children, with wholly erroneous ideas of the meaning of the word freedom, fresh from the excitement of war, a more hopeless undertaking than giving them work and teaching them to do it could hardly be imagined. It was not until the true state of affairs and the nature of the burden that rested upon Howard's shoulders was made public, through the Court of Inquiry, that a just idea of the magnitude of his task and its drawbacks was realized. A less unselfish and patient man would have abandoned a post open to assault from those who should have sustained his work ; many times, weary of ingratitude, he longed for release from its vicissitudes and vexations.

The public investigation of the Bureau management was a blessing in disguise, though at the time the necessity for it—constant misrepresentations—seemed the final humiliation which his advocacy of human rights in the interests of the colored race had entailed upon him. Generous American sentiment came to his defence when the facts were laid bare. All the difficulties under which he had labored, the work that had been accomplished, and the persecutions which had followed him—all that he would have left untold of himself, in his own honor and to his credit, the investigation brought out, and the nation's vindication came before the findings of the investigating committee. The report of this committee was concluded in these strong sentences :

"Has the Bureau been a success ? Success ! The world can point to nothing like it in all the history of emancipation. No thirteen millions of dollars were ever more wisely spent ; yet from the beginning this scheme has encountered the bitterest opposition and the most unrelenting hate. Scoffed at like a thing of shame, often struck and sorely wounded ; sometimes in the house of its friends apologized for, rather than defended ; yet, with God on its side, the Freedmen's Bureau has triumphed ; civilization has received a new impulse, and the friends of humanity may well rejoice. The Bureau work is being rapidly brought to a close, and its accomplishments will enter into history, while the unfounded accusations brought against it will be forgotten. There is a day and an hour when slander lives not. When the passions of men subside, and when the dust of time has well fallen, then comes the hour of calmer judgment. Many-tongued scandal has the briefest of existence :

A wandering night-moth,
Allured by taper gleaming bright,
Now busy, now all darkling,
She snaps and fades to empty air.

Evil is quickly forgotten ; truth alone is abiding.

"In conclusion, the committee find, on the whole case, that the charges are utterly groundless and causeless ; that the commissioner has been a devoted, honest, and able public servant. The committee find that his great trust has been performed wisely, disinterestedly, economically, and most successfully. If there be anything in the conduct of the affairs of the Bureau which could excite a suspicion, even in the breast of partisan or personal hate, it is owing to the fact that General Howard, conscious of his own purity, intent on his great work, has never stopped to think of the appearances which men of less conscious integrity much more carefully regard. Who is the inventor or instigator of these charges, it is not the purpose of the committee to inquire. Mr. Wood, of New York, as has already been stated, disclaims all personal responsibility for them. The evidence which he adduced was not evidence tending to establish the accusation, but was, nearly all of it, merely experimental—an inquiry by the person calling the witness into the details of transactions of which he seemed to have neither accurate knowledge nor information. While the examination was going on, with closed doors, under a pledge of secrecy imposed on the committee, counsel and parties, incorrect statements, purporting to be reports of the testimony, were spread extensively through the country most injurious to General Howard, and utterly without support in the evidence. It is not in the power of the committee or the House to repair this injustice, or to compensate this faithful public officer for the indignity, anxiety, and expense which his defence has entailed upon him. All that is in our power is to recommend to the House the passage of the following resolution, as expressing our opinion of the whole case, and an act of justice to a faithful and distinguished public servant :

"*Resolved*, That the policy pursued by the United States toward four and a half millions of its people suddenly enfranchised by the events of the great Civil War, in seeking to provide for them education, to render them independent and self-supporting, and in extending to them civil and political equality, is a source of just national pride ; and that the House hereby acquits Major-General Oliver O. Howard of the groundless and causeless charges lately preferred against him, and does hereby declare and record its judgment, that in successfully organizing and administering with fidelity, integrity, and ability the Freedmen's Bureau, which has contributed so much to the accomplishment of the first two of these great ends, he is deserving of the gratitude of the American people.

" SAMUEL M. ARNELL,
" JOHN BEATTY,
" GEORGE F. HOAR,
" WASHINGTON TOWNSEND,
" CHARLES M. HAMILTON,
" SAMUEL S. BURDETT,
" JAMES N. TYNER,
" LEGRAND W. PERCE."

What the Bureau had done was well told in an article in the *Old and New* (February, 1870), written by Sidney Andrews.

" Of the thousand things that the Bureau has done no balance sheet can ever be made. How it helped the ministries of the Church, saved the blacks from robbery and persecution, enforced respect for the negro's rights, instructed all the people in the meaning of the law, threw itself against the strongholds of intemperance, settled

neighborhood quarrels, brought about amicable relations between
employer and employed, comforted the sorrowful, raised up the
down-hearted, corrected bad habits among whites and blacks, restored order, sustained contracts for work, compelled attention to
the statute-books, collected claims, furthered local educational
movements, gave sanctity to the marriage relation, dignified labor,
strengthened men and women in good resolutions, rooted out old
prejudices, ennobled the home, assisted the freedmen to become land-
owners, brought offenders to justice, broke up bands of outlaws,
overturned the class-rule of ignorance, led bitter hearts into brighter
ways, shamed strong hearts into charity and forgiveness, promulgated
the new doctrine of equal rights, destroyed the seeds of mistrust and
antagonism, cheered the despondent, set idlers at work, aided in the
reorganization of society, carried the light of the North into dark
places in the South, steadied the negro in his struggle with novel
ideas, inculcated kindly feeling, checked the passion of whites and
blacks, opened the blind eyes of judges and jurors, taught the gospel
of forbearance, encouraged human sympathy, distributed the generous charities of the benevolent, upheld loyalty, assisted in creating
a sentiment of nationality—how it did all this and a hundredfold
more, who shall ever tell ?   What pen shall ever record ?"

In an article in Johnson's Universal Cyclopædia, on
the " Freedmen's Bureau," General Howard says :

" Out of the ' labor questions ' naturally came the questions for
courts—next, ' bureau courts and magistrates.' These were kept up
till the testimony of black men was received in the State and local
courts. . . . For a while, too, the subject of the marriage relation
gave rise to much perplexity. There were so very many who had
been married several times, or there had been so little recognition of
marriage at all before freedom, that the difficulties were great.
Agents saw to it that the marriage ceremony was performed, and a
careful record kept. In fact, scarcely any subject that has to be
legislated upon in civil society failed at one time or other to demand
the action of this singular Bureau. In time bureau courts gave place
to others—bureau contracts and bureau marriages to local and cleri-
cal. The pauper class was gradually transferred ; the asylums and
hospitals one after another assumed by societies or towns ; questions of land-titles closed ; in brief, all operations were purposely
reduced and transmuted into the common system of government in
this country. The last thing of importance given up were the
schools, one asylum at Washington, and the payment of bounty."

VIII.

WHILE hard at work closing up the Freedmen's Bureau in Washington, in March, 1872, General Howard was called to assume new duties in an unexpected quarter. He was appointed Peace Commissioner to the Indians of Arizona and New Mexico, including the Chiricaua Apaches, a sub-tribe of the powerful Apache Indians of Arizona. His reluctance in leaving a work in which he had toiled through so many difficulties and oppositions, and done his duty amid bitter experiences of every character, which had only endeared it the more to him, was tempered by the consideration that his mission still was to bring peace and good-will among men. The Government officials and the benevolent agencies of the country had, by their combined efforts, succeeded in establishing peace between the numerous tribes of Indians ; of the two hundred and fifty thousand tribes, it was only a few scattered bands near the Mexican frontier that had continued their predatory raids, committing the worst acts of cruelty when opportunities occurred. They had been at desperate war with the white race for more than ten years, killing and being killed, robbing and being robbed. Their homes were in the fastnesses of the Dragoon, Chiricaua, and Mogollon mountains, from which they made constant sorties upon trains of wagons, stages loaded with passengers, and individual travellers who ventured along the rough paths of Arizona. They occasionally attacked small hamlets and put villages on both sides of the border under contribution. Living on the debatable ground between the United States and Mexico, they could escape the military forces protecting the borders of either country by flying into the other. A secret friendship existed between the different tribes ; men and women of the Chiricauas were constantly going among the other bands, inciting them to acts of violence, so that outbreaks were expected at any moment by the scattered white population of the frontier. Military companies had followed Cochise and his captains into the fastnesses of the mountains, and invariably been routed and driven back. Of late they had given unusual trouble, and the civil agents and missionaries had labored in vain to conciliate them. It seemed likely that the military power would have to be invoked to wipe out this refractory band. But this last resort is always to be deplored, not only on account of the opposition of public opinion favoring peace, but also the dangers of a general Indian war.

While the authorities were deliberating as to the best course to be adopted for the settlement of the troubles without a military expedition, a member of the Indian Board, an aged Friend, commonly called "Father Lang," of Maine, went to the Secretary of the Interior, Mr. Delano, and said, "Why not try General Howard with the Apaches?" He answered thoughtfully that it could do no harm, and promised to speak to the President. When the matter was laid before President Grant his reply was, "You could not select a better man for that." The appointment gave general satisfaction, and, as it turned out, was the best that could have been

made. General Howard, however, was loath to leave
Washington ; his heart was centred in bringing to a successful and fitting termination his work on behalf of the
negroes ; but he has never allowed his personal wishes to
stand in the way of the performance of a duty.   He put
the reins of his office into the hands of a subordinate,
and receiving written instructions and personal letters
from the President to grand-division and department
commanders whose territories he had to visit, started on
his long journey to the West.   His commission extended
to the inspection of all the numerous Indian agencies in
New Mexico and Arizona, and gave him full powers.

General Howard is a man of great decision of character ; once embarked in his new duties, he surveyed the
situation with much care, and formed his plans, from
which he never departed, and which, as events showed,
were best suited to the case.   He began at the Pacific
side, went to tribe after tribe and band after band of
friendly Indians, as well as those whose attitude was
doubtful.   The Yumas, the Pimas, the Maricopas, the
Papagos, and all the worst tribes of the Apaches, as the
Tontos, Arivipas, and White Mountain bands, were in
turn visited by him.   He finally brought together in council, on the Arivipa Creek, delegates from all the bands and
tribes which he could reach, hoping thus to meet with
some of the Cochisi party and to negotiate peace with
them.   But these latter did not come.   Besides the
representatives from various tribes, there were present at
the convention General Crook, department commander,
with an escort of soldiers ; the United States District
Attorney, with Americans and Mexican-American citizens from Arizona.   With these latter were brought the
little Indian children whom white men had taken at a massacre of Indians some time before, and had since kept as

servants. The district attorney, who was not in sympathy with the peace policy, and wanted to favor those who held the children in slavery, strongly opposed their restoration to their own tribe. The white men present were not more friendly ; they believed that the best plan was to keep up tribal enmities as the surest means of " keeping the Indians down" and rendering them harmless. General Howard held that the best policy was to " begin with peace, and peace with one another." He was strongly opposed in this view ; Mexicans and Americans cursed him for his advocacy of peace ; soldiers laughed at what they called his " fanatic folly." While one side vehemently supported the retention of the captured children by the captors, the other, the Apache tribes present, vowed they would make no permanent peace without the restoration of the children.

The convention separated the first day without any decision ; that night the tired disputants lay down to sleep beside the Arivipa River, and, wearied after their long journey, soon sank into repose. While all around were buried in sleep, General Howard, a prey to anxious thoughts, held a kind of watch over his sleeping companions. The beauty of the night, which under ordinary circumstances would have attracted him, was scarcely noticed in the absorbing thoughts that banished slumber from his eyes. His companions lay uncovered on their blankets, for there was no chill or dampness in that soft, mild atmosphere. One of the number, an Indian teacher, who was asleep among the Pima delegates, he softly approached and aroused. This man, George Koch, was remarkable for his strong Christian faith and sincerity, and the perplexed general sought his advice. " Forgive me," he said, " for disturbing you, but I want your counsel ; what would you do with those children ?"

" Give them back to their relations, of course," was the prompt reply ; " that is justice."

" But that will only stir up trouble, and will not bring peace."

" It is best to do right and take the consequences," was the answer.

General Howard thanked him for his frankness, bade him good-night, and walked away. He was no nearer a decision in the matter than before, and could see no practical way to carry out such a recommendation. In his unrest and perplexity he wandered some distance off and sat down by an old fallen tree, which afforded him a resting-place. Plan after plan he revolved in his mind, but no solution of his problem could he find. He prayed for light in the mental and spiritual darkness that oppressed him, but the answer came not. At last, over-come by fatigue, he slept with his saddle for his pillow and his civilian overcoat for his cover. Unarmed and in the dress of a citizen, as became his mission, he had gone among the Indians, and his bodily comforts were as few as theirs. In all his sojourns among them he adapted himself to their mode of life, asking nothing more than the privilege of sharing with them in all the discomforts of any situation in which he might find himself.

The sun was not far up in a sky which seldom was shadowed by a cloud when he awoke next morning. In-stantly he sprang to his feet, and as quickly realized that his problem was solved. The thought that had flashed into his mind was to seek a care-taker for the children, and leave them in the care of such a third person until the authorities at Washington could consider and settle the matter. To find this person was the next step, and he could think of no better plan than to go to Camp Grant and there counsel with the wife of the commandant,

Mrs. Crittenden. Hastening thither, he found a ready listener to his hopes and plans, and one who, fortunately, could help him in his dilemma. "Did she know of a good, patient woman whom he could employ to take care of these Indian children for a few weeks?" Her reply was that there was stationed at the post a sergeant whose wife, the mother of a child frightfully afflicted with St. Vitus's dance, might be induced to undertake the task. She had been schooled in affliction, and was a patient, gentle nurse, a Roman Catholic, and hence all the more suited to have the care of these waifs, who were all converted into that faith by their present guardians. She was sent for, heard the proposition, and, as Mrs. Crittenden had predicted, said that she would accept the responsibility at a fair compensation. The delighted general went back to his post and made preparations for the grand council, which met at noon. All the morning they had waited in vain for Eskiminzin's band of Apaches, which claimed the captive children; and now, when it was mid-day, the proceedings were ordered to begin, and the leaders, with painted faces and sullen manner, came filing in.

General Howard took his place of judge, and heard again all that white men, officers of the army, Mexicans, and Indians had to say. When all had spoken he rose, and in a few simple words addressed them. Many of the Indians could speak English, and those who could not were quickly informed by interpreters. They listened attentively as he said, in substance:

"I want you all to make a good peace—tribe with tribe. Pimas and Apaches have been foes; be friends. The whites and Indians, too, have been at war, and must lay aside their differences; the Government demands peace. As to the poor children taken at the massacre, many were wounded, and were carried off by families claiming to be Christians. I decided yesterday that they ought to be returned. The new guardians cry out against it, saying, ' What, give the children we now love and are Christianizing back to the wild Apaches ? It is wrong ! ' The district attorney formally protests, and says that it will make bitterness more bitter, and stir up hate that will end in blood, and he appeals from me. All right. I will entertain his appeal. He serves the attorney-general at Washington, and, just now, I serve the Secretary of the Interior. Our common head is the President. He shall decide this matter. Meanwhile the children will remain at the agency near here ; all parties, relations and guardians, can visit them freely at will, and, providentially, we have found a Christian matron of the same faith as the Mexican guardians, who will have the immediate care and instruction of the children till the President's wishes shall be known.''

The district attorney, enraged at the decision, offered to give bonds if General Howard would let him keep the children.

"No," was the prompt response ; " bonds are not necessary. General Crook, with the army, will be security."

The joy of the Indians was instantly manifested ; they laughed and shed tears ; they embraced each other, first by the right and then by the left embrace ; Pimas, Apaches, Papagos, and all, and soon the Mexicans and Americans, catching the spirit of the occasion, mingled with the Indians, and returned their hearty demonstrations with at least a show of cordiality.

That night, intent upon making peace with those of the tribe who would not attend the council, he set out, with an aide-de-camp and several other army officers, and the agency interpreter, for the general camp of Eskiminzin's Apaches, some miles distant from the scene of the meeting. The Indians were encamped in a wild region on high banks bordering a deep ravine, near the scene of what was called "the Camp Grant massacre," where the Indian children had been taken captive.

It was General Howard's purpose to take with him a delegation of these Indians to Washington to interest them in the civilization of which they knew nothing, and to impress them, if possible, with the fruitlessness of any struggle against the Government. He hoped also by this means to keep up a friendly and influential connection with them until the wild Indians, still at war as outlaws, should be brought in and placed on a public reserve. For this purpose he made the visit, lighted only by the stars, to these Indians, who, on seeing the general and his party coming up the ravine, set up a great shout, which was followed by the gathering together of all the men, women, and children on the reservation. The interpreter explained the object of the visit, and General Howard sat down at the camp-fire of the chief. Soon the storm of voices subsided, the terms of peace explained, and arrangements were made for his Washington delegation from that tribe. General Howard was greatly helped, as he had previously been at the council and elsewhere, by the father-in-law of Eskiminzin, an old Indian (an ex-chief), whose acquaintance and friendship he had gained at a preliminary visit to the "Camp Grant Agency." At that time the general, when walking with an interpreter, saw an old Indian almost without clothing, whose magnificently proportioned head attracted his attention. The Indian was sitting on a rough bench, looking attentively at General Howard and other new arrivals. Learning the name of

the old chief, General Howard, looking kindly into his
stolid, expressionless face, directed the interpreter in
these words : "Say to Santo that I have a Father
above." It was so told him. "You, Santo, have a Father
above." This also was interpreted. "My Father and
your Father ; *He* is the same Being." The Indian's face
brightened. "Then you and I must be brothers."

The old chief quickly rose, the tears stood in his eyes,
and he went directly to General Howard and put his
hand into his. From that time this old man became
General Howard's best assistant and coadjutor among the
Indians. He was the first to consent to go to Washington, and during the trip never failed in his cordial help
to keep the Indians in heart amid their new experiences.

A month from the time of General Howard's decision
regarding the Indian children, the President had ratified
the agreement, and peace was established.

The visit to Washington was made in July, 1872, the
Indians attracting much attention *en route*. Arriving at
the capital, they were introduced to the President, who
welcomed them kindly ; to the Secretary of the Interior,
who made them presents which delighted them, and they
were taken to see the Capitol, the arsenals, the schools,
the asylums, the prisons, churches, and manufactories.
They were presented to large assemblies of people who,
in Washington, Philadelphia, and New York, were interested in them and in the efforts which were being
made to civilize them. The relations existing between
General Howard and his fellow-travellers were of the
most harmonious character ; they looked up to him as to
a father, and trusted him with the unquestioning confidence of children. He, in his turn, indulged their
childish whims, and instructed them as they travelled
regarding the country, its people, and other objects of

interest. An instance will show how perfect was their confidence in General Howard, and how they were distressed when anything told by him could not be brought within the compass of their limited intelligence. On being informed that the world was round, they turned to the general in great amazement, and begged of him not to make such absurd statements. He assured them that one of his own family had started in a ship from the port, to which he came back after a long voyage without having changed the ship's course. They repeated the same reply, and expressed the fear that their friend had been bewitched.

General Howard returned with them to Arizona, and they were delivered to their respective tribes after their long journey of eight thousand miles. Disappointed at learning, on his arrival at Camp Apache, that the parties despatched to communicate with Cochise had failed to reach him, he set out for New Mexico to visit other tribes yet to be treated with, and had almost given up hope of meeting Cochise, when he heard that there was one man in Arizona who could get to him unharmed. This man, known as Captain Jeffords, had always been spared by this chief and his people when other whites were killed, and he had penetrated at least once into the very camp of these hostiles. Unfortunately, no one could tell Jeffords's whereabouts, and General Howard reluctantly pursued his journey to the camp of a dissatisfied band of New Mexican Apaches, who were located in the western part of that country, in a wild district where they were watched by United States troops. These Indians had been forced away from the growing settlements along the Rio Grande, their beloved grounds near Canada Alamosa ; and to their new habitation among the hills he went to hear their complaints and see what could

be done for them. An Indian's love of home is one of
the strongest traits of his character, and these Indians
were homesick and unhappy. The kindly peacemaker
was in their midst, hearing their well-grounded complaints against those who had forced them to accept, in
lieu of their fertile lands, the wild region they were
in, and had been with them for a day at Tulerosa,
when Captain Jeffords, at evening, made his appearance
in the neighborhood as a guide to some scouting cavalry.
General Howard went to the cavalry camp and found
the noted scout, who, on learning his wishes, agreed to
take him to Cochise's camp, if he would consent to go
without escort. The ready assent of General Howard to
go in any way desired surprised and pleased Jeffords,
who at once set about making preparations for the trip.
General Howard was not to part so speedily as he intended, however, with the Alamosa Indians, who clung
to him, and insisted upon his visiting their old home
with a party of their tribe. This would take him a hundred miles out of his way, but the request was complied
with, as Jeffords thought it well for him to travel with
these messengers, and particularly with a young nephew
of Cochise, whom they found in the Alamosa band,
and whose presence they hoped would help in obtaining an interview with his bloody uncle, the old and
wily Apache chief. The young wife of the nephew
Chie, who was at Tulerosa, had been conciliated by
the present of a beautiful horse, which the general gave
to her.

The little party of half a dozen men, the general in
their midst, set out to travel the hundred miles, camping
in the woods by night, cooking, eating, and sleeping
together. When Sunday came General Howard notified
his companions that he would halt for the day. The

Indians, attaching no special significance to the day, proposed to have a hunt ; Jeffords told them that it was General Howard's habit to meditate and pray on the Sabbath. They were much affected at this, and at once declined to go on their hunt, saying that they would stay in camp. They had only to know the manner in which he wished them to act, and obedience was spontaneous. After the first day's march, when the dinner was ready, General Howard invited the Indians to come and dine with him. His table was a piece of canvas spread on the ground, and about it they grouped and waited in reverential silence while he asked God's blessing upon the repast. This simple act, common enough in the homes of our land, these children of the plains witnessed for the first time, and they were greatly impressed with it. Chie soon became General Howard's devoted friend, and when later they met with white men who hated Indians and threatened him, the lad rushed to General Howard for protection, and promised a reciprocal thing when the wilder Apaches should be reached.

After Alamosa, on the Rio Grande, had been visited, Jeffords desired the influence of another Indian helper, the chief of a band called Ponce. This band had just escaped from a New Mexican agency, and had been driven by Granger's troops into a wild valley about a day's journey from Alamosa. To this place General Howard, with Captain Sladen, his aide, Jeffords, the Indian lad Chie, and three others, started early one morning, and that afternoon the general, with Jeffords, who were several miles in advance of the rest of the party, came to the brow of a hill which overlooked a deep ravine and beyond a meadow-land bordering a small stream. There encamped, perhaps three miles distant, was the band of Ponce. The braves were grouped

in a circle on the ground ; the women were variously
employed, some watching the ponies that grazed near
by, others were caring for the babies, while still others
were engaged in cooking by little fires. The larger
children were busy at play. General Howard and his
companion, following the trail of a returning Indian
scout, descended the ravine at once, and when they had
arrived at the camp Ponce, who was in the circle, left
his companions and approached the intruders. Jeffords
explained their business, and General Howard won his
consent to accompany them by the presentation of a
horse to him and one to his wife, and by promising to
give protection and food to his wife while he should be
away. Accompanied by Ponce, his party now number-
ing nine persons, he turned his face again toward the
Apache Pass and the Arizona line. Ponce was the son
of a famous old chief, Ponce, who had been in his life-
time a good friend to Cochise ; he could speak Spanish,
and would be therefore of value to General Howard in
his interviews with the Indians he was to visit, all of
whom spoke the Mexican-Spanish as fluently as their
own dialect.

One or two incidents illustrative of General Howard's
methods of dealing with the emergencies which arose
during this long, wearisome march may be related here.
Over and above the dangers presented by the wild country he had to traverse, a constant source of anxiety was
the attitude of white men toward the Indians of his party.
These latter consisted, as we have seen, of Chic, the
nephew of Cochise, and Ponce, the friend of this chief.
At a small mining town, where they had encamped for
the night, a hostile demonstration was reported to be on
foot against his Indian companions. Learning the fact,
General Howard promptly called a meeting of the peo-

ple, and explained the wishes of the President and his mission to the Indians. In the assembled crowd murmurs of dissatisfaction were heard at first, but the earnest words and manly appeal of the speaker soon quieted them. When the crowd dispersed, General Howard,* considering it imprudent to risk another outburst of public feeling against the Indians under his protection, left before sunrise.

While travelling, one day, he met a party of " prospectors" armed to the teeth. One of the number, a strong, rough frontiersman, whose brother had been murdered by Indians, was particularly bloodthirsty. He had sworn revenge, and rejoiced that the opportunity had now come to retaliate by taking the lives of the Indians with General Howard. The latter was unarmed, and the assailants outnumbered his men. Resistance was useless, and moral power accomplished that which physical force would have failed to secure. Stepping in front of the Indians, he opened his coat and said, " Shoot me first." The men hesitated, when he explained to them who he was and what was his purpose in travelling with these dusky companions. The leader turned aside with an oath, and the general and his party went their way. The rest of the journey was made in safety. After tracing individual trails to larger ones, using the Indians to divine and interpret signs, they came to the foot of the Mogollon Range, where they reached an Indian outpost, with which Chie exchanged signals, which consisted in barking like coyotes, and discovered that it belonged to Cochise. A friendly greeting was accorded the travellers, who ate and slept with their hosts. The leader of this band of scouts, a stolid, old Apache, objected to General Howard going to *Shiekshah* (Cochise) with so many men. After some

parleying it was decided that the general should be permitted to proceed, accompanied by two others.

The next morning General Howard, accompanied by
Captain Sladen and Jeffords, the scout, and preceded by
,Ponce and Chie, wound their way along the trail over
the mountain range. On being remonstrated with on
the imprudence of venturing into the power of an unfriendly band with such a small company, General Howard quietly replied :

" I have considered the situation carefully, and do not
feel that I am doing wrong. This is the work given
me. ' He that saveth his life shall lose it, and he that
loseth his life for my sake shall find it.' I have laid
mine on the altar."

After a further perilous journey of a hundred miles,
crossing the second range of mountains from the
Mogollon, the travellers found themselves near the last
fastness. Here they unpacked their mules, unsaddled
their horses, and got their dinner, while Chie preceded
them, gliding down a fearful crag into a deep cut of the
huge Dragoon Range. Before sundown two Indian lads
appeared and guided them six or seven miles into a
cavernous inclosure, where natural side walls rose up
hundreds of feet, and the ingress and egress of which
could be successfully guarded by half a dozen rifles.

That night even Chie and Ponce were gloomy.
Cochise was not there, and the hostile sub-chief in charge
of the camp, mainly one of women and children, could not
tell when he would be back. When the general prepared his blankets and lay down under a tree for such
repose as would come under the circumstances, he
noticed that some of the Indian children were near by,
though the women had all gone to the slopes of the inclosing steeps. When these children gathered about him

and several lay down on his blanket beside him, he felt greater safety, and was satisfied that he and his companions would at least live until morning. Next morning the Indians assembled near him, as he consulted with Jeffords as to the best step to take ; while talking together the brother of the chief appeared riding down the ravine, and behind him followed a small, well-mounted party. It was Cochise, his son, wife, and sister, and the Indians, when they recognized their chief, sent up a great shout of welcome. He rode among them, dismounted, and seeing Jeffords, embraced him, and was then presented to General Howard, whom he eyed suspiciously. Shortly afterward a council was held ; blankets were spread for Cochise and the strangers, and the Indians, men and women, formed a circle about the group. Ponce and Chie reported the travels of the white party, and when they had concluded Cochise asked the general sternly, *what he came there for.* The latter replied, " The President sent me to make peace with you, Cochise."

The majestic-looking Indian replied in Spanish, " Nobody can want peace more than I do."

" Then we will effect it," said General Howard.

The talk that followed was a long one, the Indian warily avoiding any promise while exacting many. Finally the chief abruptly asked, " How long will you stay with me ?"

It was not a safe place for a white man to be in, but General Howard replied, " As long as is necessary."

" Well," he answered, " my warriors are far away getting their living, some in Mexico ; it will take ten days to get word and bring them in."

The general answered that he would wait ten days. The chief seemed pleased, and showed signs of trust,

when his face again clouded, and he said, " The soldiers
will kill them as they come back."

The general answered, " No ; I will send Captain
Sladen with orders." Cochise shook his head in disap-
proval, and said, " No, you go yourself ; they will obey
you. Leave Captain Sladen with me ; we have young
ladies to entertain him." At this the numerous Indian
maidens clapped their hands and shouted. It was finally
arranged that General Howard should go to Camp
Bowie, the nearest army post, upward of fifty miles
away. He asked the chief to send a guide with him,
but no Apache lad could be induced to go, certainly not
before a peace had actually been established. In the
dilemma Chie stepped out and said, " I will go." The
offer was accepted, and the two, mounted upon mules,
set out to cross the Dragoon Range and make their way
to the military garrison through a pathless wilderness.
The travellers could speak but few words that either
could understand, and the tedious journey was unrelieved
by conversation. Guided only by the stars they crossed
canyons, flanked perilous steeps, and finally reached the
rolling prairies, entering Rogers' Ranch in a forlorn
condition. The owner of this ranch was a lonely frontiersman, and a venturesome whiskey-trader, who was
finally murdered by the Indians. He took the travellers
the remaining distance in a wagon, passing en route Apache
Pass, where the father of Chie, with numerous other
Apache Indians, had been hanged by our soldiers ten years
before. This affair it was that caused the unrelenting sav-
agery and hate of Cochise and his band. As the party
drove into the ravine the young Indian covered his bowed
head, and seemed oppressed with painful emotions. General Howard comforted him with his sympathy and quieted
his outburst of feeling before they entered the camp.

Major Sumner, who was in command of the garrison at Bowie, could at first hardly believe that the forlorn-looking individual, with scratched face and ragged apparel, could be the officer he claimed to be, though he had known him previously ; and before matters were explained several exasperated soldiers threatened to shoot the Apache in revenge for one of their comrades, who had been dreadfully wounded by Indians in ambush only a day or two before. General Howard rested while wagons were loaded with provisions. Instructions were issued to restrain all garrisons and soldiers from prosecuting war against Cochise and his band until further orders. Then he returned to the stronghold of the Apaches, Cochise, Jeffords, Sladen, and a large party of Indians meeting them some miles away to welcome him back.

Thirteen days altogether General Howard and his party remained with these wild savages, utterly at their mercy. General Howard had no weapon with him, not even a pistol. With but his left hand to use it, he was as well off without a weapon as with one, perhaps better off. The instinctive liking of the children shown for him the first night he entered the camp most undoubtedly turned the scale in his favor and saved the life of himself and Captain Sladen. The absence of Cochise and the warriors made the few Indians in camp suspicious, and the spies among them, who kept close watch over General Howard, would have unhesitatingly despatched him had he returned their feelings of doubt and mistrust. But he had gone there prepared to die, and was cheerful and hopeful in consequence. When, however, they saw the feeling of the children toward the man, and observed that they were sleeping beside him and about him, their vigilance relaxed, and Cochise's coming was awaited by them without anxiety. The women liked him, and at

times, gypsy-like, made him dance with them on the
green. Two women would hold to him, one by his
hand, the other by his empty sleeve, till he had given
them some present, called the dance forfeit. He amused
himself by teaching the children to make letters, and
suffering them to teach him counting and other Apache
words. Cochise soon revered and finally loved him as a
brother. One day he said, "Don't be sad, General,
when you see the rifle of a white man here, for there has
been war." Another time he asked Jeffords how General Howard dared come there where every white man
for years had been killed. Jeffords replied, "General
Howard fears nothing." This idea that he neither
feared nor hated them won the hearts of the Indians.
Cochise would not suffer the smallest article to be taken
from him unless he gave it as a present.

At last all the warriors were in, and the council was
called for the night. The strangers were left by themselves, and they assembled on a plateau in the mountains.
After some time they were sent for, and went to the
circle, in the centre of which was Cochise, standing.
His captains were on the ground about him, sitting in
Indian fashion. Outside were the women and children.
They had begun a low chant before General Howard
and his companions reached them, and this gradually increased in sound until the high, shrill voices echoed, like
a wild scream, through the caves and canyons of the
mountain. After it had ceased Cochise spoke, and
Jeffords, the guide, interpreted his words to mean that
the spirits had been consulted and had told them that
the time had come for the Indian and white man to eat
bread together.

We can imagine the satisfaction with which General
Howard received this news ; he eagerly grasped the

proffered hand of Cochise, and then joined in the hearty congratulations with all the camp.

The next day the officers from Bowie met General Howard and the Indians at Dragoon Springs, some ten miles distant from the stronghold, and peace was established—a peace which Cochise kept as long as he lived. Our own people were the first to violate the conditions in subsequent years, and to take those lands from the Indians which were given to them by General Howard and confirmed by President Grant.

IX.

WHEN the Freedmen's Bureau act was passed in the
House, it had but one majority, its educational feature
being particularly unpopular with the representatives.
Mr. Elliott, of Massachusetts, the chairman of the Freedmen's Committee, remarked to General Howard one
day : " I rejoice at your work, but I would hardly dare,
at this time, tell my colleagues what you are doing."
This statement indicates very conclusively the tone of
feeling then existing in the minds of those who were to
make or mar its usefulness. The act creating the Bureau
was for one year, and it was the wish of its friends in
Congress to have it do its work and be brought to a final
close in that length of time. Though Republicans were
supposed to wish to make it a permanency, and engraft
another doubtful branch, like the Indian Bureau, upon
the general government, yet leaders like Mr. Morton, of
Indiana, were exceedingly anxious to rid themselves of
a measure that was not popular at the start.

This being the case, it is not surprising that during
General Howard's absence from Washington such opponents of the Bureau worked toward its abolishment. In
fact, the Secretary of War (it being a bureau of his department) promised a committee of the House to close up

its operations if it should be left to him. This promise doubtless governed the last Congressional measure and also caused that searching investigation made by the War Department into all the accounts of disbursing agents during the absence of General Howard. Though no substantial charge was raised against him directly, yet for a time several of his disbursing officers with unsettled accounts presented favorable points for partisan attacks for the framing of charges.

Smarting under these unjust charges formulated by the Secretary of War, published in all the newspapers of the country, and sent to Congress officially, General Howard wrote letters to Generals Grant and Sherman, and also to Secretary Belknap, demanding a speedy and thorough examination. The one sent to General Sherman best portrays his state of mind under the circumstances.

" WASHINGTON, D. C., November 27, 1873.

General W. T. Sherman, Commanding Army of the United States.

" GENERAL : On account of the steady confidence you have reposed in me, I write the following to you ; I am constrained to take a step that I believe I ought to explain to you and to the officers of the army affected by it. I wish to be assigned to army duty wherever it shall seem best to you to select my place of assignment.

" You have twice offered me this opportunity. My reasons for not promptly embracing the offer were twofold : (1) I was anxious to complete the work of the Freedmen's Bureau, to which I had been assigned without any solicitation on my part, but which of necessity developed into enormous proportions, and which requires time properly to close. (2) I was anxious that the university, which had grown up under my eye, and which I deemed all important as a part of the higher educational advantages I had been instrumental in securing, especially for those classes of our people whose interests were for a long time so largely committed to my care, should be put upon a secure basis in all its breadth of scope, before committing its presidency to a successor.

" I have endeavored to give it an endowment worthy of the object. Unexpected opposition, the usual misrepresentation of the motives of one engaged in such a work, and hindrances of a public and private nature have made this work slow and onerous. It is not yet done, but I am unable with my private income to continue it. I had intended to ask to be placed before a retiring board—in fact, I did so apply to the War Department. But I was sent to Arizona and New Mexico very soon thereafter, and was obliged to undertake duty equally arduous with any that I performed during the war ; on this I withdrew my application. I found myself as able to undergo fatigue and privation and all the labor that pertains to field duty as at any previous time in my life. You will remember also that the loss of my arm never disabled me from the performance of any duty demanded of me as a general officer. I have, however, often thought of retiring, hoping that my hard services during the war, and the much harder services required of me since the war, would be considered in my favor. But under present circumstances it is not prudent for me to take this step of asking to be retired.

" While many who commanded a division only for a time have been retired with the rank of major-general, I cannot lawfully be so retired, because I was wounded so early in the war, while a brigadier, commanding a brigade, and would, therefore, be obliged to retire as a brigadier.

" This might seem to be ample, and would be doubtless but for the obligations I have been forced to incur in the work providentially given me to do.

" I confess that weightier reasons affect me now than any I have given to influence my return to army duty.

" Bulletins affecting me unfavorably have gone broadcast. My integrity is officially acknowledged, I admit, and I hold letters of high commendation ; and further, my seven years of unremitting toil, anxiety, and responsibility are known, and the good fruits are seen by those who care to see and acknowledge them.

" Yet it is idle for me to try to conceal from myself the plain fact that there is a persistent effort to tarnish my record, and if not in official quarters the result is precisely the same. All the books and papers of a large bureau are transferred to other hands.

" A lengthy examination is then instituted, and whatever the results of this examination may be, from it grows public suspicion and accusation against me and the honorable officers who were associated with me.

" Now all this I wish to face. You have seen me in battle, and know how I can face death. I shall face accusation with the same fearless spirit. I wish to go to duty, to give all accusers ample time and opportunity to round out their charges, and if they see fit so to do, I wish to be tried by a court-martial as the tribunal best suited to one of my history and rank.

"Again, I have another reason for service. Should we now have a war with Spain, to free more slaves from dire oppression and defend the honor of our flag, the President would surely give me the opportunity of service. I do not wish to be shelved or crushed.

"Is it not a good thing to endeavor to preserve, and not destroy, the fair fame of men who ardently love their country, and who have in a series of successful battles demonstrated that this love is no empty boast?

"By the consideration of past service, by my earnest loyalty to my country, by my desire to preserve an unsullied record for my children's inspection, I ask for my proper place among the officers of the army.

"I am not only conscious of integrity, but of fidelity. My work was of necessity incomplete, but no wrong on the part of any officer or clerk was ever knowingly covered up by me, and I was as diligent as I could be in the pursuit of wrong-doers.

"I shrink from no danger or trial or duty, but I deprecate insinuation and suspicion. On public and personal grounds I ask your aid to restore me to the post of service and confidence that I know you to believe belongs to me.

"Very respectfully yours,

"O. O. HOWARD, Brigadier-General U. S. Army."

The Special Court of Inquiry was appointed, with General Sherman as president, and after a thorough examination of every charge its findings were as follows :

"*First.* The court is of opinion that, in matters referred to it for investigation, General O. O. Howard has not, with knowledge and intent, violated any law of Congress, regulation of the army, or rule of morals, and that he is ' not guilty ' upon legal, technical, or moral responsibility in any of the offences charged.

"*Second.* The court finds that General Howard, when charged by his superiors with a great work arising out of the war, devoted his whole time and all his faculties and energies to the execution of that work. In this he employed hundreds of assistants, and dealt with hundreds of thousands of men. In regard to the expenditure of money, it appears that his accounts are closed and settled to the satisfaction of the accounting officers of the Treasury, whose decisions in such matters are by law the highest authority, 'final and conclusive upon the executive branch of the government, and subject to revision only by Congress or the proper courts.'

"*Third.* In relation to the investment of certain public moneys in United States bonds, while the court does not hold that such investments were justified by existing laws, yet, in view of the fact that these investments were made only under the opinion and advice of the Second Comptroller, the court attaches no blame to General Howard therefor. The investment of portions of a similar fund—viz., the 'irregular bounty fund,' had previously been authorized by express law.

"*Fourth.* Some questions arising out of the sudden termination of the operations and organization of the Freedmen's Bureau yet remain to be settled, with those who were formerly subordinates and assistants to the commissioner. Some few erroneous payments made by honest subordinates, and some others made, or not made, by officers now dead or cashiered for fraud, remain to be adjusted. The adjustment of these matters belongs properly to the successors of General Howard in the Bureau ; and in these matters, as in all others brought to notice of the court during thirty-seven days of careful and laborious investigation, the court finds that General Oliver O. Howard did his whole duty, and believes that he deserves well of his country.''

This was not the result hoped for by rivals ; instead of censure the court gave General Howard high praise, and President Grant's approval was quickly affixed to its findings. Howard's long martyrdom was ended, and on the 3d of July he received his appointment to the command of the Department of the Columbia, with headquarters at Portland, Oregon.

As may be imagined, the troubles that prevented a peaceful solution of the Freedmen's Bureau problem, and cost General Howard so much personal anxiety and annoyance, reacted upon his devoted household. Soon after entering upon his duties as commissioner, General Howard removed his family from Maine to Washington, and for nine years they resided uninterruptedly there, occupying for a time a house on the corner of Pennsylvania Avenue and Twenty-fifth Street, and afterward moving to the University grounds. They had many army friends at the capital, and were happy in the reunion of family and friends after years of separation ; and but for the persecutions which were waged upon General Howard through political and personal hostility, the home-life would have been delightful. It was ever a restful and peaceful retreat after the trials of each day, and when the storm was fiercest and the future looked darkest, then did it seem indeed a veritable haven to the weary man. It was the hope of the hearthstone circle that, after his return from Arizona, he would be released from the department over which he had presided and be permitted to rejoin the army. As we have seen, he returned only to meet the mental and pecuniary drain of a trial by a military court, which he in self-justice had been forced to demand. On the day when the charges which resulted in this court were first published, General Howard, entirely ignorant of the blow in store for him, went to his office as usual, and was busy at his desk when an intimate friend entered, and, after a few remarks, inquired if he had seen the New York papers. He had not, he said, and carelessly asked what was in them. The painful task of informing him of the charges that had been sent broadcast over the land that morning was performed, and General Howard sat reading them in silent anguish, when a poor woman entered and made an appeal for help. His state of mind was such that he could hardly comprehend her words at first ; but, summoning strength, he kindly inquired into her case, relieved her wants, sent her away happy, and then went home. His wife received the papers he handed to her, and sat down beside the sofa on which he had thrown himself until she had read the cruel charges through in silence. Her ready tact and composure were never so

greatly needed, for the strong man's heart was sorely
hurt by the ruthless slanders uttered against him ; and as
she laid the papers aside she gave him encouraging assur-
ances that it would all come out right.   Long and earnest
were the silent prayers he offered, and searching was the
examination he made of himself to see that no hatred of
those who were persecuting him was in his heart.
Finally he arose and went to his desk to write the letters
to General Sherman and others, that secured the prompt
trial which resulted in his vindication.

Then it was decided that he and Mrs. Howard should
go to New York to engage counsel, and the journey was
made, the tired couple returning to Washington on the
evening of the second day thereafter.   During their absence the occasion had been taken by some of their
friends to place in their parlor a reminder of their love
and unalterable confidence in the general.

The children welcomed their parents with impatient delight, and one of the little boys urged his mother to come
directly to the parlor.   Yielding to his entreaties, she
went to the room, and found, in addition to its usual fur-
nishings, a superb piano.   On the instrument was the
sentence, " From your friends," and embroidered on the
rich cover was the verse, " Blessed are ye, when men
shall revile you, and persecute you, and shall say all manner of evil against you falsely, for my sake." *   The date
affixed was the same as that on which the charges were
preferred by the Secretary of War.

The children could give no information regarding the
donors, and, thinking that a sight of the beautiful instrument would cause great pleasure, were surprised to see
both father and mother weeping.   They were completely

* Matt. 5 : 11.

unnerved and overjoyed, and their joy was of the kind that is closely allied to pain. Years afterward, in speaking of this event, Mrs. Howard, with a beautiful light shining through her tears, said, " It came at a time when we did not know that we had a friend !" They never knew to whom they were indebted for this prized gift.

The Department of the Columbia, to which the general was assigned, included Washington Territory, Idaho, and Alaska. Here had been terrible wars with the Indian tribes of the Simcoes, Walla Wallas, Umatillas, Spokanes, and others, the last being with the relentless Modocs, where General Canby and his companions were treacherously slain. General Howard visited all the tribes and agencies ; he saw the friendly and unfriendly, and even penetrated the remote territory of Alaska, and answered earnest petitions of those Indians for teachers, by securing the attention and interest of missionary bodies for the poor red man of the far West.

Many chiefs of Washington Territory and Idaho, who had been irritated and driven to hostility by those reckless frontiersmen, who, for the sake of trade, continued to sell whiskey, arms, and ammunition, and took possession of their lands, did not scruple to betray them, were conciliated and persuaded to peace. Not a few travelled hundreds of miles to meet him, and scrupulously kept with him all their agreements. The famous Chief Moses, who reigned over a few wild lands in the extreme north-west, was once treacherously seized by white men, disarmed, put in irons, and confined in a close prison. When first surprised he ordered his followers to put down their arms and not fire, for he had so promised General Howard. In prison he continued to entreat that General Howard should be informed of his case, for he constantly averred that the instant that friend knew of

his trouble he would be released.   Moses did not trust in
vain.   He was released and restored to his place by
General Howard at the expense of much hostility and
many curses from those who were determined to annihi-
late this Indian and his tribe.   Subsequently, during the
severe wars of 1877 and 1878, thousands of Indians were
kept at peace by the help of Moses and others whom
General Howard had bound by ties of mutual trust to
himself.

In 1877, while in command at Portland, Or., and
inspecting his post of Lapwai, Id., trouble broke out
between the Nez Percés Indians and the settlers, induced
primarily by the reductions of their reservation.   The
course of the Government toward the tribe was not
based on absolute or even relative justice, and the Indians naturally resorted to retaliatory measures.   General
Howard, in his book " Nez Percés Joseph," * gives a
history of this tribe, and sets forth the true state of affairs
which brought on war and caused so much bloodshed before it was subjugated.   Speaking of the responsibility
of the Government for many of the wrongs inflicted
upon the red man, General Howard says :

" It is difficult to explain the almost uniform injustice which the
American people have practised toward the Indians.   I do not believe that we are worse than the French, the Spanish, or than our
English neighbors in British Columbia, though surely we can nearly
match the massacre of St. Bartholomew, the cruelties of the Inquisi-
tion, or the ferocity of London rioters in our dealings with the red
men.   I am inclined to believe the jar to be in our unadjustable system, which, like a machine built upon a springy soil, is perpetually
out of gear.   Our fathers, finding the Indians here, and being disposed to peace, first recognized in them the right of occupancy of the
lands.   This recognized right the Indians have always misunder-

---

* Nez Percés Joseph.   His Pursuit and Capture.   Lee & Shepard,
publishers, Boston.

stood. They have believed it to mean much more than simple occupancy.

"As our new settlements have rapidly extended, we have entered into and recorded solemn treaties, by which we have made of the numerous small tribes so many nations. Soon the national and local laws, which are constantly in conflict with the laws of these independent nations, go into active and often antagonistic operation' For example : the settler, in carrying out the homestead law, plants his stakes on the Indian's farm. A petty contest results. An Indian or a white man is killed. Close upon this follows a horrid Indian war—a war so outrageous that *bona fide* forgiveness anywhere in the neighborhood of the remembered crimes seldom, if ever, succeeds."

Blood was shed in the Nez Percés war by white men first, and the work of murder was begun ; the non-treaty portion of the tribe, who boasted that they had never killed a white man, at last went to war, committing outrages too horrible to recall needlessly. General Howard took the field in person, and continued to gather his troops and combat the Indians till he had conquered them in battles. At last the wily and able young chief, Joseph, with his braves, women, and children, and his droves of ponies, undertook a flight of more than thirteen hundred miles, in order to pass the familiar buffalo hunting grounds, get into Canada, and form junction with Sitting Bull, the chief who had previously destroyed General Custer and his cavalry. The pursuit was conducted across the continent, and General Howard was fortunate to secure the co-operation of other forces than his own, especially that of General Miles, so that Joseph and his warriors were finally defeated and the band captured before they passed the British line.

The Christian spirit which has been often referred to in these pages as the marked characteristic of this soldier of the cross, as of his country, was beautifully exhibited in this instance. He had been greatly depressed in consequence of the lack of entire success in the cam-

paign, though he had beaten the Indians in every battle
where he himself had engaged them. The work, in his
judgment, would not be completed until the tribe was
captured or surrendered. While riding along with several of his officers one day, after news had reached him
that Miles, to whom Howard had given the cue, was
pursuing the Indians, one of his officers expressed a
doubt of the latter's success. General Howard, who
had been silently asking for God's help in the case,
turned suddenly to Colonel Mason, and said they would
finally succeed ; he added that he had prayed earnestly
to God to give him the victory, even if he himself lost
the credit of the campaign. His spirits became brighter
after this prayer, and he was as confident as though the
end was already accomplished.

Dr. Alexander, at his side, said, " What is more hopeless ? There isn't one chance in a million for Miles. I
cannot see, General, where you find your hope."

" All right," was the cheerful reply ; " see if I do not
prove a true prophet."

It was as he predicted it would be. General Miles,
being apprised of the situation in time by despatches
from General Howard, gave chase, and with his fresh
troops soon intercepted the savages, offered battle, and
drove them to their deep trenches, but his work was not
completed before General Howard and his scouts, in
advance of the main body of his troops, reached the
camp. The latter used his own scouts to negotiate the
surrender ; but when the Indians came trooping in, and
Joseph and others extended their rifles to him, he waved
them off to General Miles, who received them. The
prayer renouncing all desire to have the credit of cap-
turing his enemies, if only the campaign might be
successful, was remembered by him, and he generously

gave to another the honors of the result.   But, let it be observed, he does not stint the praise due to his own troops, even in his own self-surrender.   Of this campaign and its outcome General Howard says, in the volume named :

" After Miles's march and engagement there arose all sorts of heart-burnings, reports filled with claims and counter-claims for credit. There were necessarily diversities of statement, rivalries, criminations, and controversies, such as we read of in Europe after an important battle or campaign. . . . I was sent to conduct a war without regard to department or division lines. This was done with all the energy, ability, and help at my command, and the campaign was brought to a successful issue. As soon as the Indians reached General Terry's department Gibbon was despatched to strike his blow ; then Sturgis, in close alliance, and finally Miles in the last terrible battle. These troops participated in the struggle with exposure, battle, and loss, as we have seen. They enjoyed the appreciation and thanks of their seniors in command and of their countrymen. But when, with the fulness of an honest and generous recognition of the work, gallantry, losses, and success of all co-operating forces, I turn my attention to the troops that fought the first battles, and then pursued the swift-footed fugitives with unparalleled vigor and perseverance, amid the severest privations, for more than a thousand miles, would it be wonderful if I magnified their doings and gave them, were it possible, even an overplus of praise for the part they bore in this campaign ?

" Personally, according to the covenant which I have recorded, I shall be satisfied to let another bear the crown of triumph, while my heart is deeply moved with thankfulness that the work itself was brought to a successful conclusion."

From the beginning of the pursuit until the embarkation on the Missouri River for the homeward journey, including all halts and stoppages, occupied from July 27 to October 10 (seventy-five days), and General Howard's command marched one thousand three hundred and twenty-one miles.   During this campaign, when asked one day, while the soldiers were burying the bodies of those the Indians had butchered and mutilated, if

he was not disgusted with war when looking over the
bloody field after a battle, he answered, "Yes, yes ;
disgusted, horror-stricken ; but it is the same with railway accidents, and with fire and pestilence. Indian
warfare is horrid, but Indian massacres, outrages, and
brutality, and Indian rule, which is war, are a thousand
times worse."

In this campaign he had an assembly on Sunday,
whenever it was possible and proper, for religious
services, and he says of one of these meetings, held at a
post where he stopped for supplies :

"I was glad enough to have this service of prayer, singing, and
speaking before we left. I think many besides myself felt as I did.
There is a stern reality in going from all you love into the dread uncertainty of Indian fighting, where, perhaps, the worst form of torture and death await you. It is very wise and proper to ask God's
blessing, and particularly so in these turning-points of life, when
about to plunge into the dark clouds of any warfare."

It was reported and published in the press generally,
because of a necessary halt, on one particular Sabbath
day, when time was precious, that he wasted the day in
giving religious exhortation to his command and in the
distribution of some three hundred Bibles. Of course it
was not believed, even by those who took the pains to
extend its circulation. It is a fact that in General Howard's military history he never made a halt for religious
exercises when the least necessity existed for action.

The Piute and Bannock war of the next year, 1878,
began outside the limits of his department, but worked
back through it, rolling up tribe after tribe like a big
snowball ; first the Bannocks, then the Piutes, and
finally the treacherous Umatillas, with some others,
sprang to the war-path again. General Howard took the
field and pursued them until, after several battles, they

were conquered. Then, while combing the country by numerous small columns, he managed to gather all the Indians who had dispersed and spread themselves over the country, like so many frightened birds. He gathered them and put them upon a reservation, where they could have good farms and competent teachers. In this campaign he travelled nearly two thousand miles, and when he had concluded it the Indians whom he had fought were his friends.

Bad men in not a few cases cursed his name for his lenity. One instance may be recorded. A rough frontier patriot on a steamer excited a crowd against the general, who was, so far as his friends or his officers were concerned, alone at the time. The man fiercely accused him of treachery in saving the lives of murderous savages, and the crowd hooted. General Howard walked toward him and said, "What is the matter?"

"You receive the surrender of Indians," was the reply.

"What would you do, sir?"

"I would kill them all," said the patriot.

"Then, sir," answered the general, in firm tones, "you would be a murderer. My Government and the law of nations demand that I recognize the white flag."

The man in fury began to threaten, when General Howard, facing the crowd, said :

"Sir, I have never turned a corner in my life to avoid a bullet ; what do you propose to do?"

A revulsion of feeling instantly set in as the people recognized the spirit of the soldier before them. They cheered General Howard, and the man, in approval also of his course, invited him to take a drink, an invitation which he promptly declined.

The ascendency which General Howard could exercise

over a hostile crowd was shown in another similar instance. A saloon-keeper, who had been at one time
imprisoned for crime, one day, in the streets of Portland, Or., gathered a number of roughs to do him harm.
As the general was passing, he cried out a bitter charge
of gross criminality. General Howard walked through
the crowd, faced the man, and said, " You know that
what you say is not true !" The man's countenance
instantly changed, and, to the surprise of the bystanders,
he said, " Yes, General Howard, I know you're a good
man, but you interfere with my business." Others,
standing about, ready to mob him, said, " We will not
strike him; don't strike him ; he has no arms and is a
cripple," referring to the loss of his right arm.

A Spokane chief, who had been protected in his rights
by General Howard, came six hundred miles to put
his children at school in the general's department.

On the steamer that took General Howard from that
department, in 1880, the last interview between this
chief and the general took place. The former was a
magnificent specimen of a man and a good Christian.
He seemed simple as a child as he pleaded with the general to remain among them. " We have given you our
hearts," he said ; " how can you leave us ? What
shall we do without you ?"

This sad leave-taking reminded General Howard of
his parting with the wild Cochise in 1872. As the latter
stood upon his own reserve, which General Howard had
secured to him, he said, " You must not go ; stay with
us and all will be well." The general asked him, " If
you gave orders to one of your captains to go and do a
work and then return, what would you do to him if he
disobeyed you ?"

" I would punish him," was the prompt reply.

"Well, the President has sent me, and I must obey my orders ; is it not right ?"

"Yes ; but ask him to let you come again," was the reply.

General Howard promised to do so, when the warrior approached, put his arms about and held him for some minutes against his breast. General Howard has had many wars with the Indians, but could the truth be known his influence has been nine to one for peace. His soul, instead, rejoices in schools, churches, and homes.

* * * * * *

The country learned with satisfaction of General Howard's appointment to the superintendency of the Military Academy at West Point as the successor of General Schofield, whose term had expired. His family removed thither, and soon Mrs. Howard and her younger children were established near by the little cottage in which her three eldest children, now grown up and gone from her, had played in infancy.

The position of superintendent is one requiring much hospitality on the part of the family of the incumbent. The Howards were rarely without guests, and, apart from the army circles in which they moved, there were many visitors attracted to West Point by reason of General Howard's presence there—ministers, philanthropists, members of the same denomination, who availed themselves of his nearness to New York to make or to renew his acquaintance. Parents of cadets went there to consult with the superintendent, old soldiers who had served in war time with him, and retired officers, who renewed their memories of cadet days by attending the reunions. There was never a day that some stranger was not presenting himself at the front door, and it may be imagined that the duties of host were not light.

General Howard, on assuming the position of superintendent, addressed himself to the improvement of the
cadets' mess, which had been complained of universally
by the young men.   An officer was appointed to take
charge of this important department, and the result was
a marked and a permanent change for the better.   The
quality of the food was improved, and the cadet corps
was animated by a spirit of gratitude to the new superintendent.

General Howard's solicitation being added to numerous petitions, Rev. Mr. Postlethwaite was appointed
chaplain, and in order to make his services of practical
value to the cadets he had a room set apart for his use
in the barracks.   Here he met the young men, who, at
their leisure time, would call upon him, and he became
interested in them, and they in him as they became better
acquainted.

The Bible-class and Sunday-school increased in numbers, and the church attendance was larger.   The demerit roll was a feature of the academy which General
Howard greatly disliked ; and, while he remained at the
head of the cadets he controlled its objectionable features
as far as it was possible under existing circumstances.
The system of vexatious espionage he disapproved, and
it was his determination to have broken it down had he
remained there.   He objected also to the entrance ex-
aminations, believing it an injustice to young men, who
in many instances had been ruined for life by failure
to pass an examination, which at a time of less mental
anxiety they could have met successfully.   He argued
that a great government had no right to put a blight
upon a lad's life by compelling him to meet an examination when he was enduring the strain of new associations
and some hardships not down in the curriculum.   His

experience had taught him the injustice of this course of treatment toward the youth, who, fresh from home and friends, was compelled to meet mental and physical demands before he had time, in his new surroundings, to learn to endure them philosophically.

To one who looks upon the military training as imperfect unless it comprehends the broadest moral culture, the West Point system has its faults, and General Howard was intent upon correcting them. In this he was much opposed, and finally was, for other alleged reasons, removed. In 1882 he was transferred to the command of the Department of the Platte, with headquarters at Omaha, and thither he removed his family in the early fall of that year.

From Maine to Alaska General Howard had made the circuit of the country in his military career, and had now reached the heart of the continent. With the Indians at peace and no disturbing elements to demand extra vigilance on the part of the commander, he has had time to do much literary work, and has lectured occasionally in cities adjacent to his field of labor. In his present position he has made many friends and performed much good work. As the years have passed his religion has broadened and his Christian zeal has increased. He is not, and never was, a conventional Christian ; were he such he would please many more than he has or will.

In the opinion of the world a certain amount of religion is proper and decorous, but it does not indorse the earnest, impetuous zeal of a man like Howard, who is absorbed in the thought, " I have laid my life upon the altar, and must work for the Lord." To begin the day with prayer, to read the Scriptures in the presence of his family, to select a verse that shall be the subject of

meditation during the twenty-four hours, and to live and
act to the highest light he possesses, is his idea of personal
duty. His theology has sometimes troubled the elders
because of its broadness of outline, and his constant disposition to forget the limitations of sects and creeds.
He defines his position in the orthodox church in the
following letter :

" OMAHA, NEB., November 28, 1884.
" MY DEAR FRIEND : You would like to know if there is any peculiarity in my religious convictions or beliefs—if they differ from those
of the brethren of the so-called ' orthodox churches.' I really think
not when the true and real beliefs of men and women are considered ;
but some of my convictions differ widely from those imputed to us.
"*First.* I have never trusted to the letter of the Scriptures of the
Old and New Testaments, for ' the letter killeth, but the spirit maketh
alive.' These Scriptures are the choicest mine to me, of gold and
silver and precious stones. The words, the chapters, the books of
the New Testament, are the complement of the Old, and the one is
essential to the other. As the person is made up of body, mind,
and soul, so is the Bible. The Spirit of God breathes through the
Book as you would anticipate, for the Book has been written by holy
men, who have been moved by the Holy Ghost as they have written.
Of course mistakes or slight discrepancies which exist here and there
do not spoil the Book any more than the little alloy spoils the gold,
or a little loose soil thrown in spoils the well. The best gold can be
obtained from the alloy, the best water can be filtered from the well.
Yes, go to God's Word with the right spirit, and there is no part of
it that will not yield good to the pure soul.
" As to depravity, I always say to myself, ' There is a deprivation
of original completeness.' So every man falls below the perfect man.
How to get men back to that completeness is always the problem presented. God can do it. He can bring a man up to the standard.
Giving to our God all the powers that are attributed to Him and con-
ceiving them to be unlimited, my mind does not worry over them ;
for while I know that He by His laws freezes, drowns, and otherwise
destroys men, and that His sovereignty cannot be impeached or gain-
said, yet I prefer to dwell mainly in the atmosphere of *His love.* I
assume His great loving-kindness and tender mercy.
" *The sun* in the heavens may be made a means of torture, but its
whole intention and lawful action is beneficent. *Christ* is God's

Spirit-Sun. He may be made the means of spirit unrest and poignant sorrow, but the whole intention, the whole plan, is beneficent.

" Christ is to me always the manifestation of infinite love. Jesus the man is a perfect man, the son of Mary ; but Christ the God part, the Anointed One, is not earth-born. The Christ principle—an active force—came in power ten days after Jesus ascended, and has been in the world ever since. It is the Spirit of the Living God, usually called the Holy Spirit. It restores to me, after I am born again, what I call my normal power. It enables me and any man of faith in God, through Christ, to perform miracles, not necessarily touching the body or the intellect, but touching the soul. Another soul to which I am sent may find the new birth through me, helped by this power. A man who has been all his life bad, with a hard, unkind face, may be changed by me when thus helped by the Spirit, so that his life becomes good and his face is softened and grows tender, sympathetic, and helpful. Selfishness is converted into unselfishness.

" Life, spirit life, everlasting life, it is the pearl of great price ; by my help, by the Christian's help, this life may begin in a soul. God gives this life ; has always done so. He made it plain through Christ. He reveals Himself through Christ to me.

"When I read the commandments and think, or when I meditate and watch the motions of my conscience, I know that the commandments or the laws written in my mind have been infracted. I turn from wrong done or intended with sorrow ; I purpose fully, with no secret drawbacks, to make all possible amends for the wrong done, and, further, *never, never* to do the wrong again. Even in this that spirit helps me. The Spirit shows me Christ as a loving Brother, as a tender, sympathizing Friend. The Holy Spirit cleanses me and then fills me—with what ? Peace, joy, hope, love, zeal for helping others.

" A *present* salvation is perhaps my hobby. I like the word *life* better. You, any friend I have, can have this life—should have it. How are all the helps obtained ? God has established a simple principle, so simple that it is despised ; it is only the asking-principle. As a little child asks its mother, so we—' I will to be inquired of.' Why not ?

" Again, fear God never did mean be afraid of God. I did not like to see the distress of my good mother, so I obeyed her. It is only a fear to do wrong.

" Now, as to a penalty. Let one lie down on his back and open his eyes to the sharp rays of the noonday sun ; it will give him intense pain, and no theorizing can prevent it. Put a proper shield between his eyes and the sun, and the light gives him only pleasure. This but poorly suggests the truth. I suffer so when I do wrong, and feel that the Spirit reproves me, that I want a shield—Come unto me and I will rest you. I go, then, by the asking-principle and I find my shield. How about the eternity of the *soul-penalties?* Demons (the souls of departed men not in unison with the Divine or Holy Spirit, the souls whose eyes are tortured by this intense sunlight) are not happy. They flee away from Christ, they really prefer swine to His presence. When will they seek Christ and love Him? I fear their downward tendencies grow stronger. I have only the Holy Spirit and the Holy Word to guide me in this. There is no wish in me that another shall have soul pain ; there is no such wish in the heart of God.

" Suppose I have life as a gift, and hold it out to a friend. Suppose he declines the gift. I entreat him to accept it, but he says plainly, ' I prefer not to have it,' or he says, ' If I take it, it is upon my own terms.' ' No, my friend, your terms destroy the gift itself.'

" There is in every soul a will-power. Force the will, and it is weakened. Prevail over it constantly, and it is at last destroyed. The very capacity for pure, simple, lovely, holy affections may be lost. This loss is the penalty, and the ache is tougher than some men think. God's redemption is doubtless beyond our weak conception of its power. But for my dear friends, and for all with whom I come in contact, I would rather not have them live one day in the torture of an unhappy soul—no, not even in the apathy of an un-thinking soul.

" The presenting of an obstinate and hateful face to the tenderest loving-kindness certainly is not wise ; and to trust to the spirit-land for a change when the inducements cannot be any greater than in this terrestrial land, is the sheerest folly.

" How about the atonement? That is God's part, and He has well accomplished it Himself, and made an exhibit of it in the life-sufferings, especially the spiritual or soul-sufferings of that wonder-ful Being, Jesus Christ. God never ceases to have Christ say, ' Come unto me.' Every one that heedeth the call finds the atonement all done, so far as he himself is concerned.

" I took down the names of numerous friends, after I realized the complete forgiveness of my own offences, and I prayed for them and wrote to them, or talked with them. I believe all of them came to the same healing fountain. Each one found the atonement com-plete—that is, the ability to get back to the proper spirit-condition of unison with God.

" My ultimate philosophy is very simple. Behold it in the practice : study the Scriptures ; read them daily ; have family reading and prayer ; ask God's blessing at meals ; spend the Sabbaths in seeking spiritual benefit ; try every day to make somebody happier and better ; go to the meeting for prayer to meet the Great King, and put in with others our petitions. The gathering of two or three has Christ's promise to sustain it. When people of old spoke often to one another and to Him in company, He hearkened to them ; so will He now.

" I have tried to avoid a theological way of saying things—in fact, I am not a theologian, but have been long trying in plain language to give a clear reason for the actual *hope* that is within my soul.

" You say, How with the vast outside parties—Pagans, Buddhists, Mohammedans, etc.—and how with those before Christ ? My answer is, it is a limitless God that I speak of ; all are affected through Him. Christ is His spiritual manifestation. Just how He manages in the detail with every creature, who can tell ? The Christ-Spirit has probably visited every soul in the universe. The rejection of the way, the truth, and the life was as plain in Cain and in King Saul as in Judas. The acceptance was as clear in Enoch and Joseph as in John and Philip. Without or within the circle, there infinite wisdom and love are always the same.

" Sincerely yours,

" O. O. HOWARD."

*   *   *   *   *   *

In the spring of 1884 General Howard asked for and obtained a six months' leave for the purpose of visiting Europe ; and in order to grant him an extension of time, the War Department ordered him to do duty first in Egypt for one month. He was required to witness and report upon active operations in that country, and then to visit France and report upon matters connected with the grand manœuvres of the Seventeenth Corps d'Armée. Sailing from New York early in March, he was absent until the middle of November following. His detailed report covered his visit to Egypt and the information gleaned from the staff-officers and others of the campaign of Wolseley, ending with the battle of Tel-el-

-Kebir, the battles of El Teb and Tamai, and the massacres under Hicks and Baker Pashas, with an account of
General Gordon's work in the Soudan.   He wrote and
published military articles on Waterloo, and reported
upon the French manœuvres in Southern France.

In every country he visited General Howard had interviews with the missionaries, and especially in Alexandria,
Cairo, Smyrna, and Scutari he found them doing excellent
work.   He attended the International Convention of the
Young Men's Christian Association in Berlin, and was
invited to take part in a public meeting to be held at
Manchester, England.   Wherever he went he was welcomed by the Christian people, who had long known
him by reputation ; and in England particularly, where
his efforts for the freedmen were well appreciated, he
received marked attentions.

On his return to the United States he resumed his
military duties at Omaha, and again became active in
Christian and philanthropic work.

The newspapers have from time to time reported the
wide scope of this work, and the following is an incident
that will best illustrate his benevolence.   It is from the
Omaha *Bee*.

"Some time ago a soldier was sentenced to five years' imprisonment in Fort Leavenworth for some offence. The soldier's sisters in
New York wrote to General Howard in behalf of the prisoner, appealing to him to interest himself in his case, and see if something could
not be done to lighten the sentence. General Howard had the prisoner brought before him at headquarters, as he was on his way to
Fort Leavenworth in shackles, and asked him if he had any trade.
The prisoner said he was a stone-cutter. The general had the prisoner sent back to Fort Omaha, after he had questioned him still further, and then he wrote to Washington, and succeeded in having the
sentence remitted, the only punishment being a dishonorable discharge from the army. Thereupon General Howard got him a job as
a stone-cutter in this city. The man did well, and finally went back

to New York, where he is now, a sober and industrious man. This is only one of the many kind acts that General Howard has done in a quiet way while he has been located in this city."

The Rev. Dr. A. F. Sherrill, pastor of .the First Congregational Church at Omaha, estimates in the following letter General Howard's usefulness as a public speaker upon religious subjects :

"General Howard's services as a public speaker during the war, when his wounds disabled him from field service, are well known. Ever since he has been in constant demand as a public lecturer, speaking to large audiences upon a wide range of topics, and his engagements, in the midst of regular military duties, have been only limited by time and strength. Ever since his conversion, when a young man, he has heard sounding in his ears, ' Go and tell how great things the Lord hath done for thee and hath had compassion on thee ;' and he has spoken freely and earnestly in all kinds of religious meetings, until he has a reputation, as a lay religious speaker, such as few possess. He is equally at home standing in a metropolitan pulpit before a cultivated audience, or addressing a group of young Arabs in a mission school. He can touch the highest spiritual point in the tender moments of a church prayer-meeting, or improvise a service at a post on the remote frontier, and by his hearty manner win the attention of every man as he tells the ' old, old story.' Perhaps his power of appeal is most apparent at great religious mass-meetings, where his thoughts and feelings, crowding upon his speech, rise into eloquent and impassioned utterance. The old fire of ' war and battle-sound ' is kindled, only now he is calling to enthusiasm and action in the service of the King of kings. As a speaker he possesses that magnetic power by which, as soon as he rises, he comes at once into *rapport* with his audience and holds their close attention to the end. It is not easy to analyze his speaking, but these three or four things are easily apparent :

"First, a simple style and speech. He realizes, in good degree, a recent definition of eloquence : ' Short words, in short sentences, with the ideas overlapping at both ends.' Such speech suits us all. The writer has heard General Howard addressing college students to their profit, but the farmers and children present also drank it all in, as if intended only for them. It is the use of this great simplicity of speech, in ordinary address, which enables him to tell the story of the Cross with such effect.

"Second, earnestness. This comes from his love of men and his thorough convictions of the truth. He has studied the Scriptures carefully. He has also lived out their truths. He has seen them succeed with thousands of others to whom he has brought them. He might always say, 'I speak that I do know, and testify that I have seen.' Hence there is no uncertain sound in his speech, and it carries the conviction from which it is born. He uses his personal religious experience a great deal, and very effectively ; not merely that of twenty years ago, however, but that of present daily life, of which he is always full, for he takes his religion everywhere and into all things. This makes his speech fresh and pertinent to the occasion, and gives charm and power to it. It makes him practical, and leads to homely turns of Scripture, which one can never forget. No one who listens thinks him speaking for the sake of the speech, but out of a sincere heart to do others good. He is a very appreciative listener, and I have often thought this helped him to speak so that others would listen.

"Third, his speech is personal. It is not so in any offensive sense. He is too brave and kind for that. But all the above-mentioned qualities make it certain each will feel the words were meant for him ; and so they were. 'So fight I, not as one that' beateth the air.' If the audience be a familiar one, he usually has different individuals in mind, to whom he speaks for a purpose ; but each represents a class, and so all are personally addressed. His words do not stick in the heart like barbed arrows, but are rather welcomed as 'good doctrine,' which one does not care to 'forsake.'

"Fourth, we read of those who spoke 'as the Spirit gave them utterance.' We are also told Demosthenes never ascended the bema without a prayer. General Howard has a consecrated heart. He does not desire his speech shall be with enticing words of man's wisdom, but in demonstration of the spirit that, so far as he is concerned, others' faith should not ' stand in the wisdom of men, but in the power of God.' Hence he asks earnestly for this spirit, and is at no other time so satisfied as when he can feel he was, while speaking, filled with the Spirit, suggesting thought and imparting power to his words. It is this presence of the Spirit, in response to his prayer, which chiefly accounts for the fact that men listen so attentively when he speaks, find their hearts so deeply touched, and that so many are persuaded to come to Christ. 'It is the Spirit that quickeneth.' Thus a few words spoken, or a very short prayer offered, will often go through an audience with a power which is not of man.

" Wherever General Howard lives he soon becomes a kind of general *factotum* for all sorts of public religious service and supply, to which he brings his inspired wealth of mind, and soul, and speech ; nor is he less active in his more private goings about to do good. When we remember he is also commander of a great military department, an office full of responsibility and care, we know that, as to most of us, it all would weary, wear, and soon wipe us out ; but the general seems inexhaustible ; he always comes in fresh and good as new. His face is never long, though full of care and thought, and every one hopes he will live to the age of that other hero of whom it is said, ' He was an hundred and twenty years old when he died ; his eye was not dim nor his natural force abated.' "

X.

Excerpts from letters, documents, and private diary, showing General Howard's inner life—The war, the Freedmen's Bureau, the church, and public events discussed—Anecdote of General Howard's kindness of heart—Conclusion.

THERE is no better way of obtaining a just conception of a man's character than by reading what he has written under the varying circumstances of every-day life. General Howard, the most methodical of men, has kept for many years copies of his letters and at times a diary, which is an epitome of his career. From the ample pages of his letter books have been taken the following excerpts, which show the man's nature and exhibit his religious aspect of mind at every period of life. As many of his letters have been written to the leading military men of the country, it is easy to glean from them the professional and patriotic side of his character. These excerpts have been made from a rich collection, which would yield many times the number used here, and they have not been selected as the best things he has said, but as examples of his usual expressions of opinion, hopes, and desires.

" My Bible is to me a source of comfort and strength, and I earnestly recommend it as the best companion of every human soul. On its substantial truths must rest all our hopes of good here and blessedness hereafter. . . . To my mind, with the Indians the time is near when every dollar appropriated may be made tributary to the schools. It is but little to require that people shall send their children to school. Superstitious reluctance must be made to do it ;

let it be the law to our wards, and let the law be executed. . . .
I hope Mac will cling to the *Divine Word.* This will make him
strong and wise."

To A. S. Packard.

"June 7, 1864.

". . . God is leading us through very difficult paths, and chastening us very hard, but we must learn from whom the chastening comes,
and be obedient and hopeful. I do hope and pray that this year
may end the war. . . . Every man who sets himself to the task of
working for humanity must begin by humbling himself in such
measure as to meet the wants of the poorest and lowliest. If he does
this, by the blessing of God he will be effective."

To Hon. J. G. Blaine.

"August 24, 1864.

". . . As to the brigadiership in the regular army, I should regard it as a high compliment and of material value, but I am inclined
to ask for no promotion or appointment, having already received
more than I could ask, and beyond my deserts. In times like these
it is dangerous to rise too high ; a single misfortune may topple you
over into popular disfavor. I shall exert myself in my present position with the hope of credit to myself and friends, and trust, under
God's blessing, to be of substantial service to my country. . . . How
utterly absurd it is to stand tremblingly anxious lest we lose a tithe
of liberty, when all our liberties are on the brink of ruin ! For
mercy's sake, Blaine—for our country's sake, rather—put forth all
your energies to sustain and strengthen the Government, and make it
confident and fearless in the exercise of positive power—a power
adequate to this trying ordeal, for this is the time to put it forth.

"Every family will bleed, every individual will suffer ; but if we do
our duty faithfully in this crisis, under the Divine blessing the end
will be glorious. I fear and tremble as I read the newspapers. I
fear that we have not virtue enough in this country to stand the
trial. I have no objection to peace—peace is what we want ; but let
the word ring along the lines of brave men who are giving their lives
for victory and peace."

"I would not stay to see the ' *sun dance*,' for I feared the usual tearing of the flesh and self-torture ' to appease the Great Spirit.' I told
the chiefs what I thought of this wicked barbarism. They said
that they would do what they could to keep out this bad part, but
the ' medicine men ' hold the poor people to this heathenism. It is
their hold against Christian teaching."

" A drunken agent, or a man who prostitutes his official position to bribery, I will remove at a blow."

" The feelings of hostility now existing between the two races I do not regard as permanent. The interests of both tend to decrease it."

[To a Southern Friend.

" Three hundred thousand of our brethren lie beneath the soil they have wet with their blood, to keep you from breaking and destroying the government purchased by our fathers. They have not shed their blood in vain. Your children will thank us. And would God might not give you over to hardness !"

To Hon. Horace Greeley.

" September 15, 1865.

" I notice some of the public journals are disposed to ridicule the idea of a Bureau of Refugees and Freedmen. Now, while I claim that personally I am not benefited by this administrative branch of the War Department, and not called upon to stand upon the defensive, but simply to execute a law under the orders of the President and Secretary of War, yet for the sake of a good cause I deprecate having this Bureau placed before the public in a false position. . . ."

To Rev. C. F. McRae.

" October 27, 1865.

" . . . I have noticed in the colored schools all over the country, where there were respectable teachers, that there was uniformly good attendance, and a wonderful interest manifested on the part of the children. While this interest is awakened, as if by Divine interposition, should we not, as Christians, put our shoulders to the wheel, and do all we can, by organized efforts, to open up the minds of these thousands and fill them with useful knowledge ? . . . The past is past, but if you will notice the prevalence of untruthfulness, the want of observance of the marriage tie, and the ignorance of the very groundwork of the Christian faith, you will agree with me that there is enough now to do, and enough for every laborer in the vineyard."

To James E. Rhoades.

" October 9, 1865.

" . . . Education underlies every hope of success for the freedman. This education must, of course, extend rather to the practical arts than to theoretical knowledge. Everything depends upon the youth and the children being thoroughly instructed in every industrial pursuit. Through education embracing moral and religious training, the fearful prejudice and hostility against the blacks can be overcome. They themselves will be able to command and secure both privileges and rights that we now have difficulty to guarantee. . . . Do everything you possibly can for the elevation of the freedmen. My impression is, that hundreds and perhaps thousands of Southern people would be ready to aid you, if approached in the right way. . . What are the people willing to do to secure the blessings almost within our grasp—the blessings of substantial freedom and enduring peace? Whether so or not in a political point of view, I believe every thinking man is ready to admit that we will stand or fall as a nation according as we are true to principles, according to our fidelity to trusts evidently committed to us. . . ."

"December 23, 1865.

" Order exists all over the world without the necessity of slavery. Wealth ditto. Physical condition ditto. Resources better developed where freedom has existed for any length of time.

" Slavery is a disease or abnormal condition, which always prostrates the victim, whatever the color, and he cannot always recover, and the seeds of the disease are transmitted, so that the children are often materially affected by it.

" The evil was making merchandise of a child of God ; restraining or preventing education ; keeping by force men below a certain plane, and not·allowing them the fruit of their own labor ; raising children without respecting the family relation ; keeping out industrious white emigrants—every enterprise slow in development, whether it affected manufactures or commerce, the arts or literature. In fact, a careful study of political economy will show the downhill tendency of every slavery system. You point to the chaos at Augusta, Ga.; I point you to the order already existing in Maryland, parts of Mississippi, Arkansas, Louisiana, and wherever a fair free system has actually gone into operation. You say the negro differs from other people. I admit it, yet know that he is a man, and may be led and influenced by motives as a man."

To Rev. C. Van Santvoord.

"January 3, 1866.

" Your letter has come to me inquiring as to the character of General McPherson, with regard to his religious life. While at West Point he was one class ahead of me, having entered in 1849. He was constantly at the head of his own class, and was therefore particu-

larly noticed by every cadet. He was remarkable for kindness of
manner and the sympathy he extended to any who were ill-used.
I remember a classmate of his, who is now living, and of excellent character, who was ' cut,' as they say at the academy, for some
breach of etiquette. McPherson braved the general derision, and
was always kind and courteous to him. Toward another cadet, with
like circumstances, I remember that his frank cordiality and sympathy were marked. His daily life was full of patriotic, cheerful,
Christian example. While there, I never knew a word of profanity
to escape his lips. I have seen him in Professor Sprole's Bible-
class, and always saw him in this character on the Sabbath. Again
and again I have thought of his beautiful, Christian deportment, and
wondered if he were not really a follower of Christ. After leaving
West Point I had no means of knowing his Christian example, but
found him, after the lapse of some years, the same genial gentleman
and kind friend as at the academy."

To H. B. Cadbury, Birmingham, Eng.

"March 26, 1866.

" . . . You ask what security you will have that after the freed
people have taken possession, cleared the land, built huts, and settled their families on it, they will not be disturbed. There can be
no security against lawlessness, but my belief is that interest will
soon arouse every owner of any considerable amount of property to
throw his influence in favor of law and order. No people are as ob-
noxious to the Southerners that have been in rebellion as the Union
Yankees, yet these very men have settled in large numbers in different parts of the South, and propose to remain. My impression is
that whatever policy the Government may adopt, the prejudices and
exhibitions of passion will in time wear away. There are some few
counties in the insurrectionary States where there is a large crop of
rowdies. In these it would be unwise and unsafe to settle at present. As a general rule, capital carries with it its own security. I
am anxious to have just such correctives as those you advocate mul-
tiplied. I hope there will be plenty of straightforward, fearless
men, who will purchase or aid in the purchasing of estates in every
part of the South. With such men, or the means they invest, will go
industry, thrift, education, and civilization. We are in a political
crisis, and my heart is often filled with anxiety lest we may dis-
please God by promoting or establishing some system of injustice ;
but I trust He will aid us in the exercise of that noble principle

which Mr. Lincoln so simply and plainly gave us—that is, ' Firmness in the right,'as God gives us to see the right.' . . .''

" It is customary to underrate any man's ability who tries to serve his God, and to impute to him special weakness ; but I wish you could take my administration of the brigade, division, army corps, and Army of the Tennessee, and then of this ' misrepresented Bureau,' and give to them a thorough examination from 1861 to October, 1868, and then tell me if I have not understood men, and accomplished the purposes intended. I write you this partly because I have thought you have been deceived, and because by and by I want your sympathy in a great educational enterprise. I asked the question, ' Would you not like to be a slave, if you could only be sure to have enough to eat, to drink, and to wear?' The answer is everywhere substantially the same—' I would rather be poor and free ; I would rather suffer and be free.'

" Doubtless there could be found among the degraded and among the criminals those who would prefer to be pampered slaves to being freemen ; but as far as my observation goes, the universal information is, ' My choice is liberty ;' and doubtless the expression of this choice, is the voice of God. Were it not for the color of the skin, which is like a thick veil hanging between so many of us and God's truth, how deep and how universal would be the sympathy of Christian people for these poor dependent objects of humanity, who are just struggling into the sunlight of liberty ! Let every Christian heart offer up a prayer for them, and, to the best of his ability, extend them a helping hand. . . .''

To General Brown.

" February 20, 1867.
" My freedmen's and refugees' fund will all be available for ' incorporated institutions.' Industrial is a better word than manual, I think, for it embodies hands, feet, brains, and souls. I have great contempt for Virginia prejudice ; it means Virginia sin.''

" It is undoubtedly difficult for gentlemen in the Southern States to determine the measure of their responsibility in this work of education. Yet it is important that this work, which has been so well initiated, should not cease, should not even flag—important for all the interests of the country, important in the interests of humanity, important in the light of a practical solution of the great problem of liberty for the world. Ideas drilled into us from infancy and prejudices drunk in in childhood cannot easily be changed ; but God

is just ; and if we earnestly and prayerfully wait on Him, He will not
let us go far astray.   I should not have predicted that you would
have turned against the Union, and hope you may yet be a true and
earnest friend of the Government that we once loved alike, which
nurtured and educated us together. . . .''

"I hope we may all see to it that we have the same brightness of
vision at the last when we set forth upon the journey to meet the
Lord, and our loved ones who have gone to rest in His domain,
where the prepared mansions are."

To General Grant.

"As you have always been kind to me, even when the waves of
trial rolled in upon me, so have I ever been at heart appreciative and
grateful to you.   I know that you are too strong to need or ask sympathy, but you know also in your rugged career how the dark hours
are the best test of real friends. . . .''

To A. E. E. Taylor.
"January 12, 1866.

". . . I am exceedingly obliged to you for your defence of me, but
I have been subjected to too many vexatious troubles during the
war to care much for such articles as that in the *Independent*.   I have
nothing in particular to suggest, only if you can help us along with
our work here in the Bureau, I shall be glad to have you."

"I have often spoken to children and urged them to the adoption
of right principles, no less than the love of Christ ; but I have universally entertained and spread the belief that love is shown in the
cheerful and faithful performance of daily duty."

"June 6, 1867.

"Nothing would have given me greater pleasure than to have attended your convention and participated in the enjoyments of the
occasion, and if any further inducement had been needed, you have
offered it in holding out the prospect of my meeting Sir Henry Havelock.   I read the life of his father with great interest and profit several years ago, and I trust I may ever imitate him in a straightforward Christian life.   Almost all strangers who have seen my name
associated with his are much disappointed on meeting with me, ex-
pecting to see a man of large size and advanced in years."

To Mr. E. Greble.
"October 4, 1867.

". . . You know that I have undertaken to build a church that
shall be a home for loyalty and truth, a place for our young men who

como here to find a welcome. This building will hold a people that we needed here, to quicken the good and war upon the bad—a people who have a great work to do. We have got our roof on, but are now sorely pressed for help. I will enclose you a copy of what my Brooklyn friends did, and if you could aid us a little in this, my heart will ever be filled with gratitude. This church presses heavy upon me. . . ."

To Hon. Henry Wilson.

" October 12, 1866.

" I saw a paragraph in the morning paper which said that you had publicly united with the church of Rev. Dr. Kirk, of Boston. It gave me a great deal of pleasure to read this item of good news, and I wish to hasten and extend to you a warm fraternal greeting. I trust God may make you an ornament to the church of Christ, and bless our country still further by an earnest, faithful Christian statesman. He is blessing us politically, and I trust is conducting you through green pastures of His love."

" Looking to the future, our Western States, like Iowa and Nebraska, have made ample provisions for their public schools ; nothing is placed ahead of the education of their sons and daughters. This is indeed wise ; only one thing should ever be regarded as of more importance than the training of the intellect of the youth, and that is the religious and moral foundations which we leave to the home and to the Church. Now, if we who believe in God and the Bible, in the lifting up of the weak, be it ever so little, in opposition to the atheistic theory of favoring only the stronger races—if we who regard the precept to love our neighbors as ourselves would save a remnant of the native race of this continent, we must see, on a moment's reflection, that our principal hope—nay, in fact, our only hope, lies in their complete conversion from savage to civilized methods of doing and living. Carlisle, Hampton, Forest Grove, Metla Katlah, Cœur d'Alene, and other successful schools show what can be done. Take the children, change their minds and hearts by our true, powerful school processes."

" I deprecate anything calculated to excite hostility, and ask only simple justice for the freedmen, whom I am under solemn obligations to protect. Schools had better be established on some broader basis than for blacks and whites alone. The matter of schooling for children on the plantations may be embraced in the contract which I hope every employer will make with his employés for some time to come. When left to me, the indenture of children is regulated as in

most of the free States—that is, with consent of either parent or
guardian, the officers and agents of this Bureau, or those of their appointment, being their guardians until otherwise established by law."

". . . War is devastation. As General Sherman says, it is cruelty,
and you cannot easily refine it."

". . . I love the name of Abraham Lincoln, and pray God I may
be able to live his pure, simple, honest, noble life, and contribute
something toward securing the liberty and charity he worked and
died for."

                              To Y. E. Tate.
                                             " April 9, 1867.
" . . . I differ from you in regard to the ballot. Poor men will
soon learn that it is their protection, and they will use it accordingly. They may get fooled a few times, but not perpetually. Black
men have just about as much sense as white men of the same education and advantages. . . ."

Regarding a War Monument to be erected at West Point.

" The worthy object commends itself to my judgment and heart,
and I am glad the officers at the academy are so disposed to honor
the noble men, their brother officers, who have given their lives in
this, our terrific struggle for national existence. The academy and
the regular army have had their usual share of abuse and misrepresentation during the war, but when we proudly point to the conduct
their loyal sons have exhibited—when we count over the noble records
of the killed in battle on every bloody field, every tongue is hushed.
The battle monument shall bear witness to the love we bear the
national army, the national flag, the national whole. . . .

" I am gratified that a kind Providence gave me the benefit of the
training I received under yourself and the other professors and in-
structors of the academy, and I trust I may ever be enabled to reflect
only what in faithfulness you ever strove to impart—strict integrity,
good sense, and rational sentiments."

                        To Jay Cooke & Co.
                                          "January 21, 1868.
". . . I can establish the soup-house at Memphis, and defray the
expense of it from the Bureau funds. The officers are instructed
everywhere to allow no starvation."

                          To an Officer.
" I shall have to live unending ages with human souls in some rela-
tionships or other, so that I shall be careful not to let temporary

impatience control me. A kind Providence will bring things right. . . ."

To *Hon. W. E. Dodge.*

" February 3, 1868.

". . . Your letter is just received. I have never, in all my intercourse with General Grant, seen him so affected by drink as to be noticeable from its influence ; and I have been recently assured by his own lips that he is not drinking, and has declared he shall not, during the year upon which we have entered, take even wine, and the probability is never for life. You are at liberty to use this statement privately if you desire."

To *Rev. J. W. Chickering.*

". . . Strong drink is a cruel enemy, and I trust you will meet him with promptitude, in force, and with persistence. . . ."

To *Rev. George Whipple.*

" February 12, 1868.

". . . I never threatened to leave the church, but have expressed myself willing to leave it, in the event of our brethren unanimously sustaining Dr. Boynton's celebrated sermon, and provided they should relieve me from all pecuniary obligations. . . .

"As to amalgamation being a doctrine of the Congregational Church, I have simply to say I do not think the Church is called upon to pronounce upon the subject. The pastor may have some trouble, but it strikes me that it would be well for him to wait for a case to arise, rather than call up an imaginary one. So far as the Church is concerned, I have simply planted myself upon the ground, ' Love thy neighbor as thyself.' I do not wish to see our church a German church, a French church, an Anglo-Saxon church, nor an African church, but simply a church of Christ, with its door wide open ; and I do not care an iota whether the brethren and sisters believe in amalgamation or not. I consider this subject entirely foreign to our controversy, and only put into it with the hope of exciting prejudice against me and my friends by the use of a word, in precisely the same way that prejudice used to be excited against anti-slavery by the use of the word 'abolitionist.' . . ."

To *Dr. H. Barber.*

" February 12, 1868.

" My DEAR SIR : The story has gone from your lips, with the addition that others are likely to add to stories, that I am an amalgama-

tionist. Now a letter comes saying that I threaten to leave the
church with my friends unless the church indorse my doctrine.
Now please answer me a question or two.

"1. What do you mean by amalgamation?

"2. What is your object in circulating this story?

" I never threatened to leave the church. I was willing to do so
if I could be relieved from all obligations, and so expressed myself,
bitter as the disappointment would be to me. I don't care one fig
whether people believe in amalgamation or not. In fact, I don't
know what you mean by it, . . ."

To Mr. A. H. Love.

" March 31, 1870.

" I agree with you who style yourself ' radical peace men ' more
nearly than you think. I would labor as earnestly and industriously
as any one to secure to my country peace. And really how well the
officers and soldiers performed their part during the war! It was
dreadful ; it was more terrible than you can depict, and yet I believe
sent upon us as really by divine direction as was any one of the
battles under Joshua. I have never, since I loved Christ, *hated* an
enemy ; no more do I hate a man who is to suffer death according to
law ; but protection to our country needs an army now, as your city
needs the police. I will work with you for peace, for education, for
the principle and practice of love, and am not particular about the
title of the general ; yet if Philadelphia should be beleaguered by
the British, and your families in great distress, and the permanent
peace and welfare of the whole country endangered, I should obey
General Grant's order to move with all the force I could muster to
your relief, and should avoid a battle, if possible ; but if not, I
should feel it my duty not to wear the sword in vain. Our Lord
commended the Roman soldier. It was not paradoxical for Him to
say, ' He had not seen such faith ; no, not in Israel.' Let us have
peace, but let us be true to our present duty, while we hope, labor,
and pray that our duties may be changed by the general diffusion of
the principles of peace. You would not advise drinking to the army
in order to weaken it and render our nation ignoble in the eyes of
other nations. Temperance and righteousness apply to us in the
army and navy, as individuals, as they do to you and your friends.
Human life is protected by the divine law, yet it does not mean that
the criminal shall go unpunished. God takes human life for
offences, and He has specially directed His children (in Moses' law)
to do the same ; not in revenge, not in hate, but for the purpose of

preserving life and rendering it sacred. I do daily pray for my enemies, and endeavor to entertain for them a forgiving spirit. The
men I fought were, many of them, my intimate personal friends. I
never hated them ; I grieved that they raised their hands to destroy
their government."

To Colonel D. L. Eaton.

". . . Your question of this morning perplexes me. I am glad you
asked me, however, for if I am wrong in theory or method I ought
at once to change. You say, ' General, do you think the bringing of
people in that way does much good ? ' You further say, ' I think the
proper way is by reflection.' By '*that way* ' you mean some way that
is *not* by reflection, probably by impulse, or impulse induced by excitement. My theory is that no man is Christ's till his purpose is
fixed. Now, in nine cases out of ten an impulse induced by want,
by suffering, by an exhibition of joy or sorrow begets in me a resolution, and I act upon it. A pure intellectual decision would lead
me to do differently ; yet afterward my mind indorses the impulse
and the resolution. If you should trust altogether to people's cool
reflection, the Unitarian would remain so ; those who never go to
church would not be helped—the seed would not be sown beside all
waters. If you say that excitement is not religion, I agree ; but if
you think that religion can always be without excitement, I cannot
think so. Even you throw your hat high at times. Our Y. M. C. A.
meetings have the advantage, like the Bible Society, of meeting the
strong ones of the different churches. We know that we cannot
regenerate souls nor bring a Lazarus to life, but we can roll away
the stone from many a heart. Perhaps it is pride, perhaps worldliness, vanity, false teaching, ignorance ; perhaps it is robbing Christ
by supposing that man can do all ; or perhaps the stone is apathy,
an aggregation of the accretion of years of sinning. A word, a sentence, a song, a smile, may be the leverage ; but when the stone is
away the cave of the heart is open, and the Lord's voice is heard and
heeded. We never rely upon feeling, but upon purpose, and the
test of a man's purpose is his life. Yet one never finds his Saviour
and purposes to be His forever without sacred joy and indescribable
peace. . . .''

"It is dangerous to feed people without their rendering any labor
in return."

"When we can once get a good, thorough system of common
schools in practical operation, self-supporting, with a perennial supply of good teachers throughout the slave States, the material prosperity of those States will be secured beyond peradventure."

" The school system, when once established, must be nourished by the masses of the people, and they must and will have, as soon as the schools are in practical operation, the power and the means to keep them alive."

To Mr. Frederick Douglass.

" July 10, 1870.

"My dear Sir : I read a part of your reply to the Philadelphia resolutions, copied into the *Independent* of July. Much that you there say accords with my judgment and sympathy, but I feel that you speak more strongly and sweepingly than you meant—' The church and street are about the same in point of authority and in point of excellence. Both are now on the side of popular wrong, and both are against unpopular right.' Such have not been the teachings of the branches of the Church that I have attended from my youth. That individual ministers have led astray, that people have blindly followed them into the practice and defence of crime, I admit ; but this has not been the general rule. I learned in the Church to love God. I learned to reverence the authority of His law. I found in the Church a Saviour, and my heart has been by His word and grace enlarged in its capacity to love my fellow-men, and I firmly believe that it is the operation of the teachings of the New England churches that made so many strong Abolitionists there. The great majority of ministers I have heard in Maine have been outspoken against slavery, against wrong of every kind ; and my view has been that the wrong-doing of men and women in the Church has been, not in consequence of, but in spite of the instruction they receive. ' Love thy neighbor' is the teaching. Act up to it, and slavery of every description falls. Now as to the abolition ; you do not attribute it to a miracle, not due to any special interposition of Divine Providence, but as resulting from the certain operation of natural causes inherent in the very constitution of human nature. Were this so we should be just as thankful to the Author of human nature—the Lord God, who so wonderfully arranged all things. But I think some of us who bore the brunt of the battle realized a daily aid, specially given as to a beseeching child. I cannot look upon Mr. Lincoln without regarding him as a special Providence, as much as was David. . . . Natural indeed, because God is in everything and guiding everything, and hindering even the independent will of Satan and his friends. We do not read that God is the Author of wrong—He can abolish wrong. This is the everlasting work of Christ, by His Spirit working in us and with us. He is not the Author of sin, such as slavery, drunkenness, lying, stealing, murder, hate, etc. You are a leader, have long been, and may God keep you in the forefront ; but do not let the sins of church members obscure your clear vision and hide the torches of truth that Christ and His followers have lifted up.''

To Editor Evening Bulletin.

" July 16, 1870.

" . . . My quarrel with Rev. Dr. Boynton was rather a controversy in behalf of my charge, the freedmen and their children. I had to carry the fight for them into the Church, the Sunday-school, the courts, and the legislative halls. Martin Luther contended for principle, and hate arose even against him, and did its best. Attack a popular wrong and defeat its advocate, make your own side popular, and you are never forgiven by the defeated. . . .

" Circumstances have occurred to teach and subdue my vanity, and teach me new lessons of humility, and I think I am profiting by them. Oh, that my guiding principle might be the honor of Christ ! I am so prone to forget it, and enter so heartily into things that are selfish and earthly, that I lower my spirit thankfully when God sees fit to rebuke and chastise me. . . .''

*   *   *   *   *   *   *   *

EXTRACTS FROM DIARY.

" WASHINGTON, D. C.

"*January* 1, 1871.— . . . Read two Psalms and prayed for each member present and absent ; also for Generals G. and S. and families, R. and family, Secretary of War and family (he has just lost his beautiful wife) ; also for the Church, the Y. M. C. A., and for the university ; for Brother R. and for Mrs. G. and children, little J. G. L., and the two poor men afflicted with drink ; also for God's living presence in me to help me to a purer and higher life. Cousin J. Roddy Hazard stopped over Sunday with us ; breakfast and happy morning prayer. All the family, including Irving (serving man) and the girls, present. . . . At church again to-night. Cousin Roddy and L. joined me in pew 64. Mr. R. kept our minds steadily on the text, ' Behold I stand at the door and knock,' etc. I did long to open the door wider and let Him, our blessed Saviour, in. We rode in the beautiful moonlight to the —— Stables, being without a driver, then walked home. Thus begins the year—a busy day. I told one incident, I think chiefly in self-praise, which will do no good, and may do harm. I want to guard against this besetting sin. . . . ''

"*January* 2, 1871.— . . . Mr. Lewis and his son-in-law, Captain Hall, our neighbors, called ; the latter has met with a terrible acci-

dent since I saw him, losing his left hand and his left eye. The
artificial eye looks just like the other, and moves the same as a real
one. Art is wonderful, but it is only the natural eye that can see.
He seemed very serious when I told him I must be the most wicked,
as God had to take the right arm from me. He said a colored servant told him he must be a very wicked man that God had to punish him so severely. . . Our prayer-meeting very small compared
with the size of our church-membership, yet the object was thoughtfully and humbly considered—viz., a review of the past year, an humbling of ourselves before God in view of the worldliness of Christ's
Church. I tried to recall my own record. Oh, how barren! Asked
for prayers for a better, more consecrated future ; also for my friend,
who has been so long halting at the doorway of Christ's Church. We
tried to covenant together so as to be in mood to point sinners to
Christ—this prayer-week at least—each one endeavoring to get a
clean heart. O God our Father, do not let us, in our weakness, stand
in the way of sinners coming !''

"*January* 3, 1871.— . . . Our morning reading embraced the passage, ' The blood of Jesus Christ, His Son, cleanseth us from all sin.'
I told the children of it. The little ones seem interested. . . . Busy
morning at the office. I inspected two divisions—Mr. Drew's and
General Bullock's—with a view of reduction of force. It is hard to
discharge these really good young men, who have been with me so
long and done well. I saw the appointment clerk of the Treasury,
with a view of getting some of them positions to-day. . . . We had
a good prayer-meeting for rulers, nations, soldiers, etc. I spoke for
General Grant and the Secretary of War in his bereavement, and
tried to pray. We had a crowded prayer-room and a large and pleasant sociable afterward. I hope a special blessing will follow this
work of prayer. Gracie and Jamie went with me to-night.''

"*January* 4, 1871.— . . . I tried at the meeting that night to point
out briefly the difficulties of parents and teachers, and the ways I had
been able to interest children in reading the Scriptures with them.
. . . Mr. Rankin encouraged us to labor on, though imperfect ; I
had said that I must be holier and better that, in exercise of authority,
I might not drive away our children from the blessed Saviour. . . .''

"*January* 5, 1871.— . . . Having received a mother's earnest
request for prayer for her son—twenty-five years—for *immediate* conversion, I went to the court-room and thence to the Y. M. C. A.—daily
prayer as yesterday. I spoke a few words about not *recognizing* and
not using God's Spirit when He did give it, and tried to pray. One
interesting story of the immediate answer to the request of a brother

to a praying assembly in the conversion of his brother drew general attention. . . . I am reading the life of the Claytons, by Rev. Mr. Aveling, of England. I think the book is helping me, as good memoirs of true Christian men generally do, by suggestions and recorded example."

"*January* 8, 1871.— . . . My S. S. class seemed quite impressed with the lesson. Miss B. thought it not possible that any one could be lost. I had a conversation with her after the lesson, entreating her not to let that trouble her *now*. First come into the kingdom in the appointed way, and then these things become clear. She thinks many form a wrong idea of God's character by this idea being presented. I said I did not doubt it, for all who are alienated from Him form a wrong idea of His character. . . . At a temperance meeting Mr. Buckingham (Senator from Connecticut) made a warm-hearted, Christian speech. I followed him, by special request, urging temperance as one of the *stones* that we must roll away before the Saviour would speak life to many souls. . . . I began the day with a headache ; have been busy all day, and now am quite well. Some seed has been sown. May the Lord water and nourish it, and in His own time give the increase !"'

"*January* 9, 1871.— . . . After prayers at the chapel, which I conducted, I remarked upon the passage in our reading—' For the preaching of the cross is to them that perish foolishness,' showing why it was so. They—sinners who have not been with the kingdom at all—undertake to judge of it. They undertake to pronounce on that of which they necessarily have no knowledge whatever. . . ."

"*January* 10, 1871.— . . . After a long business day we had another good prayer-meeting at our church to-night. One member of my S. S. class arose for prayer, and two others. I had a pleasant conversation with Mr. J., who has just found the Saviour."

"*January* 12, 1871.—I began to urge upon him (General Grant, at an interview at the White House) the thought that he might have kept Senator Sumner from opposition [to himself] if he had exercised his accustomed wisdom and knowledge of human character. He smiled, and finished my idea before the sentence was complete, and then told us simply how Mr. Sumner had disappointed him. Mr. Douglass, who was present, presented some thoughts about the unfulfilled mission of the Republican party, and how necessary it still is to continue it. General Grant said, earnestly, ' Yes, it is so, whoever may lead.' I plead, as usual, for *education*, presenting the idea of a full-fledged *department*, with a seat in the Cabinet."

To E. S. Tobey, Esq.

" June 27, 1871.

" . . . The despatches in the Boston *Advertiser* are contrived with a show of truth, so as to give an utterly wrong impression. For example, the one on Rev. George Whipple's testimony, and the one that speaks of ' *a whitewashing report.*'

" I cannot give my statement nor my defence until the committee reports. Now I wish you would see the editor, Mr. Stanwood, and tell him that of late his correspondent has joined my enemies. He has associated himself with one who has pursued me in the public press in a way that I can never understand.

" For three years, in at least five papers, in telegrams, he [the latter] has betrayed the most invidious, covert (now and then outcropping) malignity. In his regular correspondence he laid the foundation for, and really brought on, the investigation, under charges of conduct that belongs only to guilty and depraved men. This man has doubtless deceived and misled my former friend, the *Advertiser's* correspondent. I have tried hard, my Heavenly Father knows, to do my duty, and nothing can be gained by Republican newspapers misrepresenting me. . . ."

To Members of his Staff, for " Decoration Day."

" I shall be glad to have the entire staff, in complete ' full uniform, ' accompany me on that memorial occasion. The deeds of our honored comrades who have gone before us into rest ought never to be forgotten."

To a Friend of his Youth.

" May 31, 1883.

" . . . Don't get vexed at me, P., for I have never ceased to love you, and want you to be supremely happy, to possess beyond question the everlasting life. I cannot cease to pray for it. To come at it without the experience of the bruised soul is better—yes, is best. Twenty-seven came, with full hearts, into our church (covenant) last Sunday, among them my seventh child. She must follow her brother Harry. Of course I am more than glad. Disciple is learner. Within the children learn better than without. One needs not crime to make him an honest man. One needs not often break God's law to learn to love Him. "

" Our worn-out bodies often shut us off from the sympathy and praise which, as men, we feel that we merit ; but God looketh upon the heart, and His rewards are above human feelings and honors.

'Who trusts in God's
Unchanging love,
Builds on a rock
That naught can move.' "

". . . I am but a poor, weak, sinful man. I know that. Yet God
is good, and He hears and answers my prayers. So bless the Lord,
oh, my soul, and all that is within me, bless His holy name. . . ."

To Colonel ——.

" July 31, 1883.

". . . I write to ask if all those liquor-sellers who are getting the
soldiers into trouble have a proper license. I do not believe they
have. Can you not have the matter inquired into? And can you
not in some way legally take the offensive?"

To Colonel T——.

" August 20, 1883.

". . . I see the death announced of Judge Jerry Black. He is a
great loss to the country. His trust in God was very clearly set
forth in his last moments, and his prayer touchingly simple and confident."

To General M——.

" August 9, 1883.

". . . So another, our friend, has gone home. Let us meet him
there, where there is no sorrow. It will be more satisfying than the
acquirements of science, will it not? We there may yet roam together around brighter steppes and more charmed circles than those
we traversed together under the leadership of Dante! . . ."

To the Daughter of his deceased Friend.

" January 9, 1883.

". . . I hope you are not worn out by your prolonged work. I do
wish you and your good mamma would come and stay forever with
us. I don't think I am fair to you or your good papa, now in
heaven, not to care just as much for his child as I do for my own.
Surely I would not do less. Don't you wish I were rich? . . ."

To Mrs. C——.

" January 2, 1883.

". . . There need never be despair in America in the matter of
compensated labor. With sorrow for the temporary cloud over them,
I am hopeful for a better future. . . ."

To his Mother.

" . . . I did pray to the Lord to relieve me in His own way from
this [obligation]. I made many efforts, but all seemed futile.
[Shortly after, through a friend, the obligation was discharged.]
. . . You must join me in thanking the Lord, who put it into the
heart of one of His servants to give me this great gift."

To his Daughter.

" January 15.

" We received a good letter from James, and now, last night, another from you—yours to Harry. You say, ' Ask papa to say what
would be his answer to a man who believed in God, yet said the
Bible is no more inspired than other books—what proofs are there of
inspiration ? '

" 1. By history found within and without the Bible. What we
call the Scriptures of the Old Testament have always been received
and treated as the inspired Word, coming to Christ's time through a
regular, undisputed succession of upright men.

" 2. The prophetic parts of all Moses' writings and of other books
whose fulfilment should have taken place, has taken place in the
spirit and in the letter of the record.

" 3. The New Testament, which shows the fulfilment of all the old
types and symbols which refer to Christ and to the Church, is a beautiful counterpart and complement to the Old Testament. Our Saviour,
who is at the least admitted to have been a good man, always quoted
from the Scriptures, and showed their fulfilment in His mission and
work.

" John the Baptist and all the apostles who wrote did the same
thing.

" ' Holy men of old wrote as they were moved by the Holy Ghost.'

" 4. The Scriptures everywhere claim to be the inspired Word of
God, not in the sense of God using the English words, but in the
sense of good and true and chosen men putting the truth of God
into such shape that they may, if they wish, find it out and drink it in.

" 5. It, the Bible, can be tested like a shut-up garden. One can
go in and see ; like a fountain of pure water, one can go to it and
drink ; like a distant land, one can visit it, or talk with those who
have been there. In the experience of true men the Scriptures prove
themselves—prove that they have in them eternal life. This must
show inspiration. You cannot go to any ordinary poet for the way
of life.

" 6. Where any real discrepancies occur (I think there are very few) they are, of course, human errors. Sacred poems, like that of Job, do not need to be called historic. Symbolic language need not be worked into tales and laughed at. The Bible is like a palace of wealth ; it has in it a vast number and variety of things. But oh, what joy, what comfort, what love, what hope, what heaven, come out of it ! Its (God's) promises are absolutely sure. . . ."

To his Brother.

"November 7, 1883.

". . . Nothing could be pleasanter to me than to meet, as you suggest, in the old place or places. Every spot is crowded with associations not to be forgotten. The contrasts are painful. . . .

" The old farm and buildings running down—not even the trees that father planted for posterity cared for. He said, as he leaned on his hoe, ' Otis, I don't expect to see fruit on these trees. I plant them for those that come after me.' How I would have cherished those trees ! . . . But you cannot say too much of the wonderful landscape. Strange that you had to travel so much to understand this ! But who can look at any mountain, lake, or meadow without the eye of association and make anything of it ? I have never quite settled the matter of my burial-place, but have always felt that Maine—Leeds—would be the place. Of course, the mere tabernacle is not of much account, but still it is our habit to treat it with respect after the spirit has departed. I would not waste the money needed for the living in making superb monuments, but I would have a plain, durable headstone, good grounds well kept, and never surrounding them a tumble-down fence. . . ."

To ——.

" December 7, 1883.

". . . As I believe that God loves a truly brave man, I plead not for the teaching of business, business ! money, money ! and nothing else, but for instruction in the principles of honor. I love men who count it a pleasure to die, if need be, for the right. And men can only stand to their own and not other people's convictions. It will lift up the standard of character to the youth of our land for Mr. Coffin to show them such men, as they were, as Lincoln and Douglas, Scott and McClellan, Lee and Jackson, Chase and Jeff Davis, Grant, Sherman, Sheridan, Foote, Farragut and George H. Thomas, and a host of others who have left or are soon to leave the stage of action.

" Let them know the men of history and follow the best, fearing nothing but to do wrong."

To a Comrade.

". . . I hope that my name may be pleasantly remembered as you call over the roster of living friends. Our country is still *one*—a free nation—increasing in prosperity. There are ills which we would cure, mists which we would dispel ; but when we look back to the old days before the war and contrast them with the present, we can only rejoice and thank God. Heaven grant that the generations to come may have the virtue and the courage to maintain them ! . . ."

"It is a good motto, 'Let no day pass without making somebody happier and better.' "

To Miss D——.

"November 30, 1883.

". . . I am very grateful for your kind letter. It touched my heart, because it is the voice of a child appreciating her father.

"I was thankful for the picture of the house [the superintendent's]. West Point became irksome to me this last time for various reasons, yet I hope I left some good results."

"December 8.

"DEAR COLONEL : Since an ounce of prevention is worth a pound of cure, may I ask you quietly to look into the subject of gambling among the junior officers at your post. The reputation for gambling has gone out pretty widely, which you and I are the last to find out. Gamblers proverbially have no principle. Gambling has been leading to the many duplications of pay accounts. It is a frightful vice, prohibited by human and divine law.

"The young officers cannot afford to be found in the company of gamblers, nor to spend their nights in such utterly demoralizing occupation.

"I do not want an investigation, because my information comes from careless conversations of officers who did not really intend to apprise me of the shameful practice ; but I feel it due to you, dear Colonel, to know of the notoriety."

"December 30, 1884.

"DEAR GENERAL SHERMAN : I write you near the close of this year to give expression to my feelings of respect and affection.

"I have, as you know, great confidence in the Christian method of obtaining favors and blessings of the Great Giver—that is, to ask humbly and sincerely in the name of the Master. I endeavor always to do this for you. So when I wish you a bright Christmas and a happy New Year, I wish you a completeness of satisfaction that only

God can give. In the past *you* have been very kind to me and mine, so it is natural that I should be grateful and seek to make the best return.

"Give my best wishes to Mrs. Sherman and the children about you, and believe me ever your friend."

To the Countess de Gasparin, near Geneva, Switzerland.

"May 29, 1883.

". . . I am very glad you gave him (my son) a book to read. He will treasure its precepts and value it from you. I must thank you again for your books just received. I will study them carefully. I have used your husband's name in my addresses because he was *so* faithful and thorough in his researches, so much more so than I have been. . . ."

"My opportunity to lecture last year helped me not a little. With the Lord's blessing I am getting free from troublesome obligations little by little. I hope I shall fight a good fight and come off conqueror through Christ."

Concerning his Visit Abroad.

"Feb. 6, 1885.

"Paris and the Louvre would make a book. The glimpses into old Rome would make another.

"I had delightful interviews with the missionaries everywhere I went, and found them doing such wonderfully good work, particularly with the young girls, teaching them, as our misses are taught, that a very excellent impression has been left with me regarding them at Alexandria, Cairo, Smyrna, Scutari, and Athens. . . .

"I am fearfully depressed by the news from Khartoum. My saving thought is that it is yet necessary [in God's inscrutable wisdom] to permit treachery. I do not yet believe that Gordon is dead."

To General Morrow.

"February 4, 1885.

"General, your talk is wise ; I have no feeling now, and had better not awaken any. I invite all kindly and candid criticism, but ignore the embittered and poisoned chalice."

*　　*　　*　　*　　*　　*　　*　　*

General Howard has been an industrious correspondent, despite the disadvantage he has labored under in the loss of his right arm. He quickly trained his left

hand in the use of the pen, and finds little difficulty in
using the one usually so useless to others for this purpose.   Rarely are his letters written by others, he deem-
ing it a duty to pay his correspondents the compliment
of a personal reply.   People, in remarking upon his
facility in this respect, have frequently suggested his
forgetfulness of the fact that he ever had two arms—a
suggestion which he quickly repudiates.   He has suffered
too acutely from this cause to treat his loss lightly.
With more precision than a barometer does this mutilated
member notify him of a change of temperature, and
he can never ignore its susceptibility to exposure or
overwork.   He is constantly reminded of it also in
travel, or in streets of a city, where a jostle against his
shoulder causes prolonged pain.   But he has ever insisted that the kindness which he has received on account of his arm has overbalanced the suffering it has
cost him.   It has taught him patience—a great stock of
which he has accumulated in his life—and his dependence
upon the family circle has made him its idol.   Yet he
rides as fearlessly as before, and is capable of as continuous work with the remaining hand as many persons are
with both.

A characteristic of General Howard's which should be
emphasized is his boundless charity.   In his intercourse
with men he has remembered the assurance made by the
Master, that the greatest of all virtues is charity, and in
his constant effort to inculcate this lesson upon his mind,
he has strengthened it in himself.   In his intercourse
with his children he has systematically endeavored to
release them from the misfortune of a critical spirit, and
the subject of many of the " children's hours" has been
this important theme.   It has been the custom of General
and Mrs. Howard, for many years, to devote the hour

succeeding the evening meal to the children, and it has never been neglected. It has made the relationship between these parents and their children a beautiful one, and dignified it with a spiritual significance not common in families. In all his association with his children General Howard has, as a natural consequence, impressed upon them the child-like faith he has reposed in his Heavenly Father, and it has been no matter of surprise with them that blessings have come to their fireside. They have expected them, and have rejoiced and not wondered that they came.

Some years ago, when the Howard University was started, General Howard became responsible for a Professorship, and afterward was unable, through his heavy losses in Washington and the legal expenses of the two investigations made of the Bureau management, to pay the sum of ten thousand dollars, which was the amount he had promised to give. His inability to do so humiliated him, and he worked and prayed continuously to cancel the obligation. Time passed, and it still remained an incubus upon him, he paying the interest upon the sum, and thus maintaining the Chair. His family had almost despaired of his ever being able to meet the debt, and were often tempted to regret that he had created it ; but he met the requirements of his bond each year, and waited in patience and humility for the leadings of the Spirit in the matter. Finally, one day in the summer of 1882, in a most unexpected manner, the debt was lifted from his shoulders, and the Professorship secured to the University. General and Mrs. Howard were travelling together, and while on the cars going West made the acquaintance of two fellow-travellers, a citizen of New York and his wife, who knew the General by reputation, and introduced themselves to him. Their jour-

ney lay in the same direction for a few days, and before
they separated the gentleman, who had inquired concerning the University and its prospects, gave, unsolicited,
to General Howard a check for the entire amount, subject to the provision that his name should never reach the
public.   Mrs. Howard alone was informed, and she, too
overjoyed and grateful to observe his condition of silence,
went to him, and touchingly thanked him for the weight
he had lifted from her husband's shoulders and from
the hearts of his household.   General Howard considered it but another of the countless manifestations of
God's goodness, which he, in common with his fellow-
beings, was constantly receiving, and he humbled himself yet more in love before Him.   The incident is one
that gave satisfaction to every one who knew General
Howard, and the modest benefactor has had the silent
thanks of thousands who heard of his generosity, but may
never learn his name.   The release from this responsibility, which he was pecuniarily unable to meet, lifted a
mountain weight of care from General Howard, and will
enable him to anticipate the future without the anxiety
that would have otherwise followed him.

*   *   *   *   *   *   *   *

General Howard has now reached the summit of his
earthly fame, and rounded the pyramid of years which
marks the half century and more he has lived in the
world.   He is at his best intellectually and spiritually,
and is happy in the contemplations of the past.   Life
now has few temptations for him ; he is serene in his
strength, full sure that only good can come to him, and
ready and willing to accept whatever the Master sends to
him to suffer or to enjoy.

His attitude through life has been one of kindness

toward his fellow-men ; he has prayed for his enemies, forgiven his foes, and has not harbored hate in his heart.

*   *   *   *   *   *   *   *

Such is the record of General Howard, a man of gentle nature, kind deeds, and high Christian character, one who in his daily living has kept in view the last hour, in which he desires to say, with the apostle, "I have fought a good fight, I have finished my course, I have kept the faith."

www.ingramcontent.com/pod-product-compliance
Lightning Source LLC
Chambersburg PA
CBHW020120030726
47498CB00006B/2203